"You m... adopted?"

"No way." Brick scoffed at seven-year-old Aaron's question. "There's a picture of Mom in the scrapbook when we were in her tummy."

"She did get pregnant, but some other woman donated the eggs," Caitlin said.

The two boys stared at her. "You mean like bacon and eggs?" said Aaron.

Brick knew better. "No. People eggs."

"That's right," Caitlin said. "You know what that means?"

They didn't.

"It means," she said, "that our other mother is still alive."

"Our other mother?" said Aaron.

"Biological mother," amended Caitlin. "It has to do with genes. She's what they call an egg donor."

Brick hated it when his sister used long words. Biological had something to do with the stuff on that science guy's TV show, but what was this business about jeans? "Her pants?" he said. "Somebody gave her pants with eggs in them?"

"Forget all that." Caitlin's voice got shrill. "The important thing is that I found her name on the computer. I know who our other mother is!"

Books by Jacqueline Diamond

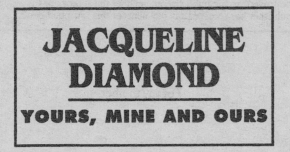

JACQUELINE DIAMOND

YOURS, MINE AND OURS

Harlequin Books

TORONTO • NEW YORK • LONDON
AMSTERDAM • PARIS • SYDNEY • HAMBURG
STOCKHOLM • ATHENS • TOKYO • MILAN
MADRID • WARSAW • BUDAPEST • AUCKLAND

For my mother

ISBN 0-373-16615-X

YOURS, MINE AND OURS

Copyright © 1996 by Jackie Hyman.

This edition published by arrangement with Harlequin Books S.A.

® and TM are trademarks of the publisher. Trademarks indicated with ® are registered in the United States Patent and Trademark Office, the Canadian Trade Marks Office and in other countries.

Printed in U.S.A.

Chapter One

When Flint Harris came down the front steps of City Hall, Robin Lindstrom was waiting for him.

Before his sharp gray eyes could register what was happening, before he could even fling up a muscular arm to protect himself, she showered him with stars.

"Beachside is a magical place to live!" Robin shouted. "How dare you try to ruin it?"

Tiny silver stars cascaded from Flint's trim brown hair onto the broad shoulders of his suit. Without a flicker of emotion, he plucked one of the stars from his lapel and examined it.

"You must be a teacher," he said.

Behind her, Robin became aware that her fellow picketers had fallen silent. Even her outspoken mother, Gigi, stood nearby frozen in concentration. Robin felt all alone in this.

"Good guess, Doctor," she said. "Did you deduce that scientifically?"

"First of all, I may have my Ph.D. but I don't use the term 'doctor.'" Flint's calm baritone did nothing to steady her nerves. "And, second, since I have kids, it was an easy guess. Teachers use these as rewards. I'm honored that you find me so worthy."

Robin felt heat rise to her cheeks. "It wasn't meant as an honor, it was meant to get your attention. The changes you want to make in this town will destroy its character. Beachside is a fun and funky place to live, and we want to keep it that way."

Behind her, people stirred, and she heard a few chants of "Save Our City!" and "Everything's Peachy in Beachside!"

"Why is a teacher leading a protest against revising the city's earthquake standards?" Flint's high cheekbones, firm mouth and tanned skin made him resemble a rancher more than a seismology expert. Robin supposed he must spend a lot of time prowling the sunbaked fault lines of Southern California.

"My mother has a business on the beachfront," she said. "You'd wipe out her sign and her facade."

"So would an earthquake." Flint had an irritating way of holding himself erect to his full six-foot-two-inch height so that he talked down at Robin. At five-foot-seven, she wasn't used to feeling short.

"You're a zealot," she challenged. "You'd have us all go back to living in caves. That would be a lot safer, wouldn't it?"

"Not at all," said Flint. "Falling rocks are a serious hazard in an earthquake. Now if you'll excuse me?"

As he brushed by, she could feel the hardness of his body. It matched the fossilized condition of his brain, Robin thought angrily. He had dismissed her arguments before she even opened her mouth.

Of course, that might be because of the stunt with the stars. Throwing them had been her mother's idea, and Robin had reluctantly agreed to go along. But she hadn't expected to end up arguing with a man so rigid and full of himself. She shuddered to think how he must treat his children.

By sound alone, Robin could trace Flint's path down the steps and along the sidewalk. The crowd's chanting rippled into a wave that peaked as he passed. After a few minutes, the normal buzz of conversation resumed, and she heard a car start in the parking lot.

Robin turned to see a squarish Volvo exiting onto the street. Naturally, she thought, Flint Harris had chosen a car renowned for safety over style. The man was so compulsive, he probably had air bags in his bathtub.

Beside her, her mother fiddled with her frizzy red hair. Gigi had been eccentric as far back as Robin could remember, and reaching her late fifties hadn't changed a thing. At the moment, she wore a riot of eye shadow and rouge, a fluffy pink sweater over a bright peasant skirt, and gold thong sandals.

"What an infuriating man," Robin said.

"Infuriating?" Gigi sounded puzzled. "I thought he had a cute aura."

"A cute aura?" Robin couldn't believe her mother had said that. "Mom, spare me."

"He likes you," Gigi continued confidently. "You made quite an impression."

Robin groaned. The problem was, her students would be making a dance presentation at the school board meeting tomorrow night. Flint and his earthquake mania were also on the agenda, and Robin knew she couldn't avoid running into him.

Maybe he wouldn't recognize her. In any case, she'd just have to tough it out.

As HE HEADED NORTH toward the suburbs, Flint mentally catalogued the hazards.

He spotted numerous oversize signs likely to topple in a strong shaker. A life-size plastic cow sat perilously atop a drive-through dairy. He frowned at an unreinforced brick building with a splashy mural of a whale painted on the side.

Flint had been hired by the City Council to make recommendations, and he was doing his job. Why did people have to get so emotional?

The issue here was safety. Flint had toured the devastation of the Northridge and Loma Prieta quakes and he never wanted to see such misery again. Running an earthquake consulting business might be a way to make a living, but it had also become his personal mission.

He detoured deliberately so his route took him by Serena Academy. Its adobe buildings sat on a tree-shaded campus, creating a peaceful image.

Several of those buildings needed reinforcement. Flint had made only a preliminary assessment, since examining the private school wasn't part of his contract with the city. He was scheduled to make a presentation tomorrow night to the school board, soliciting their business.

For some reason, an image of the young teacher at the demonstration popped into Flint's mind. Maybe it was because he'd heard that Serena hired individualistic staff members, gifted teachers who chafed at the restrictions of public school life.

The lady struck him as a prime example. The way her blue eyes lit up with fury, the impulsive manner in which she'd doused him with stars, all added up to an undisciplined nature. He wondered how she could possibly work well with children.

There was, Flint supposed, something appealing about the woman's naive energy. She deserved credit for loyalty to her mother, as well. But people who worked with children needed to keep their feelings under control.

Take, for example, his nanny. He relaxed behind the wheel, thinking about Mrs. Strich, whom his three children had nicknamed Mrs. Strict. In the month she'd worked for him, she had followed his itemized instructions to the letter and run the house like a tight ship.

She made no attempt to mother the kids, thank goodness. No one could replace the wife Flint had lost in a waterskiing accident three years ago, and he didn't want some hired housekeeper to try.

With a sense of homecoming, Flint turned in to the residential development where he lived. The two-story houses were painted in earth tones, as required by the home owners' association. All vegetation was clipped, no trash cans were visible from the street, and the only dog in sight was a Pomeranian on a leash.

He had come home to order and restraint. For the first time that day, Flint allowed himself a smile.

Then, as he reached for the garage door opener, he spotted his Aunt Maureen's Cadillac in front of the house. Had Mrs. Strich left early? Maureen was his emergency backup sitter, but Flint couldn't imagine what she was doing here today.

He soon found out.

"Maybe," Maureen intoned from the kitchen, where she stood whipping mashed potatoes, "your nannies might stick around longer if you didn't treat them like robots."

Flint pinched a couple of silver stars off his sleeve. "I thought you agreed with the way I raise the children."

"I do. But you don't hand *me* a schedule first thing every morning. And I don't have to live with you." At sixty-five, Maureen seemed to have grown rather than shrunk with age. She stood stiffly erect, only a few inches shorter than Flint. Her hair had turned a steely shade of gray, and the frown wrinkles in her forehead had etched themselves in stately parallel lines.

According to family legend, Maureen had been a sunny, outgoing girl, but she had never married and grew somber as she matured. Recently retired from her job as an office manager, Maureen would have been the perfect house-keeper, Flint reflected. He was grateful she lived nearby and was willing to help out in emergencies.

"But just to walk out like this is unforgivable," he persisted. "Mrs. Strich owed me two weeks' notice."

In the family room, he could hear the TV playing an educational tape. The children were behaving themselves, probably in hopes of escaping his fury.

"She sounded hysterical when she called." Wearing two padded mitts, Maureen removed a roast from the oven. "Brick put worms in her spaghetti at lunch."

"He's studying them for a science project." Flint couldn't believe his stocky son, the oldest of the triplets by several minutes, would have deliberately committed such a disgusting act. "They must have sneaked out."

"Caitlin's been stealing the mail again," Maureen went on. "Apparently Mrs. Strich has a gentleman friend who's working in the Middle East. He wrote her a rather personal letter."

"Caitlin read it?" Flint gritted his teeth. Dealing with a child whose IQ soared into the genius range was more of a trial than he would have expected.

"She copied it onto the Internet," said Maureen. "Then Aaron—well, you know how much he wants a puppy."

"He can't have one." Flint wouldn't have minded a watchdog, but he knew the children would spoil it to the point of uselessness.

"Well, he decided he was going to *be* a puppy." Maureen tossed the salad with crisp efficiency. Not a single leaf fell onto the counter. "Unfortunately, he kept trying to bite Mrs. Strich on the leg."

"Did she get hurt?" Flint tried to remember how much liability insurance he carried.

"No, thank heaven." Maureen began setting plates on the table. "Mrs. Strich told him seven-year-olds don't bite, so he stuck out his tongue and gave her a Bronx cheer."

Flint could feel a headache building in his temples. "How have the kids been since you got here?"

"Perfect angels." Maureen measured out the napkins and laid the flatware with military precision. "They know better than to pull that crap with me, pardon my French. I'll watch them for a few days, Flint, but you have to hire a replacement."

"I'll call the agency." Then Flint remembered that the agency had warned him this was the last nanny it would provide. The last two had suffered nervous breakdowns. "I mean, I'll advertise."

Maureen used her apron to wipe a fingerprint from the salt shaker. "Also, I can't baby-sit any nights this week. I've volunteered at the Senior Center to sit with a lady who just had surgery. Her daughter works the swing shift."

Tomorrow night, Flint had to make his presentation at Serena Academy. Who was going to watch his children then? A couple of teen-age girls lived on the block but he wasn't sure he trusted them. They'd probably smoke or invite their boyfriends over.

He was being paranoid, he told himself. Surely one of them would be fine for a few hours.

"I'll handle it," he said, and then noticed that only four places were set at the table. "Aren't you staying?"

His aunt removed her apron and hung it on a hook inside the pantry. "I help out because that's what families are for," she said. "But I prefer to eat alone."

Flint walked her to the door. "I can't tell you how much I appreciate this," he said.

"Hire a new nanny." Maureen marched down the walkway like a drill sergeant going to meet a platoon of recruits.

Flint stopped by the bathroom, downed two aspirin and then went to face his children.

They were sitting in the family room working at activities they knew he approved of. Brick was trying to induce worms to negotiate a maze. Caitlin was practicing touch-typing on the computer. Aaron lay flopped on the couch, reading a book called *My Teacher Is an Alien*.

Flint picked up the remote and clicked off the tape, which no one was watching anyway. "We need to talk," he said.

Three pairs of wary eyes flicked toward him. Caitlin's were cool and gray, like his own, Brick's a piercing shade of blue and Aaron's a light aqua.

"Dinner sure smells good." Brick dropped his worms into their box of dirt.

"We wouldn't want it to get cold," said Caitlin.

Aaron burst into tears. The other two glared at him. "We didn't mean to make her leave, Daddy! But she was so mean!"

Flint sat in his oversize recliner and gathered the little boy onto his lap. "You kids have to stop this. Maureen can't always take care of you. Now I have to hire another nanny."

"We don't want a nanny," Aaron said, snuffling against his chest. "We want a mommy."

"You can't go out and hire a mother," Brick said quickly, trying to avert a lecture. "We know that, Dad."

"On the other hand, Flint, it is time for you to think about remarrying." Caitlin's use of his first name bothered Flint, but he couldn't think of a logical objection.

He did, however, object to her point. "No one could replace Kathy. Perhaps someday I'll meet a wonderful woman and fall in love. If that happens, terrific. But it isn't something I can make happen."

"What if *we* found the right woman?" asked Caitlin.

Her brothers stared at her, Brick with disdain and Aaron in amazement. "Could we?" said Aaron.

"No." Flint set the little boy on his feet. "This conversation is over. Let's eat dinner."

When all hands were washed and everyone sat up straight with napkin in lap, they began to eat their meal in silence.

Inevitably, Flint found himself thinking about Kathy. Talking about her always brought back the memories, and they were still painful.

Intelligent, forthright, quick to laugh, she'd brightened Flint's life from the day they met in college until her death ten years later. She'd been a once-in-a-lifetime love.

What bothered him most, in a way, was that Kathy had struggled for years. Just when all her hard work was beginning to pay off, a meaningless accident had taken her life.

First she'd knocked herself out earning a law degree. Then, eager to get pregnant, she'd run into one obstacle after another. When fertility treatments resulted in her carrying triplets, she spent months in bed trying to delay a premature birth.

After the tiny trio was born two months early, Kathy had nursed them night and day until they thrived. Then, to supplement the money from Flint's fledgling business, she worked part-time at a law firm while juggling diapers and day care.

Finally his income had increased and Kathy decided to take a year off before the triplets started kindergarten. To celebrate, she treated herself to a weekend of waterskiing at Lake Havasu. Flint volunteered to stay with the children while she went with a girlfriend.

The phone call caught him off guard. A drunken boater had run square into Kathy while she was skiing. She'd disappeared into the water, and hours passed before her body turned up.

Sometimes even now he couldn't believe it had happened.

Flint gazed at the children. Caitlin was cutting her roast beef with precise slices. Brick hacked his into chunks. Aaron poked his meat as if expecting it to divide by magic.

He wished Kathy could be here to see them now. They'd grown so much these past three years. He didn't blame them for missing her, but she couldn't be replaced, and he didn't want some housekeeper to try.

He'd just have to find a nanny with more starch in her backbone.

"Daddy." Aaron pointed to his plate. "Would you cut my meat, please?"

As he helped his son, Flint felt a wave of love for the youngsters. They might act up once in a while, but they were sweet little people. He couldn't stay angry with them for long.

"Listen, guys," he said. They all blinked as if snatched from private reveries. "Tomorrow night I'm making a presentation at Serena Academy. I'm going to hire a baby-sitter and I expect you to behave while I'm gone."

"Serena Academy?" Caitlin brushed a strand of blond hair off her cheek. "Listen, Flint." Seeing his glare, she changed that to "Dad," which meant she must want something. "You've been talking about putting us in a private school, haven't you?"

"Not Serena Academy," said Flint. "It's too indulgent."

"But they have day care before and after," Caitlin said matter-of-factly.

"You mean we wouldn't need a nanny?" asked Brick.

"Yes, you would. What about all those evenings and weekends I have to work?" Besides, the idea of sending them to private school had been a casual one. The public schools in the area were fine, although to his mind not rigorous enough. "I thought you hated the idea of private school."

"Maybe we should take a look tomorrow night." When Caitlin became as intense as she was now, the freckles on her pale skin stood out. "We'd be real quiet. And if we like the place, you could sign us up."

There was something suspicious about this change of heart. "I'm not so sure," Flint said.

"Anyway," Caitlin pressed, "you wouldn't have to hire a baby-sitter."

"We'd like to watch you work," Brick said. "We might learn something."

Aaron nodded vigorously.

"I'll think about it." Flint already knew he was going to give in. He preferred to keep the children under his stern eye rather than entrust them to some teenager.

But he didn't plan to enroll them in Serena Academy. Not if it employed teachers like that disturbingly pretty young woman who bestowed her stars too freely.

After dinner, the children cleared their dishes. Aaron rinsed while Caitlin loaded the dishwasher and Brick attacked the table with a sponge.

Flint appreciated their cooperation as he settled into his recliner with a newspaper. He appreciated it even more a few minutes later when the three filed quietly to their bedrooms, leaving him to read in peace.

He bit back an impulse to go play with them. Too much fraternizing wasn't good for discipline. He'd take them all to the park this weekend. Their pitching needed work.

Confident that everything was under control, Flint resumed reading the business section.

"WHAT WAS ALL THAT STUFF about Serena Academy?" Brick asked when he was draped across the bed in Caitlin's room. "You're up to something."

"She is?" Aaron, who curled at the head of the bed hugging his favorite bear, always seemed to lag a beat behind the others. Maybe that was because he'd been born last.

Caitlin's gray eyes narrowed as she perched on the corner of a child-size table. "You guys are so slow."

Brick took a guess. "You found something in the computer."

Caitlin nodded. "Don't tell Dad." In private, she never referred to their father as Flint. "Both of you, hold up your hands and swear."

Brick didn't like letting his sister boss him around, but this sounded promising. He held up his hand and swore himself to silence, and so did Aaron.

From a chest so jumbled with toys that baseball cards could disappear into it forever, Caitlin effortlessly retrieved a crumpled envelope.

"This all started a few weeks ago," she said. "I was going through the mail and there was a letter from a medical clinic."

Brick tried to fake a yawn so his sister wouldn't see how fascinated he was, but he couldn't pull it off. All he could do was sit there bug-eyed like Aaron.

"I opened it because it was addressed to Mom," Caitlin said. "It said the clinic was closing and that under California law, Mom had a right to get her medical records. There was a little form to fill out, so I did."

"You forged her name?" Aaron was awestruck.

"No big deal," said Caitlin. "Well, the records arrived today. That's why I set up the diversionary tactic with Mrs. Strict. I needed her out of my hair."

Brick wondered how his sister could pronounce "diversionary tactic" without stumbling. He also wondered what it meant.

"You're not going to believe this," Caitlin said. "Mom had some kind of problem with her ovaries."

"Ovaries?" said Aaron.

"It means she couldn't have kids," Caitlin explained smugly.

"We're adopted?" said Aaron.

"No way," scoffed Brick. "There's a picture of Mom in the scrapbook when we were in her tummy."

"Not her tummy, her uterus, but that's right," Caitlin said. "She did get pregnant, but some other woman donated the eggs."

The two boys stared at her. "You mean like bacon and eggs?" said Aaron.

Brick knew better. "No. People eggs."

"That's right," Caitlin said. "You know what that means?"

They didn't.

"It means," she said, "that our other mother is still alive."

The boys sat in silence, trying to puzzle this out.

"Our other mother?" said Aaron at last.

"Biological mother," amended Caitlin. "It has to do with genes. She's what they call an egg donor."

Brick hated it when his sister used long words. Biological had something to do with the stuff on *Bill Nye the Science Guy,* but what was this business about jeans? "Her pants?" he said. "Somebody gave her pants with eggs in them?"

"Not that kind of jeans," snapped Caitlin. "G-e-n-e-s genes."

"She said egg doughnuts," Aaron ventured. "Is that like egg bagels?"

"You guys!" Caitlin's voice got shrill. "Forget all that. Listen to this. Mom carried us in her tummy, okay? But we started growing inside another mommy, and we're also hers. Is that simple enough?"

"But who is she?" Brick demanded. "Did the clinic tell you?"

"Not exactly." Caitlin favored him with her most superior grin. "I used the computer. Getting into their records wasn't easy, but I found out her name."

Brick was impressed. He could barely summon enough energy to tie his own shoes in the morning. On the other hand, he could see a flaw in his sister's reasoning. "There might be more than one mommy with the same name."

"That's what I thought," said Caitlin. "So I looked in the phone book and I called her."

Aaron made a mild choking sound. "You told her about us?"

"Of course not. I pretended to be looking for someone else by that name." Caitlin looked like she might burst with pride. "I said I had this aunt who was an astronaut."

Brick had finally found a good reason to scoff. "An astronaut? That's stupid."

"No, it isn't," said Caitlin, who planned to be an astronaut herself. "Besides, it worked. It got her to talk. She told me she isn't an astronaut, she's— Oh, you guys don't really want to know."

She had them where she wanted them. Brick couldn't help joining with Aaron in saying, "Yes, we do. We do."

"Okay." Caitlin beamed with delight at her own brilliance. "She's a teacher, and guess where? Serena Academy!"

Chapter Two

The beach was not an ideal place to rehearse a dance, but by seven o'clock in the evening the tourists had gone home, the punkers had retreated to fast-food restaurants and the stores were shuttered.

And, in July, there was still plenty of light. There would be lots of space and lots of privacy. At least, that had been Robin's theory when she scheduled the rehearsal here.

Their class tomorrow was going to be preempted by a fire safety assembly, and she couldn't invite the children to the school's theater at night. The building, older than the rest of the school, was set in an isolated grove of pepper trees. Robin loved the setting, but not when the campus would be deserted.

Her own apartment, despite its high rent, was tiny, and there was no room for dancers inside her mother's place. Gigi owned a small store, not very subtly labeled Fortunes Told Here, and lived above it in a cluttered one-bedroom unit.

At least she'd given permission for Robin to invite the summer school students to her beachfront address, and offered to provide refreshments.

They cavorted on the sand now, a dozen youngsters varying in size and age, playful but self-conscious in their leotards.

"Settle down, everyone." Robin tried to ignore an elderly man in a toga and long braided white hair who paused to watch. A typical beach weirdo.

The kids stopped hopping around and poking each other.

"Tomorrow night, you're going to be presenting our dance to the school board," Robin reminded them. "People will judge our whole program by your actions, so behave like ladies and gentlemen. Places, everyone!"

She turned on the boom box, and music from Vivaldi's *The Four Seasons* hummed into the evening air. The youngsters leaped and twirled until two of them collided and fell onto the sand, yowling more in outrage than pain.

Robin clicked off the tape and ran to inspect their injuries. "Everybody all right?" she said, and diverted their mutual accusations of blame by adding, "These things happen. Let's start over, okay?"

A middle-aged man in a business suit and thong sandals approached with a large black dog on a leash. The dog sniffed the boom box and lifted his rear leg, while the man stood by indifferently.

"No, you don't!" Robin planted one jogging shoe on the dog's flank and shoved. The dog and the man gave her offended glares and stalked off.

How could her mother live in a nutty area like this? But then, Robin reflected, what other kind of area would make Gigi feel at home?

She started the tape at the beginning. This time the children's prancings followed her choreography and resulted in no crashes and only a few near misses.

She supposed that, to the untrained eye, the youngsters would appear to be jumping at random. In reality, the children had to count out the movements and execute them to the music.

Dance, like life, was deceptive, Robin mused. The trick had been to capitalize on each child's strengths, compensate for weaknesses and require them to stretch themselves mentally and physically.

In her summer school class so far, one twelve-year-old girl had overcome her preadolescent awkwardness and discovered a measure of grace. One boy had stopped clowning in class and applied his outgoing nature to his dance gestures. They were growing, each in his or her own way, developing the inner discipline needed to support freedom.

Still, forced to choose between harshness and excessive exuberance, Robin would choose joy every time.

As she applauded the dancers and signaled Gigi, watching through an upstairs window, to bring the snack, Robin's thoughts swung to the annoying Dr. Harris. For some reason, his strong face and condescending expression had popped into her mind with alarming frequency since their confrontation this afternoon.

She could imagine what he would think of her students. His lip would curl, his gray eyes would turn to ice and he'd tap his fingers in impatience.

How did his wife put up with him? She hoped the woman managed to soften his rigidity around their children. Otherwise the poor kids would either turn into automatons or rebel.

As Gigi appeared with a tray of cookies and punch, the children ran whooping onto the boardwalk. Abruptly, staring at the refreshments, they fell silent.

"Purple cookies?" said a boy.

"That punch is green," one of the smaller girls observed.

"A judicious use of food coloring." Gigi handed out the cups. "It tastes fine."

A boy wrinkled his nose and sipped the punch. "It's cherry flavored," he said.

The small girl nibbled a cookie. "Ugh, grape," she said. "I never ate grape cookies before."

The white-haired man in the toga wandered up and helped himself to a cookie. The children fell back.

"Don't mind him," said Gigi. "He's the reincarnation of Julius Caesar."

"Is that like a ghost?" asked an older boy. "There aren't any ghosts."

"These cookies are okay," said the white-haired man, "but I prefer chocolate chip."

To Robin's relief, the parents arrived a few minutes later and the children departed. At least they all appeared to have enjoyed themselves.

"We're having a séance later tonight," Gigi told Robin as they waved goodbye to the students. "You should stay."

"Mom, you know how I feel about that stuff." Robin respected her mother's chosen profession, but that didn't mean she had to believe in it.

"I've been getting a strange feeling all day." Gigi ate one of the cookies, balancing the tray on her left hand. Even if Robin hadn't known that her mother had worked years as a waitress, it would have been obvious from that skillful gesture. "A spirit is trying to contact me."

"Maybe you're coming down with a summer cold," Robin said.

"Very funny," said Gigi.

Robin hadn't known whether to be skeptical or alarmed when her mother began dabbling in spiritualism fifteen years ago. It began during a trip Gigi's folk-dancing group took to Greece, where they visited the ancient oracle at Delphi.

Gigi swore the thing had spoken to her, although she would never reveal what it said. "The oracle speaks in riddles," was the most she would say.

She had tried tarot cards, tea leaves, astronomy and, finally, séances. Soon Gigi was communing with disembodied entities and making pronouncements about the future so vague that they were sure to come true.

Boom box in hand, Robin followed her mother up the steps. She didn't want to hear about the spirit, but, knowing her mother, there'd be no avoiding it.

"I think it's a man," Gigi said, ushering her daughter inside. "I think he's looking for someone. Isn't that exciting? I love mysteries."

Gigi's apartment resembled a nineteenth-century San Francisco house of ill repute, or so Robin imagined. The wallpaper was scarlet, the lamps heavily draped, the tables and cabinets made of black lacquer. A beaded screen separated the bedroom from the living-dining area.

Robin found her purse behind the gold velvet sofa. "Thanks for your help, Mom," she said. "You coming to the board meeting tomorrow night?"

Gigi shook her head. "My friend Irma is having a birthday party for her spirit guide. He's two hundred and fifty years old."

"Sorry to miss it." Robin gave her mother a peck on the cheek and fled.

GIGI WATCHED HER DAUGHTER out the window. Robin strode along the sidewalk like a young woman who knew exactly where she was going.

She has no idea, Gigi thought. *She thinks she walks through open air, when she walks among celestial entities.*

What she had told Robin was true, that a male spirit sought contact. But there were other things Gigi couldn't say because she knew her daughter would stick up her chin and comment acidly that Gigi had gone too far.

Robin had always been a private person, keeping her own counsel and holding even her closest friends and relatives at a distance. She rarely confided much about her hopes and fears, her mistakes or her triumphs.

It might be easier for Gigi to explain the feelings she'd been getting recently if she knew more about Robin's private life. There was something unresolved in the past, but

Gigi didn't know what. It had to be at least tangentially related to this new spirit. Gigi sensed that he had chosen her as his medium because of her closeness to Robin.

Forces set in motion years ago were coming together for unknown reasons. Gigi knew better than to tell her daughter this, however. Robin was likely to do the opposite of whatever Gigi suggested.

Dealing with her was going to take cleverness and subtlety, neither of which were Gigi's strong points. But she would do whatever was necessary to help bring Robin's life to the path on which it belonged.

She just wished she knew what exactly that might be.

ROBIN WAS FISHING KEYS from her purse when her fingers bumped the envelope. Startled, she realized she'd been carrying it around for weeks.

As she climbed into her aging green compact, Robin pulled it out and looked at it again. She was surprised it had reached her. In eight years, she had moved a couple of times, and the envelope bore several forwarding notations.

She'd almost forgotten about the clinic.

Robin had found it through an ad one year during college. The state had just raised tuition again, and her waitressing job wasn't going to cover her costs.

The opportunity to make extra money and help some deserving couple have children had overcome her initial reservations. In addition, the clinic had offered a free medical exam, something Robin couldn't afford at the time.

So, after the checkup, she'd taken the fertility shots they gave her, then allowed them to harvest some of her eggs through minor surgery. Afterward, Robin had walked out of the clinic with the uncomfortable feeling she was leaving something precious behind.

For a while, she'd wondered if any of those eggs had resulted in a baby. What did it look like? Was it happy? She wished there was some way to be sure the child was loved—or to know if such a child even existed. But in the past few years, the questions had faded. It had been so long ago.

Seeing the envelope from the clinic had brought back all her concerns. Still, knowing that the clinic wouldn't tell her the fate of her eggs, Robin wasn't sure she wanted to bother obtaining her medical records.

Torn by indecision, she'd stuffed the envelope in her purse. Now, starting the car, she wondered why she hadn't simply thrown it away.

In recent years, Robin had begun scheduling annual checkups, so her doctor's records were fairly complete. On the other hand, maybe someday she would need to know some detail of what had happened to her eight years before.

All right, she thought, she would send for the records. What harm could it do?

FLINT SHOVED ASIDE his newspaper and glared at his children. "Is anyone going to let me eat breakfast in peace?" he demanded.

"You already ate your breakfast," Caitlin said.

Flint glanced down at his plate. The frozen waffles had disappeared, but he couldn't remember tasting them. "Maybe," he said, "but I didn't enjoy it."

First Caitlin had nagged about wanting to enroll at Serena Academy. Then Brick had joined the chorus, claiming he hated his old school and never wanted to go back. That didn't make sense, since his marks were excellent.

The only one who hadn't pestered Flint had been Aaron. The boy was surprisingly quiet this morning.

"Here." Flint pulled a dollar from his pocket and handed it to Aaron. "You're the only one who's been good.... You aren't sick, are you?"

Aaron shook his head.

"Is there some reason you aren't talking to me?" Now that he'd vented his annoyance, Flint was starting to worry.

Aaron nodded.

"Can you tell me what it is?"

Aaron shook his head. The boy was hopeless.

"He wants to be an actor," Caitlin interjected. "Maybe you could drop by Serena and talk to the theater teacher."

"You should meet her," Brick said. "You might like her."

"As a teacher," Caitlin added quickly.

Flint lifted an eyebrow at Aaron. "You want to be an actor?"

The little boy nodded hesitantly.

"Well, we'll see." Flint had no intention of paying a call on a teacher today. On the other hand, Caitlin's suggestion had jogged his memory.

On a previous visit to Serena Academy, Flint had noticed the theater building sitting in a grove separate from the main campus. The brick structure looked older than the others and therefore potentially more dangerous, but he'd assumed it must have been reinforced at some point.

What if it hadn't? He would need to know that before he even considered enrolling his children. Besides, being able to report on a clear-cut problem would bolster his presentation to the board.

It was only seven o'clock. Flint decided to swing by the campus before school started.

Since he had no meetings until tonight, he put on casual slacks and a polo shirt. As soon as Maureen arrived, he promised again to advertise for a nanny, then drove to Serena.

Leaving his car in a central lot, Flint strolled down a pathway toward the theater building. Towering trees filtered the early morning light, providing a sense of entering a mysterious realm. He could see where the name Serena came from.

It took several minutes to reach the theater building, a two-story adobe affair. As he rounded one side, Flint found to his surprise that a modern addition had been tacked on. The glass-walled studio, its roof sloping down to one-story height, jutted onto a lawn surrounded by a tall hedge.

Then he heard the unexpected tinkle of piano music. A Scott Joplin rag, if he wasn't mistaken.

Standing in the shadows of the hedge, Flint could see someone dancing inside the studio. Judging by her well-shaped figure and graceful movements, she was too mature to be a student.

He gritted his teeth. Flint had come early to get a discreet look around. He'd planned on finding a custodian to let him inside. He certainly didn't want some instructor watching over his shoulder.

Couldn't the woman work out at a gym like normal people?

She'd left a side door ajar. It opened directly into the studio, Flint could tell, but if she didn't want to be disturbed, she should have locked it.

In fact, he thought as he strode forward, the woman was downright careless. Didn't she know that an open door posed an invitation? He hoped she wasn't as careless of the children's safety as she was of her own.

As he neared the entrance, Flint got a good view of the woman's back. The pale blue leotard and tights outlined a slim body with a nipped-in waist and gently rounded hips. Although tall, she moved with a lightness that made her appear to float.

As he stepped through the door, the woman spun around in a dance position that Flint thought was called an arabesque. Catching sight of him, she stopped dead.

From the shocked blue eyes to the honey-blond hair, there was no mistaking the nitwit who'd showered him with stars. She actually taught at Serena Academy?

Flint was glad he'd dropped by. No way on earth was he entrusting his children to this woman's care.

THE DANCE WORKOUT was Robin's favorite part of the day. The exuberance of movement combined with the invigorating music to give her a sense of peace that carried through the rest of the morning.

The shock of turning and seeing a man inside the studio sent her heart hammering into her throat. The initial panic ebbed when she recognized the arrogant face of Flint Harris, but his disapproving frown rubbed her the wrong way.

"Something you need?" Robin didn't mean to sound ungracious, but the man had a talent for irritating her.

"I'm inspecting the premises." From the way Flint's eyes roved across her body, that wasn't the only thing he was inspecting.

"Go ahead," she snapped. "Who's stopping you?"

Flint didn't move from his position. "It's not exactly safe, leaving the door open like that." With his broad shoulders and tall build, he gave the impression of blocking the exit.

"I can take care of myself," Robin said.

"And the children?" he returned. "Do you imagine you could protect them from intruders? This building is isolated."

She couldn't believe his nerve. Before her brain could click into gear, Robin found herself stalking forward until only a few feet separated them. "Try me," she said.

Disbelief twisted his mouth. Without warning, powerful hands gripped her arms and spun her around, holding her backward against his chest.

Robin threw herself into the air and kicked upward with the agility only a dancer could possess, her heel aimed right at Flint's most sensitive region. One hand loosened its grip on her arm, only to seize her ankle and throw her off balance.

With her foot held aloft and one arm immobilized, Robin felt herself pitching forward at a dangerous angle. Just as she registered the fact that she couldn't break her fall, powerful arms encircled her chest and caught her in mid-plunge.

Robin felt Flint's forearm pressing into her breasts as he held her. Worse, in this position her buttocks were positioned hard against his groin. She hadn't had contact this intimate with a man in years, and Flint Harris was the last person on earth Robin wanted to get intimate with.

"Put me down!" she said.

He gave her a final squeeze, as if to emphasize his mastery, then released her. When she stood upright, Robin discovered her ankles could barely function. She hated the sensation of being weak from relief, but if Flint hadn't grabbed her when he did, she might have suffered serious injury.

"Still think you can protect the children?" he challenged.

"I've been teaching here for three years and no one has attacked me yet." Robin tried to keep the quaver out of her voice. "At least, not until today."

"I was just honoring your request." To her fury, Flint sounded amused. "As I recall, you asked me to try you. I won't speculate about the possible interpretations of that offer."

Without giving her time to reply, he sauntered across the studio and into the interior hallway.

Only as her breathing slowed did it occur to Robin to wonder why Flint Harris was paying special attention to the theater facility.

He'd better not give her any trouble tonight. She was in no mood to put up with any more of his shenanigans.

FLINT TRIED to pretend he was paying attention as the board meeting droned on, reviewing budget items and the hiring of a new assistant principal. But his gaze kept sneaking to Robin Lindstrom.

She sat two rows ahead of him on the aisle. From this angle, he could see the soft curve of her cheek and the well-shaped shell of one ear bared by an upswept hairstyle. She'd abandoned her workout clothes for a flowing dress printed with summer flowers.

Unbidden, an image returned of her face radiating fury as she confronted him in the studio this morning. Flint had grabbed her only to demonstrate her vulnerability, and been surprised by the quickness of her response.

He could still feel the twist of her taut muscles and the unexpected pressure of her buttocks against his groin. He could trace the soft roundness of her breasts beneath his arm, the nipples coming alive at his touch.

With an inward shudder, Flint realized he was becoming aroused at the worst possible time and place. He regained control of himself by steering his thoughts to the dull discussion under way by the board.

Beside him, he heard Aaron whisper something and Brick whisper back. Flint shushed them sternly.

Caitlin leaned over to look at his agenda. Her finger traced the item right before his presentation. "A Dance to the Spirit of Learning, presented by the students of Miss Lindstrom."

She turned away and the whispering started again. Flint glared at his children until they fell silent. What on earth was wrong with them tonight?

Perhaps the auditorium itself was distracting them. The board held its meeting in the school theater, the very building he had inspected this morning.

A long table had been set up on the stage for the five trustees. Behind them, incongruously, stood a painted backdrop depicting colorful tents, an elephant and two clowns. The stage set gave unexpected humor to the proceedings.

Suddenly a group of students raced down the aisle past Flint and onto the stage, taking positions directly in front of the trustees.

Their leotards and tights were spangled with stars. Flint wondered whether Robin had used the same type of gummed stars she'd dumped over his head, and which still kept turning up in his pockets and shoes.

Robin took a position to one side and switched on a tape, and the little dancers began jumping around like hop toads. The movements probably provided them with good exercise, but otherwise Flint found the proceedings extremely silly.

He heard his offspring mutter, "She's pretty." "Kind of grumpy, don't you think?" "She's just concentrating." They must be talking about Robin, but he couldn't imagine why. He'd never known his children to take such interest in a teacher, especially one whose class they hadn't taken.

And never would take, he reminded himself.

As he watched the dance, however, something struck Flint. At first, he'd assumed the kids were flinging themselves around more or less at random.

After a while, though, he realized their movements corresponded to Robin's subtle nods. She must be counting along with them, registering each leap and twirl.

The spontaneous quality of the dance disguised the fact that it was rigorously planned and executed. Any display of discipline among young people impressed Flint, and he had to admit that he hadn't given Robin enough credit. She might be a loose cannon when it came to civic demonstrations, but apparently she knew how to manage her students.

A smattering of applause greeted the finish, augmented by Caitlin, Brick and Aaron jumping to their feet and cheering. Flint gestured them firmly to sit down and, one by one, they plopped into their seats.

What had piqued their interest? He'd suggested ballet lessons to Caitlin once and she'd snorted in disgust. Later, he'd heard her recounting the exchange to her brothers and grunting like a warthog until they fell on the floor laughing.

"Next we have a proposal from Flint Harris to analyze seismic hazards on campus," announced the board secretary, and the chairman gestured to Flint.

He carried a sheaf of papers to the microphone. "As you know," Flint began, "Harris Seismology Inc. has been retained by the city of Beachside to recommend changes in the city code. We're proud of our record . . ."

He went on to cite a few of his company's accomplishments, then noted that he had made a preliminary tour of Serena's premises. All of the buildings, he understood, had met state earthquake safety standards when the school opened twelve years earlier. Since the Northridge quake, however, scientists had learned more about how to reinforce buildings. With that in mind, Flint continued, he believed the campus was due for a reassessment.

From his position at a right angle to the board, he could see the audience, including Robin Lindstrom. She leaned forward in her seat, watching him with narrowed eyes. Wrenching his thoughts away from her, he forced himself to focus on his report.

The board members looked only mildly interested, he noticed as he wrapped it up. They might hire him on the recommendation of their attorney, but they would take their sweet time about it.

The Beachside city job would be completed soon and he could use the work. Besides, the safety of students might be at stake.

"I do have one emergency recommendation." Flint gauged the effectiveness of this statement by the sudden silence that fell over the audience and by the way several board members' eyes snapped open.

"Emergency?" said the board's attorney, who sat at the end of the long table.

"The oldest building on campus is the theater arts structure, which dates back to 1937," Flint said. "The very building in which we sit. As you know, an addition was made in 1965."

"That building was reinforced when the school opened," the chairman pointed out.

"I understand that," Flint said. "But I made a preliminary inspection this morning and found that the addition has substantially weakened the building. You see..."

He launched into an explanation of how, to survive an earthquake, structures must be able to roll with the shock waves. Any portion that reacted to stress differently from the rest of the building was likely to tear away, resulting in collapse.

"I'd recommend closing the building immediately," he said. "At least until I can make a more detailed analysis of the stresses involved." Several trustees glanced nervously at the ceiling, as if they expected imminent collapse.

The chairman thanked Flint gravely. "I think we've all learned something important tonight."

One of the two women board members took the microphone. "Mr. Chairman, I believe we should pass an emergency measure closing the theater building. This is an important safety issue."

The chairman nodded. "Does anyone wish to comment? Miss Lindstrom?"

Robin wore a stunned expression as she took the microphone. Returning to sit beside his children, Flint felt a twinge of guilt. He hadn't considered how his recommendation would affect her.

Of course, the well-being of the students came first, but he wouldn't be too thrilled if someone came in and shut down his office without warning, and he didn't expect Robin to be, either.

"Mr. Harris spent only a few minutes at the theater this morning," she was saying in a clear, steady voice. "I know because I was there.

"I'm as concerned about safety as anyone. But this building, with the addition, has stood for thirty years. During that time, Beachside has felt a number of moderate quakes."

From the mass of curls piled atop her head, a tendril had escaped onto her neck. As Flint watched, another strand slipped loose. He had the sense that they were the least of the things falling apart in Robin Lindstrom's life at the moment.

"Our campus is overcrowded already," she said. "There's nowhere to move my classes to, and spare performance space in Beachside is practically nonexistent.

"For many of my students, theater and dance are the part of school that excites them. They learn discipline because it's necessary in order to perform. They keep up their grades because otherwise they won't be allowed to take electives."

Taking a deep breath, she concluded, "I don't think an educated guess by Dr. Harris is a good enough reason to deprive my students of their classes."

As she walked to her seat, he observed Robin's hands clasped tightly as if to prevent trembling.

Had he made a mistake? Flint wondered. He didn't think so. The building looked unsafe to him. But had he been unduly influenced by his dislike of the teacher?

"Any risk is unacceptable where children are involved," the board chairman said. "Any further comment? I call for a vote."

The motion to close the theater building passed unanimously.

"I'm sorry, Miss Lindstrom," said the chairman. "You're one of our best teachers. But as you pointed out, there's nowhere else to hold your classes. I'm afraid we'll have to put you on leave until this issue is resolved."

With an uneasy feeling, Flint saw what he'd done. Although he could complete his analysis in a matter of weeks, it might take months or years to raise the funds to retrofit the building.

Thanks to him, Robin Lindstrom had just lost her job.

Chapter Three

"How could you?" The low, angry growl came from Caitlin.

Flint stared at her in surprise. Surely the children hadn't been that determined to study theater. Or, if they were, he could find another school for them.

Yet all three of his offspring were shooting murderous looks in his direction. Flint wondered if he would ever understand them.

After the meeting broke up, instead of filing out of the row, Aaron began to sniffle.

"Cut it out." Flint handed his son a tissue. "You're too old to make a scene."

"He isn't making a scene," said Brick. "You are." The boy glared at his father.

Normally, Flint wouldn't tolerate back talk, but he didn't need a hassle right now. "We can discuss this in the car."

Aaron examined the tissue as if he'd never seen one before. "Daddy, can't you hire her as our nanny?"

For a moment, the whole Harris family stared at Aaron. Then Caitlin said, "Brilliant."

What the hell was brilliant about it? "She's a teacher, not a housekeeper," Flint said. "Blow your nose and let's go."

"She needs a job," Caitlin persisted. "Maybe she'd do it for a few months."

"That's not long enough," Aaron said.

His sister poked him with her elbow. "Maybe she'll like us enough to stay."

How could he tell them that Robin was too emotional, too irrational and far too sensual? The children weren't old enough to understand the dangerous chemistry that could spark between a man and a woman.

Lifting his head, Flint spotted Robin standing in the midst of a tearful crowd of dancers, her arms draped around their little shoulders. She looked vulnerable and very much in need of a masculine protector. But it wouldn't be him.

When it came to a housekeeper, Flint needed someone dutiful and dull. Robin Lindstrom failed to fit the job description in either particular.

"I'm going to ask her," Brick said, and strode down the center aisle before Flint could stop him. Caitlin raced after her brother, and Flint was only able to grab Aaron.

"I won't do you any good," the little boy advised. "I'm not in charge here."

"Neither am I, it seems," grumped Flint, and started after his children.

THE EVENING'S EVENTS had proceeded so quickly, Robin could hardly grasp that the theater building was going to be shut down, effective immediately.

Her summer classes were just beginning to gel, and now they had ended. What would happen to her students? she wondered, and then another thought hit her. What would happen to her?

She had no money in reserve. Her finances were so drained by student loan payments that she barely made her rent each month. Public schools wouldn't be hiring teachers until September, which was two months away.

Reluctantly, she let go of her students and waved good-bye as they straggled off with their parents. She couldn't let herself break down. She had to take action. But first she had to figure out what kind of action was possible.

Robin was about to collect her purse when she noticed a young boy approaching. Despite his youth, he had a sturdy, take-charge air.

"Miss Lindstrom?" His eyes were as fierce and blue as her own. "My name is Brick and we want Dad to hire you as our nanny."

A blond girl with a precociously mature expression hurried up beside him. "We need someone to take care of us, Miss Lindstrom. My name is Caitlin. We're the Harris triplets and we don't have a mother. We're practically orphans."

"Orphans?" Robin raised one eyebrow. She knew children had a tendency to overdramatize, but this girl spoke with such adult self-assurance that it was hard to discount what she said.

Besides, if they were triplets, where was No. 3?

"Please disregard the intrusion. My children tend to be impulsive." Flint Harris strolled toward her, another boy in tow. These were his kids? No wonder they felt like orphans. The man was an emotional wasteland.

And triplets, she guessed, would take a lot of patience, a quality that Flint seemed to have in short supply.

As she regarded him, Robin realized she'd forgotten Flint's gift for giving shape and definition to a business suit. The finely woven cloth emphasized his broad shoulders and chest, while the starched collar provided only a thin veneer of civility.

The man must work out daily, she thought, probably on a computerized machine. She wouldn't be surprised to discover that he actually *was* a computerized machine.

The second little boy twisted away from Flint's grasp and ran to Robin. "Are you our mother?" he said.

The poor kid must be desperate for affection, she thought.

"Really, I am sorry." The irritated voice sounded anything but apologetic. "I don't know why my children are bothering you, but I certainly didn't put them up to it."

"Is that the only thing you want to apologize for?" Robin snapped. "The fact that your children are lonely and in need of attention?"

If she'd slapped him, she couldn't have produced a more outraged response. "For your information, my children are neither lonely nor in need of attention. What they are is headstrong and defiant. As for apologizing, if you're referring to losing your job, I regret it but I don't see what else could be done. If you weren't so emotionally overwrought, you'd see it, too."

"Overwrought?" At the moment, Robin had to admit, the description fitted her state of mind, but it was Flint's fault, not hers. Besides, with the theater now empty except for the five of them, she saw no reason to hold back. "You're a fine one to talk! I've never met a man so out of touch with his own emotions."

"I'd say you were a little *too* in touch with your emotions, Miss Lindstrom," Flint replied.

Robin resented having to tilt her head back to meet his gaze. He had no business being so tall. "You're a cold man who hasn't got a clue about human behavior. Your children are crying out for help. Maybe I do fly off the handle a little too easily. Maybe I am a soft touch for a suffering youngster. But I'll take that any day over an iceberg like you."

"What you are," Flint returned, "is a person who lacks self-discipline. You may have the credentials to work for a school, but you have nowhere near enough maturity to work for me."

"Well, I'm not working for you." Robin spun away, then paused to respond to the children. "I'm sorry, kids. Your dad and I just don't get along."

"You would if you knew each other better," Caitlin said.

Robin suppressed a shudder. "I'm afraid you're being overly optimistic."

"What's overly optimistic mean?" asked the smaller boy.

"It means thinking I can make a silk purse out of a sow's ear," said Robin.

"That's a pig," explained the little girl.

"She called Dad a pig?" said the boy named Brick.

The smaller boy bit his lip until his sister began snorting in a fair imitation of a pig, and all three burst into laughter. Even Flint chuckled.

"I didn't mean that literally," Robin said, then noticed the effect of a smile on Flint's face.

The transformation was startling. For the first time, the man appeared human. Not only human but warm, inviting, even tender. His hard gray eyes softened and his mouth curved as if inviting her to sample it.

In that moment, the space between them seemed to take on a form and texture of its own, a kind of liquid sultriness. She wondered how that hard mouth would feel pressed against hers.

Cold, Robin told herself. Like ice.

"I have to go," she said. "Kids, thanks for the vote of confidence. I hope I see you again."

"We hope so, too," said the larger boy.

"Soon," said his brother.

"We leave nothing to chance," said the girl.

"Neither do I." Flint was all hard edges again. "There'll be no television tomorrow. You kids know when you've gone too far."

As she walked away listening to their howls of protest, Robin wondered how a stuffed shirt like Flint Harris had managed to produce three such expressive kids. In some ways, their spontaneity reminded Robin of herself.

She imagined the trait drove their father crazy, and profoundly hoped so.

WHOEVER COINED the expression "You can't go home again" must have had living with Gigi in mind, Robin reflected two weeks later. Moving in with her mother had been a mistake, but one that she was powerless to rectify.

It was a Friday afternoon and she'd just returned from interviewing for a job at the new experimental school, A Learning Place for Children. It didn't surprise Robin to find the Fortunes Told Here store crammed with her mother's tarot-reading students, but she hadn't expected to run into more people upstairs.

The living room, which had doubled as Robin's bedroom for the past week, was filled with an odd mixture of people, all sitting cross-legged on the floor murmuring variations on "om," such as "um" and "hum." One old lady seemed to be meditating on "tums." Robin wondered what she'd eaten for lunch.

At the front of the room, the toga-clad man with long white braids sat with crossed arms and legs on the coffee table. Above his head hung a blackboard on which was scribbled "Higher Consciousness Class. J. Caesar, Instructor."

His "om" had mutated into a motorlike "vroom vroom" and, eyes shut, he held up two fists, palms down, rotating them as if driving a motorcycle.

Robin spotted the résumés she'd left on the coffee table now lying in one corner of the room. Several had been crumpled beyond repair.

Moving in had seemed like a good way to save money. So had taking a part-time job as a waitress. Now Robin's shoulders and back ached from carrying heavy trays and her life felt as if it were rocketing out of control.

At least she could afford to meet her student loan payments, she reflected. But if a teaching job didn't materialize soon, she didn't know what she was going to do.

Not stay here, that was for sure, she mused grimly as the white-haired man peered up and winked at her. "Got any beer?" he asked.

"The only spirits we have around here are dead ones," she told him.

The other students were eyeing her in disapproval, so Robin went downstairs. Gigi wasn't much of a businesswoman, but she was probably charging these people something, and Robin didn't want to interfere.

As the tarot class began breaking up, Robin helped herself to a cup of coffee from the urn and waited until her mother was free. Gigi fluttered over to her, past racks of New Age books and mystic paraphernalia. "How did it go, darling? Did you get the job?"

"I won't know for weeks, maybe longer." Robin rubbed her legs, sore from wearing high heels to the interview. In two hours, she would be hefting a heavy tray again at the coffee shop. "Mom, do you think it's wise, letting a nut like Socrates teach students?"

"He isn't Socrates, he's Julius Caesar," Gigi reminded her. "You know, he renounced all his worldly goods to pursue a life of meditation."

"Meditation and beer," corrected Robin. "By the way, I'd appreciate it if you'd ask him to be more careful of my things. I can't afford to keep printing résumés."

"No need for résumés. The right job will present itself." Gigi nodded sagely. "Fate is taking a hand in your life. Recent events have made this clear."

Something in her tone made Robin set down her coffee cup. "Mom, what's going on?"

"You'll see for yourself." As if on cue, the front door opened with the tinkle of wind chimes and in blew Gigi's friend Irma.

Irma couldn't have been more than seventy-five, but thanks to heavy smoking and hard living she looked as if she'd recently awakened from a mummy's tomb. Small and wizened with clawlike fingers, she was a whiz at frightening children on Halloween even without a witch's hat.

"We'll have to move up the séance," she told Gigi. "I can't make it tonight. My grandson is being bar mitzvahed."

"I knew you'd come early," Gigi said. "That's why I dismissed my class ahead of time."

Irma looked impressed.

The thump of footsteps on the outside stairway told Robin that the meditators were departing. She hoped Julius would go with them.

"It's a bit early in the day for a séance," Irma observed, "but I think we can make it work."

Gigi put up her Gone to Commune with Spirits sign and closed the shop. The two of them went upstairs, Robin tagging along.

Her chief worry ever since her mother got mixed up in the occult was that at some point Gigi might go off the deep end. Her second concern was that her mother would get caught up in something dangerous. Whatever her mother and Irma were doing, Robin wanted to keep an eye on them.

She wasn't reassured to find the white-haired man still in the apartment, wolfing down a tuna fish sandwich at the table. "Meditating makes me hungry," he explained.

"Good," said Irma. "You can help us create a strong energy for Mortimer." That was what Irma called the spirit guide who supposedly spoke through her during séances.

"Wait a minute." Gigi faced her friend. "It's *my* guide we're going to use. Horatio is the one who brought us Frederick."

Frederick, Robin supposed as she helped clear Caesar's lunch dishes from the table, must be the restless spirit her mother had mentioned a few weeks ago. Gigi had learned in a later séance that he was searching for a woman from his past.

That wasn't a lot to go on. Probably, Robin thought, because Frederick was a figment of her mother's imagination, like Horatio the spirit guide.

"Now, dear," Irma said, "Horatio is a fine guide, but he's so young. Only—what—a hundred years old? Whereas Mortimer, as you know, recently celebrated his two-hundred-and-fiftieth birthday."

"Frederick won't come to Mortimer." Gigi planted her hands on her hips.

"It can't hurt to try, can it?" countered Irma.

Robin wished the two women would stop trying to one-up each other. She also wished her mother had some normal friends.

"Well, I've only got a couple of hours before work, so we'd better get started," she said. A séance could drag on for a long time, depending on who was conducting it and how chatty the guide felt.

The blinds were already shut against the mid-afternoon sun to accommodate the meditation class. When Gigi turned out the lights, the room sank into a yellowish gloom.

The four of them sat around the table, Gigi at one end and Irma at the other. Robin was glad she didn't have to hold hands with Julius, although she felt his foot bump hers more often than necessary.

Irma began to work herself into a trance. Gigi had stopped fighting the older woman's attempt to seize control, Robin observed, and wondered if there was a rule of etiquette about hogging a ghost that had been discovered by a friend.

"I call upon my spirit guide. Oh, Mortimer, speak to us...." Robin relaxed and let Irma's voice wash over her. She'd participated in a couple of séances before and found them entertaining, if silly.

Suddenly Irma's voice deepened and took on a pseudo-English accent. "Yes, I am here. I come to advise and guide you. I am Sir Mortimer."

Irma's face and manner changed until she almost physically became an elegant man of a previous century. The power of self-delusion, Robin mused.

What happened next surprised her.

"But I should not be here," said Mortimer. "There is another guide, Horatio. I call upon Horatio."

Irma' s muscle tone slackened. Robin felt a jolt of electricity pass through her and then, without preamble, Gigi spoke from the other end of the table in the Southern-accented tones of Horatio.

"I have before me the spirit of Frederick. He is deeply troubled. He seeks your help."

Her mother's acting skills deserved a more worthy forum, Robin thought. A person might almost believe Horatio was real, if the whole idea weren't so preposterous.

"What kind of help? May we speak with him?" Gigi asked, this time in her normal voice.

Abruptly, her manner changed yet again. She stiffened, her jaw tightened, and she seemed to Robin to grow taller. "I am Frederick." The voice was hesitant but definitely masculine, without an accent. "Please help me. I must find the woman I love."

"Who is she?" Irma asked.

"There is a link," said the spirit called Frederick, speaking through Gigi. "A link to someone here. Someone named...Roberta. Or Rose."

"Could it be Robin?" suggested Irma.

Spare me, Robin murmured to herself. Why on earth did her mother want to drag her into this foolishness?

"Yes, it is someone—not close to Robin—but someone she will meet soon. She must help.... I am called away.... I must go," said the voice of Frederick, fading fast.

Had his celestial beeper gone off? Robin wondered, indulging in a little sarcasm. Or might there be a spiritual pizza deliveryman at the door?

The voice of Horatio returned. At Gigi's request, he tried to find Frederick again so they could continue the questioning, but the other spirit had departed.

Gigi fell quiet. Gradually her facial muscles relaxed, and then she opened her eyes.

"You see?" she told Robin. "I wanted you to hear that."

"Why?" Robin said. "You know I don't believe in that stuff."

"Well, you should," said Irma.

"You need to keep your eyes open," Gigi added. "Frederick said you would meet the woman soon."

"I meet lots of women at the coffee shop. What am I supposed to do, ask every one of them if she has an ex-boyfriend who's dead?"

"You'll figure something out," said Gigi. "You're smart."

Robin heaved a sigh. The story had been so vague—like everything else that emerged from her mother's otherworldly dabblings—that she doubted even Sherlock Holmes could have found a useful clue. Furthermore, Robin had enough to worry about at the moment without chasing down some woman who probably didn't exist.

Irma departed to dress for the bar mitzvah, and Julius wandered out to the beach, where a volleyball game was under way. With a sigh, Robin went into the bedroom to put on her waitress uniform.

When the phone rang, Gigi ran to answer it, calling, "It's about Frederick's lover! I can feel it!"

The caller turned out to be the coffee shop manager. "I'm sorry," he told Robin when she picked up the phone. "We had a little accident and we have to close the restaurant for a couple of weeks."

"A fire?" she asked in dismay.

"No," he said. "If you can believe this, a man was trying to make a U-turn and his accelerator stuck. He crashed through our front window and took out a row of booths. Fortunately, no one was hurt."

The man promised to call Robin when the place reopened, and hung up.

"Fate," crowed Gigi when Robin told her the news. "The spirits want you to work elsewhere."

"Then why don't they offer me a job?" she grumped.

She couldn't believe she'd lost two jobs in two weeks. Now what was she going to do?

With a sigh, Robin pulled on her bikini. Until her benumbed brain clicked into gear, she might as well get some exercise.

THE VOLLEYBALL GAME was a pitiful mismatch, Flint noticed as he strolled along the boardwalk. Two young men, a middle-aged woman in cutoffs and an old man in a toga were beating the daylights out of two young women and a boy of about thirteen.

He checked his electronic notepad. The address given him by the academy belonged to a fortune-telling shop, which had an oversize sign and a flimsy facade.

Maybe Miss Lindstrom rented the apartment above it. How typical that she would unthinkingly pick such a dangerous place in an earthquake. Beaches had sandy soil, which magnified the intensity of the shaking. Not only would that sign and the false front collapse, but the whole building might go.

The volleyball flew past, and a woman from the losing team darted past to swoop it up. She had pink hair to match her torn T-shirt. It featured a spider on the front, which, in turn, matched the spider tattooed on her shoulder.

"You're a bit out of your league, aren't you?" Flint observed as the player trotted by.

She surveyed him from the tips of his jogging shoes up his slacks to the polo shirt. "We could use some help. How about it?"

Flint was about to beg off when he noticed the other woman on the redhead's team.

If Robin Lindstrom looked good in a dance studio, she was nothing short of a knockout on the beach. Honey-colored hair floated around her shoulders, and her skin gave off a golden sheen, every bare inch of it, from her lively face down to her long, slender legs.

Her bikini left very little to the imagination. No need to speculate about the rounded fullness of her breasts or the slimness of her waist. A man could almost feel how she would melt beneath him.

Flint took a deep breath. He had come to offer Miss Lindstrom a job, not to seduce her.

Chapter Four

"You people need to get organized," Flint said as he removed his shoes and joined the team.

Robin shot him a look of pure horror. He supposed that, from her point of view, he deserved a measure of dislike, but Flint didn't take much interest in other people's points of view.

He knew what mattered—hard work, responsibility, achievement. When life threw you a curveball, you learned to hit curveballs.

These people couldn't even hit a volleyball headed straight toward them. "Fan out," Flint advised. "You're leaving half the court uncovered."

"There is no court," grumped Robin, moving as far from him as possible.

"Picture it regulation size," snapped Flint. He had no patience with foot-draggers.

They managed to keep the ball in play for several volleys, but the skinny white-haired man in the toga moved like greased lightning. "He's amazing," Flint admitted as he chased the ball. "What does that guy eat?"

"Chocolate chip cookies, tuna fish and beer," Robin said.

After a while, they rotated positions, which gave Flint a better view of Robin. He tried to keep his eye on the game, but beach volleyball was a sport with many interruptions. Dogs walked across the court, kids ran after beach balls and oblivious strollers failed to notice the players until they came nose to nose with the net. He had plenty of time to ogle Robin.

It must have been her dance training, because she had a body like no one else on the beach—tighter muscles, slenderer thighs, firmer breasts. Flint tried not to remember how she'd felt in his grasp, hard against his groin and soft beneath his arm. He tried not to imagine how she would look if that bikini bra vanished—something any strong wind could accomplish—or how her blond hair would fan out across a pillow.

He'd become involved in only one affair since Kathy's death. The woman had been an executive who hired his company's services. Her interest in his personal services had been confined to lunch-hour trysts.

Her no-nonsense approach to lovemaking had appealed to Flint at first, but finally he realized that he'd chosen her because he wasn't ready for any deeper attachment. The affair ended when the woman was transferred to another city, and neither of them regretted it.

He had a feeling that if he followed his instincts where Robin was concerned, they might both regret it very much.

The light began to fade. Although opinions varied as to the score, the volleyball game ended in an obvious victory by the other side, and the players dispersed.

The pink-haired woman thanked Flint for his help and gave him another thorough examination. He excused himself and went to Robin.

Her lips were pressed together as she regarded him. "Have you come about the sign?"

"The sign?" Flint repeated.

Angrily, she pointed to the fortune-teller's shop. "My mother's sign. It violates your earthquake codes, you'll remember. I suppose you want us to pull it down."

"I don't enforce the city codes, which by the way haven't been approved yet," Flint said. "I'm just an adviser. No, I came about you."

Sunlight gleamed off the smooth curve of Robin's throat and flared in her blue eyes. "This better not be personal."

Flint couldn't believe her nerve. "If I want something personal from a woman, I don't ask permission first. Frankly, I don't need to."

"That's right, I had a demonstration of your caveman technique at the studio, didn't I?" She tossed her mane of blond hair. "I suppose some women find that impressive."

Flint could feel his hands flexing with an urge to grasp this maddening woman and give her another sample of his caveman abilities. He wished he knew why, within minutes of encountering Robin Lindstrom, his entire body tingled with desire and his temper steamed on the verge of a full boil.

Coming here had been a mistake. He couldn't possibly hire her as a housekeeper, no matter how desperate the situation.

"Obviously, this isn't going to work..." he began, when an apparition floated toward them through the twilight.

Silvery folds of gauze fluttered in the breeze as an ethereal being coasted across the boardwalk. Ghostly arms spread wide as the creature swooped with inhuman grace.

Nearby, a toddler stood frozen in fright and a dog whined. Beachgoers stopped in the midst of collecting their gear and stared.

The vision in silver jerked abruptly, flailed through the air and collapsed onto the sidewalk. "Oh, spit!" it exclaimed in a woman's voice.

"Mother, please." Robin strode to the creature and helped her up. "Don't you think you're a little old for this sort of thing?" A veil had fallen to reveal shocking red hair and a rouged face that Flint recalled from the City Hall demonstration.

"I was just getting the knack of these things," the woman said, lifting the edge of her gown to reveal in-line skates. "Some bozo left trash on the sidewalk and I tripped over it."

What kind of mother zoomed around wearing a ghost costume and in-line skates? Flint wondered. The same kind of mother who operated a fortune-telling shop, he supposed.

At least Robin Lindstrom came by her eccentricities the honest way.

"I'd better be going," Flint said, and was about to depart when the red-haired woman skated over and nearly collided with him.

"I'm Gigi Lindstrom," she said. "How nice to see you again, Dr. Harris."

"You aren't worried about your sign?" he said, and immediately regretted the wisecrack. "Sorry. Your daughter seems to think I'm following her around trying to make her life difficult."

"You do tend to have that effect." Robin tried to pull her mother away. "Mom, it's time for dinner."

"You came to offer her a job, didn't you?" Gigi said.

"Actually..." Flint stopped himself on the point of blurting that, in his opinion, Robin was unsuited to work for him or anyone else.

He'd been acting on impulse ever since he arrived, joining the volleyball game and trading barbs with Robin. It was time he regained control. Or at least a measure of proper manners. "You're a very perceptive woman, Mrs. Lindstrom, but..."

"I knew it!" Gigi crowed. "The spirits have been predicting your arrival."

It struck Flint that a logical connection was missing in this exchange. Gigi had no way of knowing why he'd come. He certainly didn't believe any spirits had told her. She must be a victim of wishful thinking—or worse.

He was about to set her straight when Robin said, "Dr. Harris didn't come to offer me a job, Mother. The only job he has available is for a nanny, and Dr. Harris believes I am the last person on earth who's qualified to care for his children. Did I leave anything out, Dr. Harris?"

What she left out, Flint reflected, was the fact that for two weeks his children had made his life a misery. Aaron sulked, Caitlin wheedled and Brick had resumed a childish penchant for throwing temper tantrums.

The respondents to Flint's want ad had included three women who spoke no English, a man with shifty eyes, an eighteen-year-old girl with no experience and an older woman who wore biker boots and chewed tobacco.

The only likely prospect had been chased away by the children's rudeness. He'd never seen the triplets so determined and so unified about anything. Then Maureen announced that she was going on a trip to Hawaii next week and he would have to shift for himself.

The only possible salvation that came to mind was Robin.

Flint had reminded himself that Robin was well-liked by her students. His check with the school had produced a glowing recommendation, and he decided to give her a chance.

Surely, with a little guidance, she could learn to uphold his high standards. Flint knew how to supervise employees, and he was certain he could make Robin Lindstrom shape up.

Nothing had really changed during the volleyball game, had it? The children still wanted her. The school still recommended her. Maureen was still leaving.

"The fact is," he said, "I did come here to offer you a job. As my housekeeper and nanny. The pay is less than what you received at the school, but room and board are provided, plus benefits after a trial period of two weeks."

"You'd expect me to live with you?" Robin said. "Dr. Harris, under no circumstances could I possibly—"

"Wait!" cried Gigi, waving a hand for silence. "Did you hear that?"

"What?" said Robin.

"There's someone in the apartment," she said.

Robin shrugged. "It's probably Julius, snarfing down a sandwich."

"I'll investigate," Flint offered. "Wait here, Mrs. Lindstrom."

"No, no." Gigi blocked his path. "If you would just walk me to the foot of the stairs, I'll go up. Sometimes, you see, I am visited by mischievous spirits. If a stranger were to enter, there's no telling what they might do."

"Honestly, Mother." Robin expelled an exasperated breath. "You can't expect a scientist like Dr. Harris to believe such hogwash."

Flint was pleased that Robin didn't share her mother's metaphysical leanings. However, he didn't mind humoring the old lady. "I'll walk you to the stairs, if it will set your mind at rest."

Gigi smiled at him, linked her arm through his and pushed off on her skates so fast that Flint had to lope to keep up.

At the foot of the staircase, which ran between her establishment and a surf shop, she sat and removed the skates. Then she skipped upward, the skates bouncing over her shoulder, and disappeared.

From where he stood, Flint could see Robin tapping her foot impatiently on the sidewalk. He marked it as a good sign. Perhaps she wouldn't tolerate nonsense from his children, either.

It puzzled him for a moment that he found himself wanting to hire her when a short time before he had rejected the idea. Was it only the memory of the last two weeks of nanny wannabes that had inspired the change?

With an inward smile, Flint realized his true motivation. He was going to save Robin Lindstrom from herself. Growing up with such a scatterbrained mother, it was no wonder she'd turned out so unpredictable.

But inside, he believed, dwelt the soul of a schoolmarm. He would help her to achieve her true potential, and she in turn would guide his children. He would take this undisciplined woman and teach her how to make use of her talents.

If only he could persuade her to accept the job.

A moment later, Flint received help from an unexpected source. Upstairs, he heard Gigi call out, "No, you mustn't!" and then a lace-trimmed teddy soared out a window.

"Mom, what are you doing?" Robin raced forward, snatching the undergarment from midair. "That's my stuff!"

"It's the spirits, dear," came her mother's quavery voice. "They're in a terrible mood!"

Two blouses and a skirt heaved themselves out the window next, followed by the flowered dress Robin had worn to the school board meeting.

"Do stop! Do stop!" cried Gigi overhead, not very convincingly, in Flint's opinion.

As Robin ran about collecting her clothes, two leotards and a pair of tights followed. Flint debated whether to embarrass her by helping, then decided she couldn't be any more distressed than she already was.

Soon his arms were filled with a pink nightgown, a pair of jeans, a Joffrey Ballet T-shirt and a pair of low-heeled pumps.

"Stop now! Stop!" cried Gigi inside the apartment as more items came fluttering down. "Oh, dear!" She stuck her head out. "Is everything all right?"

"I'll never forgive you, Mother!" Robin yelled, her arms piled with clothes.

"It isn't me, it's the spirits!" Gigi waved her hands in distress. "I'm so sorry! I'll clean it all up, I promise!"

Robin bit her lip, tears of frustration glimmering in her eyes.

"I wouldn't want you to accept the job under duress," Flint said. "But I do think you should give my offer serious consideration."

She sucked in a long, shuddering breath. "Well, Dr. Harris, it appears the spirits want me to take the job. Or at least, my mother does." She grimaced as a pocketbook came flying toward them.

Flint executed a catch worthy of his football days at the University of Southern California. "Yours, I presume?"

"Let's go dump this stuff in my car," Robin said with what dignity she could muster. "Then, well, I suppose it wouldn't hurt to go talk to your kids."

ROBIN PUT ON SHORTS and a camp shirt over her bikini. She couldn't believe she was getting dressed in the parking lot—and in front of Flint Harris.

She also couldn't believe her mother had pulled that stunt. Restless spirits, indeed!

It soothed her temper to watch the military precision with which Flint folded her clothes into the trunk of her car. His strong hands aligned and positioned each dress and blouse to leave it wrinkle-free. Left to her own devices, Robin would have stuffed everything inside and regretted it later.

Only when she noticed Flint manipulating her lingerie did it occur to Robin that this was getting too personal. "I'll do that." She moved forward, brushing against him in her hurry to reach the undergarments.

His mouth tweaked into a smile. "I do have a daughter, you know. I'm not easily embarrassed."

"Well, I am."

Flint swung aside to provide access to the trunk, but at this close range she could feel the heat rising from his skin. It occurred to Robin that she hadn't finished buttoning her camp shirt, which hung open to give a candid view of her bikini bra.

Well, it wasn't anything he hadn't already seen, was it? she reminded herself as she poked her underwear into a semblance of order.

"My mother is a bit on the flaky side." Talking about Gigi made her less self-conscious about Flint's powerful frame looming inches from her body. "I never know what she's going to do."

"Does she actually make a living telling fortunes?" he asked.

"In a sense." Robin made a mental note that at least her mother hadn't pitched down the résumés, probably more from a desire not to litter the beach than from any concern for Robin's feelings. "She holds classes and sells books and trinkets. People are fascinated by the occult."

"Are you?" Flint's breath whispered across her neck. Why did he have to stand so close? Was he trying to intimidate her?

"I'm interested in the fact that people are fascinated by the occult. We all seem to have a need for something deeper than everyday life. But I certainly don't buy all this gobbledygook about spirits." Intent on her words, Robin turned toward him, only to discover that Flint was even closer than she'd thought.

His thigh pressed against hers, his throat was level with her lips, and she caught a whiff of after-shave lotion mingled with musk. It penetrated directly to her brain, leaving her powerless to withdraw.

"So people feel a need for something deeper," Flint repeated in an amused baritone. "How about you, Miss Lindstrom? Are you looking for something deeper?"

Annoyed that he was toying with her and even more annoyed with herself for responding, Robin slammed the trunk so hard that Flint winced. "Is this some kind of power play, Dr. Harris?"

"Excuse me?" One eyebrow lifted.

Had she misunderstood? Maybe he hadn't intended any sexual connotation. "You're purposely putting me at a disadvantage, looming over me this way," she finished lamely.

"Let's just say that as a seismologist, I enjoy shaking things up." With a low chuckle, Flint led the way to his Volvo. Robin fought off an impulse to stand her ground defiantly. It wasn't as if she had anywhere else to go.

Still, as she strapped on her seat belt, she wondered what on earth she was doing here. She had no serious intention of accepting a job that involved living in the same house with Flint Harris.

On the other hand, she needed a cooling-off period before she returned to confront her mother.

He put the engine into gear and headed out of the parking lot. Despite the car's roominess, there was barely enough space for Flint. He filled it with a muscular form that seemed designed more for wrestling mammoths than for steering a Volvo.

Robin had never met a man so irritating, or so enticing. With her blond hair and long legs, she'd attracted her share of guys over the years. The cute surfers tended to come up short in the brains department, and the more solid business types treated Robin like a trophy. She'd survived a few semi-serious relationships, but in the end she'd always chosen freedom.

No one had challenged her mentally and physically the way Flint did. If he weren't so rigid, she might actually be attracted to the man.

That admission bothered her. What she needed now was a job, not a boyfriend. Not even a boyfriend who was offering her a job.

But then, Flint had given no indication of wanting any romantic involvement. Robin tried to picture the kind of woman who would appeal to him and kept coming up with Sigourney Weaver in *Working Girl,* a hard-as-nails executive with the instincts of a killer.

She felt a wave of sympathy for his children. They really were cute kids. If they belonged to anyone else, Robin would love to take care of them.

A few minutes later, Flint turned down a side street that led into a homogenized housing development. Robin remembered when it had been built, during her teenage years. All those cookie-cutter structures going up at neat intervals had made her want to run in the opposite direction.

She had to admit now that the homes were attractive, modern with a hint of Spanish influence in the stucco walls and tile roofs. If only they weren't painted such boring earth tones. If only the vegetation appeared to have grown here naturally instead of having the clipped look of nursery transplants.

She wondered if children were allowed to play kick the can on these manicured lawns, and doubted it. They probably spent all their spare time at organized soccer matches and Little League games.

At the touch of a button, a garage door opened and they pulled inside. Robin wondered how she would differentiate this house from all the others, and then reminded herself that she wouldn't need to.

Flint unlocked a small door from the garage. It led into a hallway.

For a moment, Robin thought no one was home. It was hard to imagine three children occupying a place in such utter silence.

"This way." Flint escorted her into a family room.

Except for a low couch and a television set—turned off—the place looked more like a laboratory than a den. A desk had been set up with a computer, and a table was covered with a maze and a glass box of dirt that probably housed some form of insect.

"Where are your kids?" Robin felt a twinge of concern.

Flint frowned into the air. "Do you smell anything?"

She sniffed. "It smells like something burned."

Before she could finish, he strode past her to the kitchen.

Following, Robin saw a woman standing with arms folded, glaring at the stovetop. Dressed in a shirtwaist buttoned from throat to mid-calf, she appeared almost as large as Flint and, if possible, sterner.

The stovetop was covered with black goo. "During my afternoon nap, Brick chose to conduct a scientific experiment on the stove," the woman announced. "It does not yield to conventional cleaning materials."

"I'm sorry." Flint let out an exasperated breath. "I was hoping they wouldn't get up to their old tricks. Aunt Maureen, I'd like you to meet Robin Lindstrom, our new nanny."

"I didn't agree to—" Realizing that Maureen had thrust out her hand, Robin hurried to grasp it. The grip was brief but bone-crunching.

At the same time, the older woman gave Robin a disapproving once-over. Her gaze didn't miss one detail of the bikini bra straps or the tiny shorts, which had seemed perfectly appropriate at the beach.

"My airplane leaves in three hours," Maureen said. "I've been planning this trip to Hawaii for months and I don't plan to miss it. Pleased to meet you, Miss Lindstrom. I trust you'll dress more suitably in future."

With a crisp farewell to Flint, Aunt Maureen headed for the door. Robin regarded her with a measure of awe. The woman appeared capable of outgunning even her intimidating nephew.

Flint lifted a note attached to the refrigerator by a magnet. "Tom will be here at one tomorrow. Leave a key under the mat," he read. "Tom's our handyman. But what are we going to do without a stove?"

"We could microwave," Robin suggested. "I mean, *you* could microwave." The house felt surprisingly empty, considering how many people were supposed to be here. "Where are your children?"

"In their rooms, I presume." Flint glared at the stove. "Damn. She didn't even cook dinner."

The housekeeper was expected to cook, too? Robin grimaced. She knew how to make two things—spaghetti and macaroni. Both required packaged mixes.

"We'll just have to order pizza," she said.

Flint's gaze traveled from the stovetop to her. "Pizza?" he said.

Robin planted her hands on her hips. "Don't play innocent. There isn't a parent on earth who hasn't sent out for pizza."

"Miss Lindstrom." Flint drew himself up. In a kitchen designed at woman height, he towered. "In my house, we do not order pizza. We make it from scratch, using healthy, low-fat ingredients."

"If you want scratch, you'd better find a housekeeper with an itch." Robin indicated the wall clock, which was edging toward seven o'clock. "Now I suggest we locate your children. They've been awfully quiet."

The first room they inspected belonged to the two boys. Equipped with bunk beds, a large bureau and two small desks, it was noteworthy for the number of paperbacks crammed into a bookcase and the odds and ends visible through the half-open sliding doors of the closet—polished rocks, Legos, a magnet and several test tubes. Robin imagined there might be small animals living in that closet, possibly of the amphibian persuasion. Plaques engraved with the names Aaron and Brick indicated which bunk belonged to which.

There were no children in sight, however.

Caitlin's room next door had been decorated with pink flowered wallpaper and lacy curtains. On a window seat, a Raggedy Ann doll flopped on a stack of computer manuals. There was no one else around.

The youngsters had obviously fled either from their aunt's wrath or from the boredom of being sent to their rooms. Or both.

With a muttered oath, Flint stalked through the house. "Where the hell did those kids go?"

For a man with a strict nature, he didn't have much control over his offspring, Robin reflected. Of course, children had to suffer the consequences of their actions when they misbehaved. At the same time, her teaching experience had taught that discipline worked best when children were offered a carrot along with the stick.

But at the moment, the issue was where to find the runaway children, not how to handle them. "Do they have friends nearby?" she asked.

Flint shrugged. "I have no idea. Let's go see if their bicycles are missing."

There were no bikes in the garage, and a side door had been left unlocked.

"How far are they allowed to ride?" Robin asked.

"Two blocks in any direction," Flint said. "Let's go. It'll be dark soon and I have no idea how long they've been gone."

As they cruised the streets in the Volvo, Robin felt herself softening in response to Flint's obvious worry. He even stopped to ask a couple of pedestrians if they'd seen the children, but no one had.

At the farthest edge of the search area sat a small shopping center. Flint swung into the parking lot to turn around.

"Look." Robin indicated a shadowed corner by a gift shop that had closed for the evening. In the twilight, she could make out the shapes of bicycles.

Robin felt her heartbeat slow in relief. As for Flint, judging by the way he clenched his jaw, his anxiety was rapidly turning into anger.

As he parked, she noticed light pouring from a pizza parlor that advertised arcade games. "Do your kids get an allowance?"

"If they do their chores," Flint said grimly. "And there's nothing they love to spend it on more than games."

Robin told herself that this whole affair was none of her business. She hadn't accepted the job, and she couldn't possibly live with Flint. She would have to put up with Gigi's offbeat ways for a little longer, she told herself as she hopped out of the car and trailed after Flint.

Inside the pizza parlor, a family of four sat in a booth eating and a man waited at the take-out counter for his order. Otherwise, the only occupants were three small figures hunched over a video game, their backs to the door.

Caitlin occupied the driver's seat. As she twisted the joystick, her brothers whooped and bells rang. Even from behind, their small figures vibrated with enthusiasm.

In a flash, Robin saw that all the scoldings and punishments in the world would never dissuade these youngsters from treating themselves to a good time. Especially not when what waited at home was a cheerless housekeeper and a politically correct dinner.

Still, they couldn't be allowed to defy authority and get away with it.

As Flint started forward, Robin placed a hand on his arm. "Why don't you let me handle this?" she said.

"I don't know why you think you can succeed where—" He stopped himself in mid-sentence. "Very well, Miss Lindstrom. This should be interesting."

Interesting indeed, thought Robin. She hoped a plan came to her quickly, because at the moment, she didn't have the slightest idea what she was going to do next.

Chapter Five

"Congratulations," Robin said from behind the children. "You're the big winners."

The trio swung around with expressions that were almost comical in their astonishment. Three pairs of eyes, remarkably dissimilar for triplets, swiveled first to her, then to their father, then back to Robin.

"It's her," said the smaller boy, who must be Aaron. "Are you really our mother?"

"Nanny," corrected Brick. "He's kind of dumb sometimes."

"Don't call names," Caitlin said primly. "And of course she's going to be our nanny. Didn't I tell you?"

"That remains to be seen." Robin found herself reluctant to tell the children she wasn't staying. Besides, she didn't want to get sidetracked. "Your father's been worried about you. We searched all over the place."

"Oh, nothing's going to happen," said Caitlin. "We're careful." She indicated three bicycle helmets awaiting them on a table. "We always follow the rules."

"Which rules?" snapped Flint from behind Robin. "The ones you make up?"

Robin glared at him. "You promised."

Flint gave a tight nod, his eyes narrow with the effort of reining in his temper. "All right."

The children's jaws dropped. Apparently they'd never seen their father squelched before, at least not by anyone other than Aunt Maureen.

Robin pretended an interest in the score flashing on the video screen. "That's impressive," she said. "You kids didn't spend all your money on games, did you?"

"Oh, no!" Brick pulled a crumpled envelope from his pocket. "I've got four dollars left."

Caitlin patted the breast pocket on her denim shirt. "I've got six."

From his pocket, Aaron pulled a worn leather wallet that must have once belonged to his father. "And I've got eight!" he crowed.

"He hoards it," explained Brick.

Robin breathed a sigh of relief as inspiration struck. "Well, I think it's nice of you kids to treat your father and me to pizza."

"Treat?" said Caitlin. "In your dreams." Realizing she'd just addressed Robin the way she would talk to one of her brothers, she said, "I mean, we're kids. We don't pay for stuff like that."

"I presume that stunt with the stovetop was no accident," Robin said. "What was your aunt planning to cook for dinner?"

"Ugh. Liver and onions," blurted Aaron.

"Well, you children fixed it so she couldn't cook dinner," Robin said. "Some parents would make you pay for the stove repair, but I'm afraid that will cost more than, let's see, eighteen dollars. However, we could get a large pizza and a pitcher of sodas for that. Maybe a salad, too."

"No salad," said Brick.

"Salad," said Flint.

The children's shoulders sagged. Robin almost felt sorry for them.

"I guess so," said Caitlin.

"If there's any change, can I have it?" said Aaron. "I'm putting up the most money, so it's only fair."

"Sounds reasonable to me." Robin had to fight back a grin as the other children grimaced at their brother. Apparently Aaron wasn't as much of a pushover as he appeared.

Soon the kids were absorbed in choosing the toppings. Half the pizza had to have pepperoni and mushrooms, while the other half featured olives and—at Robin's suggestion—pineapple. After their initial distress, the children became excited about the fact that they were paying for it themselves.

Flint wore a bemused expression as he rounded up plates and flatware. He approved of her disciplinary tactic, Robin could tell. The children weren't sulking, yet they'd learned a lesson.

The challenge of finding a creative way to deal with the children reminded Robin of the excitement of being a teacher. She would never have sought out a position as a nanny, but it definitely beat waitressing. As a temporary position, this job might not be so bad after all.

How long was Aunt Maureen going to stay in Hawaii? she wondered. Surely she wouldn't go all that distance for less than two weeks.

That was the exact length of the trial period. Robin didn't believe the spirits had arranged things this way, but she did appreciate the coincidence.

She could help Flint by staying for two weeks, and help herself at the same time. By then, she might hear from the experimental school or land more interviews from the résumés she'd sent out. If not, she could always stay longer if the job proved bearable.

Besides, the children needed a new approach to discipline, since whatever Flint was doing obviously didn't work. Robin didn't imagine she could psych them out all the time—they were smart little rascals—but she hoped to teach them to regulate their own actions instead of trying to outwit authority figures.

The most difficult part would be getting Flint to see things her way, but Robin figured she could handle him. How could one man be any harder to manage than a whole classroom full of children?

WATCHING ROBIN with the children filled Flint with conflicting emotions.

She had a gentler manner than any of the other nannies, and the kids seemed to respond. But once her newness wore off, he felt sure, contempt would set in. Maybe she needed to learn the truth the hard way—that if you gave children an inch, they'd take a mile.

When bedtime came, Robin's inexperience showed. She averted her eyes in embarrassment when the boys ran around naked, and she didn't inspect their teeth-brushing closely. But those lapses were to be expected in someone unused to parenting.

The only problem, from Flint's point of view, arose when Robin read the children a Magic School Bus book for bedtime. Aaron crawled onto her lap, Caitlin drooped against her shoulder and Brick curled around her feet. They hadn't acted that way since Kathy died.

He didn't want anyone, even Robin, to come here and take Kathy's place. Already, he worried that the children were forgetting their mother. They took less interest these days in the scrapbook full of her pictures, and Caitlin had stopped playing the tape of children's songs that Kathy had made, accompanying herself on the guitar.

Flint wandered to a window and stared into the night. He felt as if he should apologize to Kathy for bringing this stranger into their house.

Then, gazing into the darkness, he remembered the fear that had gripped him earlier as he searched for the children. Worse than anything would be to let harm come to his youngsters. For at least a few weeks, Robin would keep them safe. He had to accept her until Maureen returned.

And probably by then the children's usual high jinks would have returned full force. Now that he thought about it, Flint supposed one reason he didn't get too angry was that the escapades were never directed at him. And, in a way, the fact that the children flouted their caretakers proved that deep in their hearts, they still wanted their mother back.

He turned to observe Robin. Lamplight bathed her and the children as they clustered on the couch, creating a bright oasis in the dimness of the family room.

Oddly, she and the children resembled each other. Brick's eyes were the same shade of blue. The curve of Caitlin's cheek and the delicate shape of her ears were quite a bit like Robin's, and as for Aaron, his eager expression matched hers twinkle for twinkle.

It must be a trick of the light.

Robin read with animation, varying her voice and widening her eyes to stir the children's interest. She didn't look much older than they were.

Images crowded into Flint's mind—Robin leaping for the volleyball, unselfconscious in a bikini. Robin running around in front of her mother's shop, catching clothes and nearly crying in frustration. Robin pressed between him and the trunk of her car, making his breath come fast.

Living in such close quarters with her might be tempting fate, but Flint could deal with it. The fact that it was the first time in three years he'd experienced such sharp desire only meant that he was finally healing. It certainly didn't mean he intended to pursue a relationship with someone as incompatible as Robin Lindstrom.

The story ended, and he went to kiss his children goodnight. Then, before calling a cab to take Robin home, he drew up a work contract that ensured she would belong to him for at least two weeks.

ALL THE WAY HOME, Robin wondered if she'd done the right thing.

The contract had caught her by surprise. There was nothing objectionable about it—it simply set forth the terms of her employment, her wages and day off and the fact that she agreed to work for Flint for a two-week trial period. After that, either of them was required to give two weeks' notice for termination.

She hadn't been expecting to sign anything, but why not? As soon as she'd scribbled her name, Flint had handed her a key and instructed her to move in at ten o'clock the following morning.

On her way out, Robin had noticed that her room was on the far side of the house from the other three bedrooms. That would give her a measure of privacy, but then, having any bedroom to herself was an improvement over living at Gigi's.

Flint had paid the driver in advance, but Robin tipped him extra when they stopped at the beach. She knew how hard cab drivers, like waitresses, worked for their money.

And housekeepers, she told herself. The contract called for meal preparation and light cleaning. A service came in biweekly during the summer to vacuum and mop, Flint had said, since she could hardly be expected to perform those chores with the children underfoot.

It was the meal preparation part that bothered Robin, but she put it out of her head as she strolled along the sidewalk toward her mother's shop. What could be hard about tossing a few dishes on the table, in this age of frozen chicken nuggets and instant mashed potatoes?

Robin debated about retrieving some clothes from her car, but decided to borrow one of Gigi's caftans to sleep in. Her mother could hardly object.

"Well?" Gigi challenged when she let herself into the apartment. The older woman, wearing an embroidered kimono and full makeup, sat at the table eating ice cream.

"I start work tomorrow morning." Robin tossed her purse aside and began opening the couch into a bed.

"I knew it!" Gigi crowed. "Want some ice cream?"

"No, thanks."

"You always sleep better on a full stomach," her mother said.

"I have a full stomach. Mom, about that stunt with my clothes..." Robin wasn't sure what to say next. She knew her mother had meant well. But it was the sort of trick she would expect children to play, not a woman approaching sixty. "Anyway, I hope you're not matchmaking, because you're going to be disappointed," she finished.

"Matchmaking?" said Gigi. "Not at all. I'm thinking of Frederick."

"The ghost?" Robin retrieved her pillow from a closet.

"He wants you in this position, I'm sure of it." Gigi downed a bite of chocolate ripple. "I'll help you get to know the neighbors. The children's friends and their families, too. I'm sure we can find that woman he's seeking."

This was an angle Robin hadn't figured on, that her mother would want to get involved in Flint's household. "No way," she said. "You don't know my new boss. He runs a tight ship."

"Sounds like he'll be good for you," Gigi observed. "I've always said you lack discipline."

This remark was so completely out of sync with reality that Robin didn't know how to answer.

Ever since her father left them when she was twelve, she'd virtually raised herself. Gigi had been too busy working to provide more than basic necessities and occasional advice. Robin had worked part-time during high school, then put herself through college with hard work and long hours. If anything, she'd had too much self-discipline for a girl so young.

But her mother could be counted on to do or say the unexpected. That was exactly what was worrying Robin at the moment.

"Frederick or no Frederick, you're not going to camp out at Flint's house," she told Gigi. "The kids and I need time to get acquainted."

And Flint needed time to see that Robin could manage the job, she reflected. The man might even learn a few things about how to work with children. On the other hand, with his thick skull, he probably wouldn't acknowledge that he'd ever been less than perfect.

"Don't worry." Gigi waved a hand dismissively, splattering drops of chocolate against the wall. "I'll give you a while to get established." She peered into the ice cream container. "You know, there's not enough here to save, but I'm full."

Robin hadn't intended to eat any, but she considered it a sin to waste ice cream. "I guess I could eat it," she said, and fetched a spoon along with a paper towel to wipe up the mess.

Only when she had finished the container and caught the grin on her mother's face did Robin realize she'd been manipulated. It gave her the uncomfortable sense that it might not be easy to keep Gigi from getting involved in the Harris household, or from doing anything else her mother wanted.

The very thought of Gigi invading Flint's turf gave Robin the cold shivers. Or maybe, she told herself, it was just the effects of the ice cream.

FLINT WAS channel surfing from bed when he glimpsed something on the local cable station that made him stop.

It was the demonstration at City Hall from several weeks ago. The programmers must be in the summer doldrums, he reflected, if they were rerunning boring news in case anyone missed it the first time.

But something about the scene wasn't boring at all. Right in the foreground, Robin marched beside Gigi. The older woman waved a placard that read, This Medium Isn't Happy.

Now, how had Flint managed to miss that?

The camera lingered on Robin. Flint hadn't noticed what she was wearing at the time, but now he saw that she'd thrown a wraparound skirt over her usual leotard.

The woman moved like a dancer, even during a protest march, and the camera admired every inch. In fact, the cameraman must have developed an instant crush, because the picture played from a shot of the two women to a close-up of Robin, then trailed down her throat and dwelled on the soft swell of her breasts beneath the stretch fabric.

Flint was about to make a protesting phone call to the station when he realized the cameraman had been focusing on Robin's necklace. From it dangled silver letters that spelled out, Save Us.

No slogan had ever received so flattering a display.

Flint lay back against the pillow, trying to tell himself that having Robin living in the house wasn't going to bother him. He'd passed adolescence long ago.

She was pretty, of course, but he could resist that. He could resist her impish grin and the way she lifted her chin defiantly, and her tenderness with the children, and her well-toned dancer's body....

As the camera moved on to other marchers, a dream slipped beneath his eyelids, one of those reveries that almost passes for reality. Flint and Robin were standing in a grove of trees, alone on the school grounds, and she was showing him her necklace close up.

The silver letters kept falling beneath the scooped neck of her leotard, so he pulled the cloth down, revealing full breasts tipped in pink. For some reason, neither of them seemed to think there was anything odd about Flint examining Robin's bosom along with her necklace.

He was about to bend down for a better view when music interrupted his concentration. Startled, Flint heard "I Wanna Hold Your Hand" and was debating its meaning in the context of Robin's breasts when he realized the TV picture had changed. The shots of the demonstration had been replaced by changing placards announcing upcoming city events, accompanied by the music from an oldies radio station.

Damn it, he'd been dreaming about Robin like a schoolboy. Disgusted with himself, Flint switched to a sports channel and finally fell asleep to highlights of a Dodgers game.

THE MAIL ARRIVED early at Gigi's place. Robin hurried downstairs when she heard the creak of the mailbox, hoping to find a response to one of her résumés.

Her mother was finishing a breakfast of Pop Tarts and coffee when Robin returned, sorting through bills and circulars. "Anything interesting?" Gigi asked.

Robin handed her a copy of *ESP Today* and a wad of advertisements. It was amazing how many products were manufactured about the occult, from books and tapes to special lighting supposed to enhance the odds of spotting a visitor from the Beyond. Gigi must be on every mailing list.

At the bottom of the stack, a thick manila envelope bore the return address of the fertility clinic. Robin glanced at it, realized that it contained her medical records and set it aside.

"Mom." She wanted her mother's full attention, so she sat next to Gigi and stared her directly in the eyes. "I did some thinking last night. Very hard thinking."

"Did you eat breakfast?" Gigi asked. "I didn't see a dirty plate. It's the most important meal of the day, you know."

"I'm not hungry." Robin refused to be distracted. "Listen. It's about Flint Harris and that ghost of yours."

"Not mine," her mother protested. "Horatio brought him."

"Horatio, Mortimer Snerd or anybody else, I don't care," Robin said. "I don't believe in ghosts. If you want to, that's your privilege. But there is no way I'm letting you disrupt my new job. I have a responsibility to Dr. Harris."

"Last night you referred to him as Flint," said Gigi.

"I don't care if I referred to him as Count Dracula," Robin said, "the point is, I've made up my mind. I'm happy to bring the kids here if you want to meet them, but I don't want you visiting me there. It's inappropriate."

"I can't visit my daughter in her own home?" Gigi squeaked. She looked genuinely distressed, but Robin knew her mother possessed considerable acting abilities. How else did she manage that show-and-tell business with Horatio at the séances?

"It isn't my home, it's my place of employment," Robin said. "I don't recall you feeling the need to observe me at school, did you? I have Sundays off and I promise to visit. You can call me if there's an emergency. Otherwise, Mom, I mean it. No pestering Dr. Harris *or* his kids with any of this ghost nonsense."

"I wish I could persuade you to believe." Gigi rested her pointy chin in the palm of her hand. "From the very beginning, you've been a skeptic, haven't you?"

"I think I've been remarkably tolerant." Not for the first time, Robin felt as if their roles were reversed and that she, not Gigi, was the parent.

"I didn't invent Horatio," her mother went on. "I feel him inside me. I don't know what all this is about. Maybe there's some scientific explanation and we just haven't discovered it yet. But the ghosts are real. I'm convinced of it."

Robin clasped her hands together, hanging on to her patience. "I know you're sincere. And as long as you're dealing with other people who share your beliefs, that's fine. But Flint doesn't. I can't let you disrupt his household, interview his neighbors and interrogate his children's friends. And I refuse to do it for you."

Gigi's mouth twisted in disappointment. Robin knew her mother wouldn't take no for an answer, not for long, but maybe she'd keep her distance for a few weeks. "If you insist."

"I do insist, Mom," Robin said. "Now I'm going to pack the few items you didn't toss out the window."

"Not me. The spirits," Gigi corrected.

"Whatever."

Her mother tapped her fingers rapid fire on the table but apparently couldn't think of anything to say that might change Robin's mind. "I'll go open the store a little early. I have a feeling that's what I ought to do."

"Sounds good to me," said Robin. "And Mother, I love you."

"I love you, too," said Gigi. "But I don't know how I ever got such a pigheaded daughter."

After her mother left, Robin made a quick check of the premises, rounding up her toothbrush and cosmetics and some china figurines of dancers that she'd collected as a teenager. It was amazing how the spirits had managed not to throw anything breakable out the window.

As usual, her mother had left the blinds in an almost shut position, casting a filtered gloom through the apartment. Robin felt as if she were suspended in a twilight time, an unrecognized period between night and day.

You could almost believe in ghosts, living here, she thought as she stripped her sheets from the bed. She collected her towels and threw the lot into a compact washing machine off the kitchen.

Standing in the tiny utility room, Robin scribbled a note reminding Gigi to put the laundry in the dryer. Then she checked her hair in an aging mirror and tweaked her bangs into place. An oxidized film dimmed the glass, making it hard to see clearly.

The haze seemed to deepen and swirl, as if there were something within it. Robin shook her head and looked again. She hadn't been mistaken. The diffuse shape of a face was appearing in the mirror, like something from a scary movie.

Now she understood why people pinched themselves to see if they were dreaming. But she was standing square on her feet and she could hear the washing machine churning behind her, although her head did feel a bit light.

Robin wouldn't put it past her mother to engineer some special effects. She reached out and touched the hard glass. It felt solid.

The face, a man's face, became more clearly defined moment by moment. He couldn't have been older than thirty, his hair close-cropped in a style that reminded Robin of the 1950s. He stared at her with dark, pleading eyes.

"Who are you?" she asked.

He seemed to be searching for words, and then his lips began to move. He repeated the same phrase over and over, until she understood.

He was saying, "Help me."

"Help you?" Robin couldn't tear herself away. "Help you how?"

The vision in the mirror faded. She put up her hand but encountered only cold glass. There was nothing before her but a flat surface marred by her handprint.

The face belonged to Frederick. Robin knew it with a chilling certainty. Or could this be a trick of Gigi's?

Carefully, she removed the mirror, which hung by a metal wire from a nail. The frame was thin and didn't appear to contain any inner works. There were no trick wires, and no sign of anything electronic.

Had Frederick's ghost really just appeared to her? If so, she'd been wrong about a lot of things.

Robin didn't like to think about what Flint might say. On the other hand, there was no reason he had to know.

Still undecided whether to trust her own eyes, she replaced the mirror and went to the living room to pack her few remaining possessions. Robin was about to slip the manila envelope from the clinic into her suitcase when she decided to open it.

If it contained anything of interest, she'd keep it. But if, as seemed likely, it only described a basic examination and the unremarkable results, there'd be no point in hanging onto it.

It felt good to have something ordinary on which to focus her scattered thoughts. Robin tore open the envelope and scanned the contests.

A brief letter explained that this was in response to her request, and so on. There followed a few pages with her slim medical history and the exam results, including a negative Pap smear.

Another form listed the drugs she'd been given to stimulate her ovaries, and there was a notation about the surgery to retrieve the eggs. Reading it made Robin feel queasy. How young and naive she had been, eight years ago. She couldn't imagine submitting to such a procedure now unless it was to have children of her own.

The last page of the records was the one that surprised her. A brief handwritten note had been photocopied, apparently by some inexperienced clerk, because Robin knew as soon as she read it that had never been intended to reach her eyes.

The note said: "Successful triple implant; recipient Kathleen Harris."

Chapter Six

Robin stared at the paper in her hand. She couldn't absorb what it meant.

Could Kathleen Harris be Flint's late wife? She wasn't sure. Then it occurred to Robin that the name Caitlin might be a variation of Kathleen. Besides, how many women named Harris could have borne triplets in Beachside seven years ago?

This was all speculation, she told herself, stuffing the envelope into the suitcase. It might be a coincidence.

Her mind in turmoil, Robin decided to stop at a coffee shop for breakfast. It would make her late to Flint's house, but she needed to calm down.

Besides, she'd already begun to blame hunger pangs for the apparition in the mirror. In her woozy state, the conversation with Gigi about ghosts must have implanted the idea in Robin's brain.

Implanted. She didn't want to use that word, not in any context.

Suitcase in hand, Robin hurried to her car. She refused to let herself think about anything except starting the engine, pulling out of the lot and finding a place to eat.

En route, she passed the café where she used to work, its window boarded over where the car had plunged through.

Had the spirits really engineered this whole business just to ensure she worked for Flint?

And if so, had the spirits done so for Frederick's sake, or for the children's?

You're cracking up, Robin told herself. *This is all nonsense.*

She stopped at a Coco's, found a booth and ordered breakfast. With the reassuring sensation of hot coffee trickling down her throat, she let herself mull over that shocking notation on her medical form.

Caitlin, Aaron and Brick might be *her* children. Impossible, unthinkable, out of the question. Robin liked them and she enjoyed working with youngsters, but she wasn't prepared for an instant family.

She certainly wasn't prepared for one that belonged to Flint.

The obvious course of action would be to telephone and explain that she'd changed her mind about the job. Unfortunately, she'd signed a contract, and Flint wasn't the sort of man to let her break it.

Maybe the kids weren't hers. Maybe his wife's name hadn't been Kathleen. Maybe the birth date would prove to be too early or late. She didn't know anything for certain.

And if she did, should she tell Flint?

He'd be furious at the invasion of privacy. Worse yet, those smart kids would eventually ferret out the truth. It would turn their world upside-down, and when Robin left, they'd be losing their mother all over again.

She had to keep this to herself.

Beginning to calm down, Robin reminded herself that this was only a temporary job. And, whether these children had grown from her eggs or not, she wanted to make sure they were safe and happy.

It would be especially important, she told herself as she spread jam on her toast, to make sure Flint nurtured the children's creativity. After all, if they were hers, Robin owed them that much. And if they weren't, well, they needed a chance to discover their potential anyway.

As she picked up her purse, she saw that she was going to be half an hour late to meet Flint. Not the best start, but it couldn't be helped.

Robin stood up, squared her shoulders and left a large tip.

HE SHOULD HAVE KNOWN she wouldn't be on time.

Sitting at the kitchen table, Flint rattled the newspaper in annoyance. He'd already wasted half the morning, and the children's schedule had been ruined.

Their constant queries about when Robin was going to arrive had nearly driven him up the wall. Finally, he'd sent them across the street to play with a boy and girl who were visiting their grandparents.

Flint tried to remember the grandparents' names. They'd lived across from him for eight years and often waved hello. Was it Andrews? Anderson?

His digital watch clicked to 10:36 as Robin's green compact pulled into the driveway. Flint restrained the urge to stalk out and confront her.

He opened the door as she was reaching for the bell. "I'm sorry I'm late," she said before he could speak.

"Very late." Flint stepped aside to let her in.

"Well, not *that* late." Robin brushed past him. She'd worn jeans over a leotard, not the sort of outfit he expected of a nanny. "I had to stop for breakfast. I didn't feel hungry earlier, and then I got dizzy. Where are the kids?"

"Across the street, playing." Flint knew he must seize control of the conversation immediately. "Miss Lindstrom, my children are supposed to follow a schedule, and you have disrupted it."

"It's Saturday." Robin carried her suitcase into the back bedroom, which in earlier years had served as Flint's office.

"I'm aware of the day of the week." Flint followed, wishing he had thought to carry the suitcase. Not that he was concerned about manners—he just didn't like the sense that Robin already felt free to make her own way through his house.

"On Saturdays, children are supposed to play." She clicked open the suitcase. There was hardly anything in it, Flint noted—a manila envelope, some knickknacks and a few cosmetics.

"Are your clothes still in the trunk?" When she nodded, he said, "I'll help you bring them in. Then we'll go over the schedule."

"You weren't kidding?"

"You don't know me very well, Miss Lindstrom."

Those blue eyes shot him a look of pure impishness, worthy of Brick at his worst. "Well, Dr. Harris, why don't you educate me? And could we cut this last-name business? If we're going to be living together, shouldn't it be Flint and Robin, or at least Daddy Flint and Nanny Robin?"

She began to chuckle at the absurd sound of the names. When Robin laughed, her face glowed and her body shook. The movement brought Flint's eyes to her throat, or rather to her necklace.

It resembled the one from the demonstration, except that this time it featured a silver pendant in the shape of a ballerina. The charm dangled into cleavage revealed by her low-cut leotard, and with a jolt Flint recalled his sensual dream of the previous night.

"Robin and Flint will do," he said. "But you're going to have to change your clothing."

"Excuse me?"

"What you're wearing is inappropriate." He marched to the double-width closet. Sliding open the doors, he indicated a half-dozen dresses. "These were left by some of your predecessors."

"They left their clothes?" From Robin's wide-eyed stare, he gathered that she might burst into laughter all over again. "Did they flee in that great a hurry, Dr. Harris? I mean, Flint?"

She wasn't far from the truth. Nannies had a way of beating a quick retreat from the Harris household, leaving no forwarding address to which he could send the clothes that had been overlooked in the laundry. Undergarments had gone to Goodwill, but Flint was glad now that he'd saved the dresses.

"I can't account for the slipshod packing of my previous employees." He wished he didn't sound so stuffy, even to his own ears. "Find something you like and put it on, please. I'll be back in a minute."

Flint hurried through the house and retrieved the computer-printed schedule that he'd left on his bureau. He hadn't meant to make an issue of it today—Robin and the children needed time to get acquainted. But her late arrival had underscored the importance of getting off to the right start.

He detoured outside and found, as he suspected, that she'd left her car unlocked. Popping open the trunk, Flint fetched an armful of clothes.

The garments had picked up Robin's fragrance, Flint noticed as he headed into the house. The light floral perfume brought every graceful inch of her sharply to mind. He wished now that he had paused to enjoy the sound of her laughter and the sight of her enlivening the back bedroom with her presence.

That, Flint told himself, was because he had no intention of allowing himself to enjoy Robin Lindstrom's presence in future. There would be no leotards, no silver pendants dangling into cleavage and, he admitted with a twinge of silent regret, probably not a lot of laughter.

He strode into the bedroom and dropped her clothes on the bed. "Let's go over the schedule," he began before he noticed what Robin was doing.

Stripped to her leotard, she stood in front of the mirror holding up a long, shapeless dark dress. "What do you think?" She twisted her blond hair into a semblance of a knot. "Maybe I could find one of those witch's hats they sell at Halloween."

Flint tried not to focus on the shapely body displayed before him. "I asked you to change your clothing, not parade around in a state of undress."

She tossed the dress aside. "Flint, I've danced in front of audiences wearing no more than this. We're going to be sharing the same house. I don't intend to put on a long robe and a veil every time I go to the bathroom."

"You have your own bathroom," he returned. "And I'm not employing you as a dancer. Are you under the impression housekeepers parade around in leotards?"

"For a man who hoisted me through the air and twisted me like a pretzel, you're pretty uncomfortable with your own body, not to mention mine," she snapped.

"I'd rather not mention yours." Flint surveyed the items on the bed.

"Don't tell me," Robin said. "Mentioning my body would be 'inappropriate,' is that right?"

"Put this on." He handed her a blouse. "And your jeans, of course."

Robin shrugged and took the garment. With what he could have sworn was deliberate provocation, she eased her arms into the sleeves and took her time fastening the front, leaving the top three buttons open. Then she yawned with a stretch that drew the fabric taut across her breasts.

The view made Flint yearn to rip the damn blouse off and teach this woman exactly what her seductive manner did to a red-blooded male. He decided that would be a bad idea.

"Here's the schedule." Flint thrust the printout at her. "They work on projects from nine to ten—Brick is testing worms in a maze, Caitlin is practicing touch-typing, and Aaron is learning to play the keyboard. That's on Tuesdays, Thursdays and Saturdays. They have alternate projects on other days. I'll give you a full week's schedule on Monday."

Robin opened her mouth as if to ask whether he was kidding, then appeared to think the better of it. "What about ten to eleven?"

"Bike riding. However, in view of last night's outing, I've allowed them to skip that today." Flint was proud of the schedule. He didn't believe children ought to waste their summer vacation in unstructured play, but he didn't want them turning into bookish nerds, either.

From eleven to twelve they performed household and garden chores. At noon, they ate lunch. From one to two, he'd scheduled lessons using workbooks.

From two to three the children were to read. At three o'clock they reported for a gymnastics class at the community center next to City Hall, followed by swimming lessons. At five, they returned home and watched an educational video while Robin prepared supper.

The program was thorough, balanced and productive.

"When do they have fun?" asked Robin.

"In the evening, we play games," Flint said. "Uno, jigsaw puzzles, Monopoly, checkers. Games that help with spatial development and mathematical reasoning. My children have good minds, and I intend to see that they develop them."

"What about art?" said Robin. "Self-expression?"

Flint didn't like to concede that she had a point, but he was willing to be flexible. "If they wish to paint, they can substitute that for quiet reading a few days a week," he said. "I'm not entirely rigid, you know. I allow them to play with friends instead of riding bikes once in a while, as you can see."

"Impressive," murmured Robin.

"You know where the community center is," Flint said. "I expect them to be on time this afternoon."

"Maybe we should synchronize watches." She flashed him a smile, then turned to tuck clothes into a drawer. "Did you bring my shoes?"

"Not yet." Realizing he'd left the trunk open, Flint hurried out and finished carrying in her possessions. "I have to drive to Claremont to do some work," he said. The city was located about an hour's drive inland. "I'll be back for dinner. We eat promptly at six."

"Yes, sir." Robin's arm twitched as if she was fighting the urge to salute.

Flint wished he felt as confident about her as he had about Nanny Strich. He decided he might come home early today, just to make sure everything was on track.

ROBIN CARRIED the printout with her as she crossed the street. She couldn't believe anyone would dream up a plan as strict as this for three seven-year-old kids on summer vacation.

Hadn't Flint ever been a little boy? Hadn't he spent hours lazing with a book or playing with friends around the neighborhood?

Robin knew there had to be a balance, that children needed adequate supervision. But among her students these last few years, she'd noticed a trend toward overscheduling. The poor kids were always being whisked off to some class or organized sport, with no time left for independent play. They ended up overstressed and dependent on others to entertain them.

She glanced at the schedule. Flint had gone to a lot of work to draw this up. She supposed she ought to give it a try.

When she introduced herself to the older lady who answered the door, the woman explained that she was Sarah Anders and that she and her husband were planning to take their grandchildren to the beach.

"I'm afraid we can't go." Robin consulted the schedule. "Eleven-thirty. It's almost time for lunch."

Mrs. Anders laughed. "Is he on that kick again? Every nanny he hires goes crazy trying to follow that thing."

Her husband, a short, merry fellow named Marty, poked his head in the doorway. "Did I hear you say lunchtime? Well, why not take a picnic to the beach?"

"I'd prefer to get off on the right foot," Robin was explaining, when the triplets ran whooping into the room.

"Robin! Robin!" they called and flew into her arms.

Brick, Aaron and even Caitlin seemed intent on all hugging her at the same time. Robin felt her knees wobbling and nearly collapsed beneath their combined weight.

Feeling their warm little bodies snuggling against her, she experienced a pang of disbelief. These might actually be her children. They might carry in their bodies the genes that shaped the history of her family and the same personality traits that guided her own life. She wanted very much to deserve their affection.

"Whoa!" She staggered against the door frame. "Hey, little guys. What's going on?"

"I've never seen them like this," said Sarah. "Usually when the nanny shows up, they barely acknowledge her."

"Except to put frogs in her pockets, I gather." Robin gave each child a light squeeze. "I'm flattered."

"You're not like *them*," said Brick.

"You're special," said Aaron.

"We're going to the beach, aren't we?" said Caitlin.

Robin exchanged glances with the Anders couple. "I think I get the picture. They're buttering me up."

"No, listen," said Caitlin. "We'll take our workbooks and our reading books and we can do all that stuff in between playing. I mean, there's nothing in the rules that says we have to study at home, is there?"

Robin had to admit there wasn't.

"We could take our gym clothes," said Brick. "And we'll wear our swimsuits."

"The community center is right on our way home," noted Caitlin.

"Please, Robin," said Aaron.

Sarah Anders gave her a knowing smile. "I'd say that was an offer that's hard to refuse."

"There goes Dad," Caitlin added.

Robin turned and waved as Flint's Volvo churned reliably down the street. "As long as we follow the schedule, I don't suppose it matters where we are."

She knew in her heart that Flint wouldn't approve, but darn it, today was Saturday, and how often did the kids have a chance to go to the beach with their friends?

She shepherded the youngsters home to change into beachwear and collect their towels. The three peppered Robin with questions and with accounts of the games they'd been playing that morning.

It amazed her that they accepted her so readily. Despite maintaining a friendly air, inwardly Robin wasn't sure she was ready for this cozy a relationship.

The more she looked at them, the more the triplets resembled a cross between her and Flint. But that might be her imagination. She didn't know anything about their mother's appearance.

While the kids disappeared into their rooms, Robin inspected the family room. She hadn't paid attention before, but one wall bore a dozen photographs of the children at various ages, and of their parents.

The late Mrs. Harris had a lovely face. Superficially, her coloring was similar to Robin's—blond hair and blue eyes. Unbidden came the thought that of course the clinic would have tried to match them.

But where Robin's eyes were bright blue, Flint's wife had eyes of a lighter shade. Her hair was ash light, not honey-colored like Robin's. Neither of those distinctions helped much, since the children showed a range that might simply reflect the genetic traits of both parents.

More telling was the fact that Mrs. Harris's face revealed sharp bone structure, possibly indicating Scottish descent, while Robin had the broader cheekbones of Scandinavian ancestors.

When the three children walked into the room, she could see her cheekbones echoed in Caitlin's and Brick's faces. Aaron showed signs of developing the more chiseled features of his father.

"Your mother was beautiful," Robin said. "What was her name?"

"Kathleen," said Caitlin.

Robin had thought she was prepared, but hearing the name spoken aloud sent a shiver up her spine. She felt a surge of sympathy for the woman in the photograph, the woman who had given birth to these precious children and had loved them so much.

"She must have been very special," Robin said.

"Daddy talks about her a lot," said Aaron.

"He doesn't want us to forget." Brick planted himself, legs apart, arms wrapped around a beach ball.

"Did you fix our lunch?" Caitlin said.

With a start, Robin realized she hadn't given it a moment's thought. "We'll buy something at the beach."

"Daddy doesn't like junk food," Aaron announced, only to be shushed by his siblings.

"He makes exceptions," Caitlin assured Robin.

"All the time," said Brick.

Robin couldn't help laughing. "Just this once," she said. "We really do have to follow the rules, you know. Everybody got their gym clothes and books? Let's go."

They squeezed into her small car and rattled to the beach, caravaning behind the Anders's sedan. Robin found it ironic that she parked not fifty feet from the space her car had occupied overnight.

As they joined the Anders family on the sand, Robin discovered how unprepared she was for dealing with children.

First Aaron pointed out that she'd forgotten the sunscreen. Fortunately, Sarah had brought plenty.

Then she realized she didn't have a blanket to sit on, either, so she settled for planting her jeans bottom in the sand.

Within five minutes, the children were complaining of hunger as they watched their two friends munch sandwiches. After treating them to hamburgers and sodas all around, Robin discovered that feeding four hungry people on fast food was a lot more expensive than buying a quick meal for herself.

If she kept this up, she would spend her entire salary before she received it.

When, after half an hour of romping in the surf, the children declared they were thirsty again, Robin wasn't about to cough up money for another round of soft drinks. Vowing to bring a thermos of lemonade next time, she left the triplets with Sarah and Marty while she trudged over to Gigi's apartment.

Naturally it proved impossible to escape without detection. As Robin came down the stairs with a bottle of fruit punch, her mother darted out of the shop, and Robin found herself filling in the details of the morning.

"Life is a perfect circle." Gigi closed the shop and hung her Gone to Commune With Spirits sign. "I knew the spirits would bring you here."

"The spirits had nothing to do with it," grumbled Robin as her mother followed her to the picnic scene.

The triplets bounded over immediately. Unlike most children, who never seemed sure whether Gigi might not be some kind of weirdo, the Harris triplets found her fascinating.

"Can we call you Granny Gigi?" asked Caitlin. "Our grandparents all live far away."

"Would you tell my fortune?" Aaron pleaded.

"What did you bring us to drink?" said Brick.

Delighted as always to find herself in the spotlight, Gigi agreed to be called Granny and told Aaron that his palm showed he was a very smart little boy. Finally the kids scampered off to build sand castles with their friends.

Robin's hope that her mother would go back to work were dashed when Gigi plopped herself on the Anders's blanket and began interrogating Sarah.

"How long have you two been married?" she asked, and went on to pose such questions as, "Did you ever know a young man who died?" and "Did you ever have an unhappy love affair?"

Sarah's frown lines deepened as she grew more and more confused. Robin was relieved when her mother's friend Irma arrived and called Gigi away to hear the details of last night's bar mitzvah.

"Your mother is an interesting woman," Sarah said tactfully.

Believing the truth to be the best policy, Robin explained about the mysterious spirit.

"I wish she'd asked me that outright." Sarah shook her head. "Marty and I were childhood sweethearts. Whoever this ghost is looking for, it isn't me."

By the time Robin thought to check her watch, it was after two o'clock. She called the children over and made them tackle their workbooks, although privately she agreed that it was a waste of sunshine.

The trio made short work of their math problems and handwriting exercises. Then they waved goodbye to their friends, piled into her car and read at least a few paragraphs of their books en route to the community center.

As they dashed into the building, gym clothes over their arms and sand flaking from their swimsuits, Robin calculated that they had exactly five minutes to change in the rest rooms. But they'd made it.

Her sense of relief lasted until they rounded a bend in the corridor and ran straight into Flint.

Chapter Seven

"There is, I presume, an explanation?" Flint said.

Robin's heart thudded into her throat. The way he towered over her was downright intimidating.

"Children, go change for gymnastics," she said.

Her stern tone did the trick. Without protest, the triplets vanished.

"Well?" Flint forced out the word through clenched teeth. "I left you a simple task, Miss Lindstrom. A simple schedule, I would have thought, to follow."

Robin pulled the crumpled page from her pocket. "Right here," she said.

Flint snatched it away. "I see workbooks at one and reading at two. No mention of a beach. That is, I presume, where they got the sand."

"You don't specify the location." Robin was determined to stand her ground. "If you check my car, you'll find the children completed several pages in their workbooks."

"At the beach?"

"At the beach."

"What about reading?" he demanded.

"I'll admit, it got short shrift." Robin refused to lie. "You did promise to be flexible."

"I did?" Flint's forehead puckered. "I don't seem to recall—"

"I remember it clearly," said Robin.

Caitlin hurried around a corner, wearing gym shorts and a T-shirt. "You didn't fire her, did you, Daddy? She was very strict. We wore our seat belts and she put on sunscreen, and we chewed our food like we're supposed to."

"What exactly did you eat?" demanded Flint.

Caitlin blinked and realized her mistake. "Uh, I had some lettuce and tomato."

"That would be on your hamburger?" said her father.

The little girl nodded unhappily.

"Believe me, I won't be buying them any more fast-food lunches," Robin assured him. "I can't afford it." In response to his dubious look, she added, "I forgot about packing a picnic. I'm not used to being a nanny, but I'm getting there."

Brick appeared, with Aaron tagging along. The boys, less interested than their sister in the interactions of grownups, grabbed Caitlin and dragged her off to class.

"Why don't you guys go have coffee?" the little girl called. "Spend some time together."

The boys hauled her out of sight.

"I don't believe it," said Robin. "She's matchmaking."

"It must be a little-girl thing." Flint shook his head. "All right, Robin. I'm not going to make an issue of today, since you did get them here on time. But in future I expect you to toe the line."

"Yes, sir," said Robin.

As she met his gaze, a troubling thought jolted her. *This man and I have had children together.*

It was a startlingly intimate realization. Normally, that would mean they had made love. In an odd way, Robin felt as if they had.

In another way, she couldn't imagine making love with Flint. He was too hard, too controlling. His mouth would torment hers, his hands would claim her with relentless ferocity, and the demands of his body would drive her beyond the safe limits she'd always maintained with men.

Robin didn't want to be possessed. Not by anyone.

"Let's go watch the children," she said. "I'd like to know what they're learning about gymnastics."

Flint gave a short nod and pressed one hand on the small of her back to guide her toward the gym. From the shallowness of his breathing, she thought for a minute he must have read her mind.

Or maybe he was simply controlling his annoyance about the disrupted schedule.

BY FIVE O'CLOCK, the children were so wiped out from their athletic activities that Aaron dozed off in the car. Flint considered pulling over and waking the boy, since he didn't believe it was safe for a child to ride in that slumped position, but he decided it wasn't worth the disruption on such a short trip.

He'd insisted the three kids ride with him. Robin's car was too small and, in his opinion, not solid enough to protect the children. He hadn't considered that issue when he hired her. Well, he didn't suppose she'd be driving the children around very much.

Perhaps it hadn't been such a bad idea to take the triplets to the beach, he had to admit. They'd made only a few expeditions to the ocean this summer, despite living so close, and being accompanied by the Anders family meant extra supervision.

None of the other nannies had brought Robin's freshness and energy to the job, he conceded silently. Despite her flaky approach, she cared about the happiness of her charges. That was definitely a plus.

None of the other nannies had filled out jeans and a blouse the way Robin did, either. Flint clamped his jaw tight and tried not to think about her supple movements or the color that flooded her face when they argued.

No wonder the children reacted so positively. Her enthusiasm was contagious, even if sometimes misplaced.

He'd been right to hire her, after all. He doubted Aunt Maureen would agree, but she was in Hawaii for two weeks. Besides, Flint could run his own household without anyone's interference.

At home, he stationed the kids in front of a *Bill Nye the Science Guy* broadcast and took out the ingredients for dinner. At the supermarket earlier that afternoon, he'd purchased food for a week's worth of nutritious meals, and he decided to get started on the cooking himself.

Tom the handyman had arrived on schedule and, after paging Flint for permission, replaced the stovetop. Flint had to admit the shiny almond-colored replacement was an improvement over its scratched avocado-green predecessor.

Tonight's menu called for stir-fried beef, rice and a salad.

Flint had learned to cook after Kathy's death, tutored by Maureen and a series of books. On the housekeeper's day off, he did his best to dazzle the children with his culinary finesse. Their response was usually on the order of, "Can't we have spaghetti instead?"

He had a feeling Robin would suit them fine.

By the time she let herself in with her key, Flint had started the rice and begun chopping the meat into thin strips. "Get lost?" he asked as she leaned in the doorway, watching him.

"Nope. Got dessert." She held up a half-gallon of chocolate chip ice cream. "Is this enough?"

"I allow one hard candy apiece for dessert." Flint realized how coldhearted that must sound. "But we make exceptions for special occasions, like tonight."

"What's so special?" Robin went to put the ice cream in the freezer.

"The arrival of our new nanny," he said.

"I'm honored." She peeked into the family room. The children must have been settled, because she turned around and asked, "Need some help?"

He didn't, but Flint wanted to keep her in the kitchen with him. He wanted to feel her presence as they moved around, preparing food, chatting idly, doing the casual friendly things that bring a couple closer.

They weren't a couple. But since they had to live together, they might as well act like one.

He handed her a head of lettuce and some tomatoes. "Why don't you fix the salad?"

"No problem." She retrieved an apron from the pantry, then poked around until she found a wire twist tie to pull back her hair.

Flint liked the way she checked the cupboards and drawers instead of interrupting him to ask where he kept things. Other housekeepers had driven him to distraction with their constant queries.

The kitchen did seem smaller than usual, however. Although it was spacious, they kept bumping into each other. Robin would have to reach across him to retrieve a knife, or he would discover that she was standing in front of the spice rack, forcing him to lean over her to retrieve the ginger.

Each slight touch became magnified in Flint's awareness. He could have sworn his nerve endings registered every air current that moved between her body and his.

Robin rinsed and dried the lettuce, then tore it by hand. "Wouldn't the salad taste better with some croutons or a little cheese?"

"The kids wouldn't eat it," said Flint as he stir-fried the beef.

"They're that picky?"

"Pickier."

She flipped a strand of hair. "I never realized how little experience I have with kids and food. As a teacher, it's easy to fix a special snack, but celery stuffed with peanut butter wouldn't exactly make a good meal."

"Celery stuffed with peanut butter?" Flint had never come across that one. "It sounds healthy but disgusting."

"Maybe we can try it sometime." She tossed the salad, picked up a tomato slice that fell onto the counter and threw it back in.

"Shouldn't you rinse it?" Flint said.

"Why? Didn't you clean the counter?"

"Yes, but I didn't sterilize it."

"I washed my hands but I didn't sterilize them, either," Robin said.

"Hands are different."

"Why?"

Because my instinct tells me so, he wanted to retort, but knew that wasn't scientific. "We don't wash our hands with the same kind of chemicals we use on the counter," Flint retorted.

"But our skin is continually shedding cells." Robin found the ranch dressing in the refrigerator and set it on the counter. "Aren't you worried about skin cells getting into the salad?"

"Are you always this stubborn?" he asked.

"I'm not—" She stopped in midsentence. "Am I?"

"I've never met a woman who argued with everything I said, until you."

She beamed at him. "Aren't you lucky? And I don't even charge extra." Before Flint could think of a reply, she called, "Whose turn is it to set the table?"

All three kids swarmed in, even though it was Brick's turn. The table got set in record time, and Flint pretended not to notice that a couple of napkins were crumpled and the forks were on the wrong side of the plate. Not even he could expect perfection from seven-year-olds.

As the five of them sat down to eat and he gazed at the shining faces of his children, it occurred to Flint that they felt more like a family than they had in a long time.

And as Robin had said, she didn't even charge extra.

ROBIN AWOKE at seven-thirty on Sunday morning. She stretched, noticed the time, then pulled the sheets over her head and went back to sleep.

Someone shook her awake an instant later. "Go away," Robin said. "It's Sunday."

"I wanted to ask you something." Flint sat on the edge of her bed. Robin checked the clock and realized half an hour had passed. "We agreed that you get Sundays off. I thought, however, that you might want to make an exception today, since you're just getting to know the children. We could arrange another day off when you need it for a teaching interview."

That sounded like a reasonable proposition. "Okay." Robin sighed. "I'll get up in an hour."

"We leave for church in forty-five minutes," Flint said.

"Don't they have a later service?" Robin yawned, then realized that one strap of her silky black nightgown had fallen, baring a considerable portion of upper chest. She slipped the strap into place.

"There's only one service and it starts at nine." Flint removed himself from the bed.

Robin groaned and dragged herself into the bathroom. She showered, wincing at the hot water, then put on a dress and stockings.

She couldn't remember the last time she'd arisen this early on a weekend. But she would need a day off for a job interview, if anything came up. And she devoutly hoped it would.

Still, yesterday hadn't been so bad. Flint had mellowed after their confrontation at the community center. She'd actually enjoyed cooking dinner with him.

At the moment, he was loading the dishwasher with a preoccupied expression on his face. To Robin's relief, she found the coffeepot half full and poured herself a cup. In her current state, she knew she'd never locate the cream and sugar, so she drank it straight.

The first draft was only halfway to her befogged brain when Caitlin said, "Where do you usually go to church, Robin?"

The little girl was reading the comics in the breakfast nook, wearing a starched dress and a navy straw hat. As Robin staggered to the table, she wondered if Flint would expect her to starch the dress.

"Sometimes I go to Buddhist services, Protestant, Baha'i, Catholic, Jewish—whatever," Robin said. "I don't have any regular schedule."

Flint leaned over the counter from the kitchen. "In my experience, a regular schedule promotes self-discipline."

Robin set her cup down with a clunk. "I thought the purpose of church was to promote spirituality, not discipline."

Flint retreated, and she chalked up one round for her side.

Breakfast, Robin found, consisted of frozen whole-wheat waffles. She wondered why anyone would bother making junk food out of whole wheat. Even under a thick coat of syrup, the waffles tasted like wood chips.

Brick and Aaron ran in from the den. "Brick's hitting me!" Aaron wailed.

"I am not!" Brick shouted, then decided to hedge his bets by adding, "anyway, he hit me first!"

"Both of you to your rooms!" Flint snapped. The boys pulled long faces and stomped away.

In the bright light of a Sunday morning, Robin decided that these children couldn't possibly be hers. No descendant of Robin's would possess that much energy at such an hour.

She realized that the issue had been roiling around in her subconscious all night. It was hard to dismiss the notation in her medical records, but her brain was trying. After all, if these children were hers, she either owed them more than she could possibly give or she ought to leave at once.

The note hadn't listed her name on the same page as Kathleen Harris's. Maybe the memo had been stuck in her file by mistake. Perhaps that was why the clinic was shutting down. Its sloppy record keeping must have produced a lot of lawsuits.

She couldn't think about it any more. Her head was starting to ache.

Robin's morning wooze didn't wear off until after church. She was glad no one quizzed her about the contents of the sermon. She remembered an anecdote she'd read about President Calvin Coolidge, a man of few words. One day when his ailing wife missed church, she asked him what the subject of the sermon had been. "Sin," he replied. When she asked what the minister had said, Coolidge answered, "He was against it."

Robin assumed that Flint's minister was against it, too.

They ate lunch at a soup-and-salad cafeteria that offered enough variety to satisfy the children, especially when they discovered the muffins. Then they changed clothes and headed for the park.

"The children need to work on their pitching," Flint explained. "Aaron has been getting teased at school."

"He throws like a girl," Brick said.

"Not like me." Caitlin sniffed. "I throw overhand."

"You couldn't hit a cow in a tunnel," Brick sneered.

"You stop it!" Caitlin's voice rose to a shriek. "You're always trying to make me look bad in front of Robin!"

"I don't have to make you look bad, you just do it naturally!" Brick said.

"Stop it now!" Flint's voice boomed through the air, silencing all dissent. "Brick, you have a fifteen-minute time-out."

At the park, Brick sat chafing on the sidelines while Flint worked on Aaron's throw. The boy had a hard time getting his movements coordinated and kept stamping his feet in frustration.

Robin and Caitlin found a swing set. As they floated back and forth, Caitlin plied her with questions. Where had she grown up? Did she have a boyfriend? Could Gigi really tell fortunes?

Aaron's complaints finally brought his lessons to an end, and Flint called to Caitlin that it was her turn.

"I'm swinging!" she shouted.

"Come here now!"

"I already know how to throw a ball, Daddy!"

"Caitlin!" The ominous note finally drew the little girl from her perch.

Aaron, meanwhile, had collapsed near Brick. Within seconds the two were throwing handfuls of grass at each other. Robin tried to get them to join her on the playground equipment, but Aaron whined that his arm hurt and Brick protested that he was still having a time-out.

Robin didn't hear whatever smart-aleck remark Caitlin made to her father, but a short time later Flint stormed over and dragged them all to the car.

They hadn't been at the park half an hour. How could so much go wrong in so short a time?

Robin was determined to stay out of this. She was only the nanny, after all. These were Flint's kids, and he knew them better than she did.

At home, Flint sent the children to their rooms. "I can't understand it," he said as he and Robin retreated to the back patio with the Sunday paper. "I schedule time to play with them, and all they do is complain."

Robin busied herself working the crossword puzzle.

"I don't want Aaron getting teased about his pitching," Flint went on. "And Caitlin's losing her athletic interests. I don't want her to buy into that stuff about girls not playing ball. She won't admit it, but I think that's what's going on."

Robin tried to think of the answer to nine across, a group of islands in the Atlantic. She wasn't sure where the Azores were located, but they fit the spaces, so she filled them in.

"I was going to plan a party for their birthday, but they're so negative about everything, I'm not sure that's a good idea," Flint went on.

"Birthday?" Robin could feel her ears perking. "Their birthday is coming up?"

"August fifth. Well, fifth and sixth," Flint said. "Brick was born just before midnight. Caitlin was born one minute after midnight, and then came Aaron. He's the youngest and he acts it, doesn't he?"

Robin had undergone her procedure during Christmas vacation. That would mean the triplets had been born a little over seven months later. "Were they full term?"

"Nearly two months early," Flint said. "They were such cute little things. When did they get so cantankerous?"

Robin could feel her self-imposed remoteness poofing away like a popped balloon. How could she go on pretending the triplets were someone else's children? She heard herself admonishing Flint, "At seven, kids enter a new developmental stage and they need freedom to make their own decisions."

"Freedom has to be earned," he said. "I won't tolerate irresponsibility."

"Look at it from their perspective," Robin said. "Did they want to practice pitching? Did you ask them?"

"It's something they need to work on. I want our time together to be productive," Flint grumbled.

"And was it?" she challenged.

He leaned forward in his chair. "After twenty-four hours on the job, you know more about my kids than I do?"

"I know about kids because I've taught a lot of them," she said. "A teacher has to change her tactics to suit the children's learning styles. Each class is different. You figure out what works for them, and build on it."

"Oh, really?" From the angle of Flint's chin and the narrowing of his eyes, she could tell he didn't intend to lose this argument. "I don't believe in catering to children's whims. They have to learn to fit into this world on its own terms."

"But in the real world, each of them has choices," Robin stated.

"Fine." Flint stood up. "It's time for you to fix dinner. We're having the liver and onions that Maureen couldn't cook, because if it sits in the fridge any longer it will spoil. Let's see how much choice you can give the kids about that."

It was a direct dare. Robin stood to face him. "As long as I fix the liver and onions, you won't interfere?"

"No sending out for pizza."

"I don't have to cheat," she said.

Standing so close, Flint loomed above her. Robin refused to let him rattle her.

"It's a deal," Flint said. "Do it your way. I could use a good laugh."

As she went to fetch the children, Robin wondered if she'd bitten off more than she could chew. Or perhaps, she mused, she was preparing to cook more than she could bite off.

She gathered the triplets in the boys' room. "You guys get to help me make dinner," she said. "But we have to fix the liver and onions."

The boys groaned.

"Give us a break," said Caitlin.

"What else are we having?" Aaron asked.

"Let's go find out." In the kitchen, they discovered that Flint had set the ingredients on the counter. The side dish was lentils—more groans from the kids—with frozen peas for the vegetable.

"This is the most disgusting meal in the history of the world," said Brick.

"Let's make it more disgusting," said Robin. "But you guys have to eat it."

"What do you mean, more disgusting?" asked Caitlin.

"We can add anything we want," Robin said.

"I like chocolate chips." Aaron gave her a sly grin that reminded her of Gigi.

"Hard-boiled eggs," Caitlin added.

"Sugar," said Brick.

"Let's go to it." Robin had sworn to give them choices, and now she had to live by her decision. "First, everybody wash hands."

An hour later, when they called Flint in to dinner, the children proudly served up their dishes—lentils with chopped eggs, peas flavored with sugar and liver and onions sprinkled with chocolate chips.

Chapter Eight

At the sight of Flint's horrified expression, the triplets burst into laughter.

"Are we really going to eat this?" he asked.

"You promised," said Robin.

Flint transferred some liver to his plate and poked at a chip. "Is this what I think it is?"

"You have to eat the whole thing," chortled Aaron.

It was far from the most dignified meal in history. Even Flint couldn't resist making faces as he downed his dinner, and the children shouted with glee as they ate their own concoctions.

"Anybody want to make this again tomorrow night?" Robin asked.

With one voice, the four Harrises said, "No!"

"This is fun." Aaron beamed.

"It's like having Mommy back," said Caitlin.

The humor faded from Flint's face. "That was inappropriate, Caitlin," he said. "No one can replace your mother. Ever."

"Of course not," Robin said quickly. "You must miss her a lot. I'll bet you had lots of fun when she was here, didn't you?"

The youngsters agreed, and Flint's grim expression eased. He didn't broach the matter again until after the children were in bed.

"I suppose you've gathered that I don't want my children forgetting their mother." He and Robin were finishing the newspaper in the family room. Two lamps glowed in the summer evening.

"I wish I could have known her," Robin said. "She must have been special."

He told her how Kathy had earned her way through law school, struggled with infertility and helped support the family while he established his business. "She deserved better from life than she got," Flint said. "She hadn't even begun to reap what she'd sown when she died."

He'd never recovered from his anger at her death, Robin realized. "You have a strong sense of justice. It outrages you when life isn't fair."

Flint drummed his fingers against the business section. "I never thought about it that way, but it's true. People who play by the rules ought to be rewarded."

Robin wanted to ease his obvious tension. "Speaking of rules, do you have any games we could play? You mentioned Uno and checkers, I believe."

"Too tame." A gleam lit up his eyes. "This calls for War."

"I don't think I know that one." Robin watched dubiously as Flint crossed to the closet and removed a game box from a high shelf.

"It's simple. Each person tries to take over the world. The fighting gets vicious, and then I win." He opened the box and set the game board on the coffee table.

"Excuse me?" Robin challenged. "You expect to win, do you?"

"Against an inexperienced player? Not to mention a do-gooder like you?" He grinned as he taunted her. "You'll be so busy protecting your countries, you'll never be aggressive enough to win.''

"Try me," snapped Robin, then remembered what had happened the last time she issued that dare.

Flint must have been remembering, too, because he shot her a smile of such masculine arrogance that Robin ached to take him down a few pegs.

"Here's the rule book." He tossed it to her. "Let me know when you're ready."

The game was simple. Players challenged each other, massed their troops and rolled dice, wagering one or more soldiers in a battle to take over country after country. It was designed for three or four players, which meant the weaker competitors could be eliminated until two finalists squared off.

In this case, there were only two players to divide up the world. Robin would have preferred a less dog-eat-dog game, but she had to show Flint that she could whip him.

That wasn't quite the way it worked. Robin held on to South America and Africa for a long time, even making incursions into Europe and Mexico. The problem was, she realized as her armies dwindled, that she didn't possess Flint's willingness to risk huge numbers of soldiers on one throw of the dice.

With a sinking heart, Robin retreated toward the South Pole. The world was slipping away, and to a self-centered, destructive warlord like Flint!

She threw her forces together and took a couple of big risks. It proved to be too little, too late. Before she knew it, Flint had conquered the earth.

Which, Robin reflected, was what he probably figured he deserved in real life, as well.

"I'll beat you next time," she threatened.

Flint laughed. "The only one who ever beats me is Brick, because he doesn't know the meaning of fear. I'm not looking forward to his teenage years. By the way, the loser picks up the pieces.''

"And what does the winner get?"

"He gets to gloat."

Robin made a face but swept the pieces into the box without comment. Then, as she stood to put the game away, she stretched painfully. Leaning over the low table had cramped her back.

"Are you all right?" Flint returned the box to the closet. "Next time we'll use the kitchen table."

"I'm fine." Robin tried a few stretching exercises and discovered soreness in a few muscles she'd forgotten she possessed. "I may have to call in sick at work tomorrow, though. I'm not looking forward to it—my boss is a real slave driver."

"We can't have that." Flint stopped behind her and ran his hands up her back. "Where does it hurt?"

"Low down." Robin braced herself against the wall and let him press the aching muscles. His thumbs found each knot and teased it out, then moved upward to provide delicious relief between her shoulder blades.

"You have delicate bones." Flint's hands spanned her rib cage. "Graceful, which is what I'd expect from a dancer."

"Offstage, dancers aren't graceful at all," Robin said as he completed his massage and stepped back. "We run into things because we're accustomed to lots of space to move around in. Like this."

As she spoke, she pirouetted toward him, making a wider turn than she'd intended. Although she hadn't meant to demonstrate her clumsiness, Robin succeeded in bumping him hard in the hip.

Flint caught his balance by reaching past her to the wall. They both realized at the same time that he'd trapped her within his arms, and Robin was about to apologize when she saw that his eyes were hooded with desire.

Flint's mouth caught hers without warning. Hard and demanding, it was indeed the mouth of a conqueror who takes what he has won, a man who doesn't need to ask permission for anything.

Unprepared, Robin yielded beneath his onslaught, her arms encircling his neck. She felt an answering hunger flood her veins as Flint's tongue invaded her mouth and his hands claimed her waist. She'd never known a man so fierce or so primitive. She could no more resist him than she could stand against a force of nature.

Was this really her? Where had her feisty independence gone? Robin wondered dazedly.

Flint drew away for a moment, stroking her hair as he regarded her in the dim light. He turned her slightly, manipulating her to a better angle for him to explore her lips and teeth.

Robin could only give him what he wanted. And it was rapidly becoming what she wanted, as well.

With a deep groan, she pressed against him. Fire burned through her, a raging response that she had never felt with a man before. There had always been a part of Robin that held back, that stayed apart from her physical responses. That part was gone.

Where had it come from, this yearning to merge with Flint? He was too strong, too dangerous to play with. All her life Robin had fought to be self-sufficient, and for the first time she sensed that someone might be able to rip away her independence and make her want him beyond reason.

Her skin flamed with a longing to be touched, caressed and crushed. Robin wound her arms tighter around Flint and melted into him.

Then she felt him draw back. Slowly he released her, his breath coming ragged through the cool air. "I didn't mean to..." He caught his breath. "This was an unfortunate lapse. It won't happen again.'' Without waiting for her response, Flint stalked out of the room.

Robin sank onto the couch, trying to absorb what had happened. In their embrace, she'd discovered a side of herself that had lain dormant until now, an urgent need that surpassed her good judgment.

As she gazed toward the spot where moments before he had savaged her senses, she saw what must have struck him like a blow—a family photograph on the wall, Kathy's face shining as she held three babies on her lap. Even through his passion, the sight of it had torn him away from Robin.

How could she possibly compete with a dead woman?

But that wasn't the issue, she told herself. She didn't want to compete with Kathy. True, growing up in such an unorthodox household, Robin had sometimes longed for a stable, reliable husband. But not for a rigid figure like Flint. Not for a man who would gladly fill the world with time clocks for people to punch, whether they were attending church or taking their children to the park.

She couldn't deny that she found the man attractive. He had an elemental male strength that aroused an instinctive response in Robin. But he had come much too close to stripping away her defenses and tearing apart her self-protective shield.

He was right—they couldn't let this happen again.

A noise from the bedrooms pulled Robin from her thoughts. At first, she assumed it came from Flint's room, but after a moment she identified the low noise as a child crying.

Hesitantly, she started toward the sound. Flint's bedroom lay just beyond those of his children, but he had closed his door. Apparently a father's ears weren't keen enough to hear the faint whimper.

It came from the boys' chamber. Robin stepped inside, noticing how a night-light threw odd shadows that intensified rather than softened the gloom. Still, it helped her see that Brick snoozed undisturbed in the upper bunk.

In the lower, Aaron lay curled into a ball, sobbing into his teddy bear. Robin ducked to avoid the overhead bunk and sat beside him.

"Bad dream?" she whispered.

He gave a barely perceptible nod. "I have nightmares. Like a baby. Don't tell anybody."

"Doesn't your father know?"

"He comes in sometimes," Aaron admitted. "But don't tell Brick and Caitlin."

"I won't. Besides, everybody has nightmares once in a while, even grown-ups." Robin gathered his small shape into her arms. He nestled against her, his instinctive trust filling her with warmth.

My child. Robin had had a hard time grasping exactly what that meant until this moment. Now she felt his heartbeat ripple through her veins. She ached at the thought of his unhappiness, as if their nervous systems had forged a connection.

"Can you tell me about it?" she murmured.

"I was—I was lost in this dark house, and I kept hearing voices, but whenever I got close, they went away." Aaron snuffled. "I miss my mommy, even though I don't remember her much. Caitlin says you could be our mommy."

Robin hadn't suspected the precocious girl of that much sentimentality. "I'm glad she's fond of me, but I'm afraid there's more to being a mother than getting hired as a nanny. For one thing, I'd have to marry your father, and I'm afraid that's not going to happen."

"Why not?" asked Aaron, distracted from his tears.

"Because he's still in love with your mother." That seemed the simplest explanation. "But, Aaron, you don't need to have these bad dreams. Your daddy is here to take care of you, and I'm here, too."

"Are you going to go away like the others?" the boy said.

"Not like the others," Robin heard herself say. "I'll take care of you, Aaron. Now go to sleep."

A short time later, his breathing quieted and his body relaxed. The boy had fallen asleep in her arms.

Why had she promised that she would take care of him? Robin wondered as she slipped him onto the pillow and tucked him in. Was it only because cradling him that way had aroused her maternal instinct?

Or was it because the children obviously needed her?

She recalled what Flint had said earlier about dreading Brick's adolescence. What about Caitlin and Aaron, as well? The youngsters needed nurturing and a sympathetic ear. Guidance and discipline had to be tempered with understanding. As teenagers, they would rebel against a tyrannical father, perhaps sacrificing their best interests in the process.

Robin could never turn her back on the children. Whether she stayed as their nanny or left, she would always feel a sense of obligation to them.

More than obligation. Love.

As she checked on Caitlin and then retreated to her own room on the other side of the house, Robin reflected that she and Flint had created these young lives together, even though they hadn't known each other at the time. If Kathy were here, things would be different. Robin respected and admired the woman who had given birth to these children, but she was no longer available to counterbalance Flint's harshness.

Robin wasn't sure how she would manage to remain a part of the children's lives after she no longer worked here. At some point, she would have to tell Flint the truth. She shuddered to think how he would react.

Once thing was for sure. Before she told Flint, she wanted to devise a plan for how the two of them could work together for the children's benefit.

Changing into her nightgown, Robin tried to convince herself that it was a good thing she'd discovered her own vulnerability to Flint. Now she had time to figure out how to steel herself against him for the inevitable moment of confrontation, whenever it might come.

As HE FLIPPED his bedroom calendar to August, Flint wasn't sure where the week had gone.

Had it been only ten days ago that Robin moved in with him? He'd plunged into his work after their close encounter in the den, putting in evening hours that often kept him away at dinner time. Somehow, along the way, he'd lost track of the days passing.

Last Monday, Flint had landed the Serena Academy contract, and he wanted to get off to a running start. Then the City Council had asked him to prepare an updated report for this afternoon's study session. Knowing that protestors would turn out in force, he'd needed to make sure he could bolster every recommendation with facts and figures.

Flint's thoughts returned to Robin. To his surprise, she hadn't made an issue of their passionate embrace and his sudden withdrawal. She'd appeared calm at breakfast the next morning and had never referred to the incident.

In the past week, Robin had adhered, more or less, to his schedule. She'd even shown initiative by suggesting that the hour between nine and ten be devoted to planting a vegetable garden.

She'd pointed out a backyard bed of summer flowers dying in the heat, and explained that, according to an article in the newspaper, this was the right time to plant fall vegetables such as sugar snap peas and broccoli. Flint, who tried to avoid any lengthy conversations with Robin, had agreed that the project offered both scientific and exercise benefits.

In addition, she'd instituted a new discipline plan. The kids received a check mark for bad behavior, although serious offenses could also result in time-outs or suspension of privileges. Five check marks in one day cost them a quarter out of their three-dollar weekly allowance.

When none of the children received a single mark all day, they got a treat at night—a special dessert, extra time to play video games, permission to watch a noneducational TV show. It had worked better than Flint would have expected, although he entertained doubts about how long the cooperation would last.

After knotting his tie, he checked his watch. It was almost ten o'clock, a late start. He'd spent part of the morning on the phone, getting information about recent tests to locate new faults in the Los Angeles basin.

Scientists had set off underground explosions and tracked the sound waves to create a seismic map. The results weren't final, but enough new data had been gleaned to support Flint's contention that Beachside needed to prepare for more frequent earthquakes than previously anticipated.

It was always better to know the worst, he told himself, but he doubted the town's businesspeople would agree.

As he slid his wallet into one pocket and his keys into the other, he heard the back door slam, and children's voices filled the house.

Their excited shouts gave Flint pause. He could just picture them stomping across the carpet with muddy shoes and dribbling fertilizer onto the furniture from their dirty clothes. Stepping out of the bedroom, he was preparing to issue a warning when the children giggled past him, stripped to their underwear.

The three scattered for their bedrooms. Flint couldn't suppress a chuckle himself. For some reason, kids always thought nudity and underwear were funny.

He found Robin in the laundry room by the back door, stuffing dirty clothes and towels into the washer. Four pairs of canvas shoes, freshly hosed off, sat drying in one corner.

"I see you've figured out how to keep them from tracking in dirt," he said. "Very clever."

Brushing aside a strand of honey-blond hair that had escaped its ponytail, Robin turned to meet his gaze. From her dirt-streaked face to her rueful expression, she looked like a child herself.

"That garden is going to be unique." She closed the washer lid and pulled the knob to turn it on. "They've got radishes and onions mixed with the peas and broccoli. Caitlin claims she read somewhere that they'll serve as a natural pesticide. Aaron insisted we plant nasturtiums, which are edible flowers, and Brick wanted tomatoes, even in winter. I figured it couldn't hurt to try."

"Ever gardened before?" Flint asked.

"I grew a lemon tree in a barrel at the beach once," Robin said, "but people kept stealing the lemons."

He realized that he shouldn't stand here staring, but damn it, he'd missed her. Yesterday—on Monday—Flint had gone to Ventura, an hour and a half away, to bid on a contract, and hadn't returned until nearly ten. Before that, on Sunday, Robin had taken her first day off.

Flint hadn't expected to miss her so much. It was the first time he'd realized how Robin filled the house with energy. The air had felt dull in her absence, and the children had moped about.

They were growing attached to her, and she to them. Flint wondered why Robin hadn't mentioned anything further about finding a teaching job.

Perhaps there were things she wasn't telling him. With a start, he realized that he'd come to expect that Robin would always speak her mind. Had she started holding back? A new job prospect, perhaps, or—well, he couldn't begin to guess what might be in her thoughts.

Watching her wash up in the laundry-room basin, he wondered why the idea bothered him so much. After all, he was proud of the way he'd kept his distance this past week. Why shouldn't she be holding back, as well?

"Got any special plans for today?" he asked.

"Not really." Robin groped for a towel and he hurried to hand it to her. Standing this close, he could smell the light fragrance of her shampoo mingled with an earthy tang that had survived her post-garden scrub.

"What's for dinner?" Flint probed. He'd allowed Robin to choose the week's menu and given her a blank check to shop for groceries on Saturday. However, so far he hadn't had a chance to evaluate her choices. "Liver and chocolate chips again?"

"Spaghetti," said Robin. "French bread and salad."

"Always a safe choice."

She nodded. Damn it, he couldn't even get a simple conversation going.

"What are we eating tomorrow night?" Flint asked.

Robin pulled the rubber band from her hair and regarded herself in a mirror over the sink. "Burritos and corn on the cob."

"Are burritos one of your specialties?" Surely he could draw her out if he kept at it long enough.

"I found it in your recipe box. Caitlin suggested it." Robin opened a utility drawer and took out scissors. She proceeded to trim her bangs into the sink.

Flint wasn't going to give up easily. Besides, he was surprised to see someone cut her own hair, especially with paper scissors. "What did you normally eat, at home?"

"Take-out," said Robin. "And Stouffer's."

"Frozen food?"

"I heated it up before I ate it."

He wasn't going to get anything more than a terse response, and Flint had to concede that this was no coincidence. Robin must have made up her mind to play the game according to his rules. Like a good nanny, she was avoiding intimate contact. It made perfect sense.

For the first time in his life, Flint didn't like something that made perfect sense.

"I'll be home for dinner," he said. "The council study session should be over by five."

"I'll make plenty of spaghetti." Snip, snip. Tiny bits of hair freckled her nose.

Flint walked out of the room. He called goodbye to the children, but it sounded as if they were taking a bath together in their oversize tub. Laughter flew through the closed door, and he could hear the water running.

By habit, he paused before the picture of Kathy and the babies. Although Flint stood behind her in the photograph, his figure seemed shadowy by comparison. She had glowed so brightly.

A soft noise made him look up as Robin walked in from the laundry room. She stopped when she saw him.

A shade of sadness swept across her eyes, and then she gave him a sympathetic smile. When she passed through to the kitchen, he noticed that particles of hair still clung to her cheeks.

Flint picked up his briefcase and headed to work with the sense of having left some business unfinished.

Chapter Nine

So far, her plan was working, Robin reflected as she changed from her gardening clothes into clean shorts and a T-shirt.

She'd decided last week that her focus should be on the children. If Flint wanted no further closeness, that suited her fine. She would be a good nanny and stick this job out as long as she needed to.

By then, she would have won Flint's respect. When she left, she would tell him the truth, and there was at least a slight chance he'd agree to allow continuing contact with the children.

After leaving, she would function as a doting aunt, Robin decided. She'd be someone the kids could bring their problems to, a safety valve for their growing pains.

Still, she'd felt rather heartless today, returning only the briefest of responses while Flint plied her with questions. She knew the man had a heart beneath all that muscle and bone, even if he kept it locked away, and she knew he must get lonely.

Maybe eventually he'd find an ice maiden who could live with his personality flaws and his undying devotion to his late wife. With Robin close by to help the children, everyone would be satisfied.

Sure. And maybe pigs could fly.

She checked the schedule she'd posted on her bedroom wall. Ten to eleven, bike riding. Well, the hour was half gone, but Flint hadn't objected. By the time the kids were finished washing, they'd be ready for eleven o'clock chores.

Robin intended to have them clean their rooms, which were dense jumbles of toys and books. Then they could help her fix lunch.

Why did Flint have to make things so cut-and-dried? She was always having to bend the schedule here and there simply to allow the children to live normal lives. She supposed she was lucky he hadn't installed a school bell to blare out the changing of the hours.

And imagine his nerve, quizzing her about the menu! What did he think she'd planned, hot dogs and canned chili every night? Well, okay, so she'd been tempted. But she'd resisted.

It occurred to Robin as she brushed her hair that the children's birthdays were coming up at the end of the week. Flint hadn't mentioned anything about a party. She'd have to ask him how he wanted to celebrate the event.

It would be the first birthday Robin would spend with her children. Her heart clenched as she contemplated the significance.

She decided not to dwell on it. After all, she didn't want to reveal to Flint that the day had any special meaning for her.

The rest of the morning passed smoothly. Excited about their garden, the children didn't bother to torment each other. They helped fix sandwiches and whooped with joy when Robin proposed a picnic on the front lawn.

By the time they finished the corn chips, it seemed like half the neighborhood had dropped by. The triplets knew almost everyone and advised Robin on which youngsters they liked and which were too rowdy.

To Robin's delight, one older lady from down the block brought them Chinese pastries she'd purchased while visiting relatives in Taiwan. "These are very special," she advised, sitting beside Robin on a blanket. "The bakery that makes them, there's nothing like it in this country."

The children took tentative nibbles, then downed the baked goods as if they were starving. Robin thanked their visitor, whose name was May Sung.

"I've bought pastries in Chinatown, in L.A., but they were never as good as this," Robin said. "How kind of you to share them."

"I always see the triplets out riding their bikes, but I never see their mother," May explained. "I am pleased to meet you."

"Oh, I'm just the nanny," Robin said.

The older woman slanted her a knowing look. "Only the nanny? I don't think so."

"Do you have the second sight?" Caitlin asked. "Robin's mother is a psychic. She tells fortunes."

"What's the second sight?" said Aaron.

"It means she wears glasses," Brick retorted smugly.

"She doesn't wear glasses," said Aaron.

"Second sight means that people can see beyond, to another dimension," said May. "Your mother is a psychic?"

"She thinks she is." Robin sighed.

"What can she see? Ghosts?" asked Aaron. "Do they really exist?"

"Don't you know?" taunted Brick. "I thought you were the expert on that stuff." Aaron, the bookworm of the three, was currently reading a science fiction novel entitled *I Left My Sneakers in Dimension X*.

"Now, boys," Robin said in a warning tone. "We don't want any bad marks today, do we?"

"Who's that?" Brick pointed toward the street.

A Taurus station wagon painted pink with lavender trim halted in front of the house. A door flew open and Gigi hopped out. She pulled some signs from the back and dropped them facedown on the lawn.

"Bye, Irma! Thanks!" she called, and the station wagon pulled away.

How like Irma to buy the world's most conventional car and paint it pink, Robin thought. It was kind of her to give Gigi a ride. Robin's mother didn't own a car and was usually stuck riding the overcrowded buses at the beach.

But what was Gigi doing here? Robin had specifically asked her not to meddle in Flint's affairs. She didn't want to argue in front of the children, however, so she decided to let her mother reveal her agenda at her own pace.

"Hi, Mom." Robin gave her a hug as the children called happy greetings. "We were just talking about you."

"I knew it!" Gigi beamed. "I could feel it." She plopped down next to May, and Robin introduced them.

"You are a very unusual woman, I can tell," May said.

Gigi regarded her with the glee of a spider spotting a fly in its web. Robin remembered that her mother was on a quest to discover Frederick's lost lover.

About to insist that her mother leave the neighbor in peace, Robin halted as she remembered Frederick's face in the mirror.

She could almost swear the apparition had been a hunger-induced hallucination. But she remembered the pleading in his eyes with startling clarity.

On the other hand, it seemed a trifle suspicious that he had turned up in Gigi's mirror. If he really existed, why didn't he show his face in one of Flint's mirrors?

As the children listened intently, Gigi said, "So you're from where? Hong Kong?"

"Taiwan," said May. "You are very curious about me. There is something particular you want to know, is that not so?"

"Well, yes." Gigi chewed her lower lip, obviously disappointed at having her thunder stolen.

"My mother believes she's contacted the ghost of a man who's seeking his former girlfriend," Robin explained.

Gigi glowered. "Some matters are best expressed indirectly."

"What does that mean?" asked Caitlin.

"You mean you don't know?" said Aaron. "There's something you don't know?"

"She just *thinks* she knows everything," scoffed Brick.

"This man is Chinese?" asked May. When Gigi shook her head, May said, "Then I am sorry, but all my old boyfriends are Chinese."

"Maybe he was in love with you but you didn't know it," Robin suggested, then wondered why she was meddling in this nonsense.

"If a man falls in love with me, I know it," May said.

"She's in danger," Gigi volunteered.

The children leaned forward. "What kind of danger?" asked Aaron.

"Mom, where did this come from?" Robin demanded. There'd been no mention of danger when she visited her mother on Sunday.

"We had a séance last night." Gigi glowed with satisfaction at having news to break. "Frederick came and, oh, he was terribly distraught. He said he must find this woman because of the danger. Irma was so jealous I thought she'd burst. You know, Mortimer never brought her anything as interesting as this."

For the next half hour, Gigi explained to her rapt audience about spirit guides and the contest between her and her best friend to make the most impressive contacts.

Finally May had to leave. "I am so happy to meet your mother," she told Robin. "She has many ideas in her head. Perhaps someday I will come to her shop."

"I'd like that very much," Gigi said.

After May left, Robin discovered that it was almost two o'clock. The children had missed workbook time, and Flint was sure to check.

When she explained to Gigi, her mother volunteered to help. They spent the next fifteen minutes supervising the children's rapid scribbling, then sent them to change for gym class. Reading time was abandoned altogether, but Robin told herself that meeting a lady from Taiwan had been educational in its own right.

"So you're going to City Hall. That's perfect," Gigi said when they were alone in the living room.

The off-white decor accented with blue showed no traces of fingerprints or dents in the furniture, testimony to the fact that it was off-limits to the children. Robin hardly ever came in here, but the light streaming through the front window had a mellow cast that attracted her. Somehow it seemed natural to wait here with Gigi.

She had the feeling Kathy had been saving this room for some distant day when the children were older and it became possible to entertain with elegance. She felt a sharp sympathy for the woman who had planned and worked so hard and enjoyed so little benefit from it.

I'll keep everything safe for her, Robin thought. *Except Flint. He'll have to keep himself safe.*

"You need a ride?" she asked her mother, then remembered that Flint was addressing the City Council's study session this afternoon. "You're not going to protest, are you?"

"Why not?" said Gigi. "They're trying to ruin my store. Honestly, the sign and the facade are practically made out of cardboard. Even if they did fall, they wouldn't hurt a fly."

"Mom, that's kind of awkward, don't you think?" Robin hoped the children would take a long time changing. "I mean, you're marching against my employer."

"You still have freedom of speech," her mother reminded her.

"Me?" Robin said. "I'm not going to protest."

"Well, you *could*," Gigi argued. "Anyway, the meeting started at two, and there's no telling when your Mr. Harris will finish his presentation. He's not the only item on the agenda, you know. So we'd better hurry."

"Mother," Robin said between clenched teeth. "Let me make this clear. I am not going to protest against my employer. That's why you came here, isn't it? You actually believed I would join you. Did you expect the children to march, too?"

Gigi heaved a melodramatic sigh. "You always were strong-willed. Well, all right. But I do need a ride and you're going to City Hall anyway."

"I don't suppose I have much choice," said Robin. She didn't mean to be churlish, but her mother could be infuriating at times.

The children piled in from the bedrooms, wearing their gym shorts and shirts. Robin collected their swimsuits and towels for their second class of the day, then remembered the signs her mother had left on the lawn.

"Mom, I don't think your stuff will fit in my car," she said.

"Of course it will." Without a backward glance, Gigi hurried out to the driveway, and the children scurried to keep up.

Her mother did manage to stuff all the signs into the tiny trunk, although they had to borrow Caitlin's stretchy bicycle hooks to hold the hood partway shut. Then the five of them crammed inside, hip to hip, and off they went.

With luck, Robin decided, they could drop her mother at City Hall and park next door at the community center without attracting attention. She had to admit, she felt a bit awkward about not supporting her mother in the protest. Robin had agreed that the earthquake standards were unreasonably strict. As the businesspeople pointed out, they had to make a living. And the town had withstood numerous shakers over the decades without serious mishap.

As usual, Flint was applying harsh standards that would prove more destructive than helpful, Robin told herself. His attitude toward his work mirrored that toward his children.

On the other hand, she couldn't march against him. Especially not during work time. Although the children would be in their gym class, she didn't want to get involved in a conflict of interest.

She wondered if Flint would appreciate her dilemma. Of course not, she reflected as she turned into the parking lot. He wouldn't understand why anyone would think twice about doing what was right.

If only right and wrong were always that simple.

Unfortunately, the spaces close to City Hall were all filled. From the car, Robin could see several dozen protesters on the march, but there was no sign of Flint.

Over her mother's protests, she refused to double park. Instead, she drove to the community center next door.

"It's almost three," she informed Gigi firmly. "If you want to haul your signs over there yourself, go ahead. Otherwise, you'll have to wait until I escort the children to their class."

Gigi clucked. "You're making a mistake. Think how educational this would be. They could witness democracy in action."

"Could we?" Aaron gazed eagerly toward City Hall, where the marchers were distantly in view.

"Don't be a Daffy Duck." Caitlin planted hands on hips. "They're protesting against Dad. If we get him mad, he'll never take us to Disneyland for our birthday."

Robin couldn't suppress a smile as she ushered the children indoors. "Disneyland, is that what you want?"

"We haven't been in years," Brick told her as they clattered through the entryway.

"Dad says it's silly," Aaron noted.

"Mom loved to take us there." Caitlin's answer explained a great deal. Apparently returning to Disneyland had been too painful for Flint to contemplate.

Robin wondered if he'd be able to handle it this year. For the children's sakes, she hoped so. They shouldn't be barred from the amusement park forever.

Not until the class began and the children were involved in stretching exercises did Robin depart with Gigi. Even though this time was her own, she had an uncomfortable feeling about the whole business.

She helped her mother lift the signs from the trunk. They were too heavy for Gigi to move herself, that much was obvious.

"Why not just leave them here?" Robin asked, surveying the four posters. "You don't need all these."

"Some of them belong to other people." Gigi braced two heavy signs on her shoulder. "We had a paint-in yesterday afternoon at the store. It was fun, and good for business, too."

How like her mother to promise to bring the banners when she didn't even have a car, Robin reflected. She wasn't sure whether she admired her mother's cavalier approach to life or resented the assumption that someone—usually her daughter—would always be around to pick up the slack.

As they trudged across a grass median to the City Hall lot, Robin said, "You mean a lot of merchants wanted their fortunes told?"

"Absolutely," said Gigi.

"And you charged them full price?" Her mother might be a good businesswoman, but she had a soft heart toward anyone who could even loosely be defined as a friend.

"We swapped," said her mother. "I've got free coupons for pizza, dry cleaning and VCR repair."

That sounded like a good deal, Robin had to admit.

Some of the protesters waved as they approached, and a couple of men came to help. Robin handed her signs to the owner of a drive-in dairy, thanked him and said, "I'd better be leaving."

"Hold on," he said. "I haven't got a good grip on these." He leaned one into her hands.

At that precise moment, Flint stepped out of the building. Gazing down from the head of the stairs, he must have had a clear view of Robin's sign.

Cold fury flashed from his gray eyes. Alarmed, Robin peered up.

The sign read, Let's Embarrass Harris.

Chapter Ten

Flint couldn't believe he'd been such a damn fool. In the past week and a half, he'd begun to believe Robin had reformed. She'd appeared to settle into normal life, behaving responsibly and sensibly.

But no employer could stomach this kind of disloyalty. Even though he knew the children must be safely tucked away in their gymnastics class, it was unbelievable that Robin would attack him in public this way.

He strode down the steps, his body tight with fury. Flint hardly noticed the dozen or so merchants clustered around, shouting at him with red faces. If ten they had anything reasonable to say, they would have said it during the council study session.

Everything had gone smoothly until now. His recommendations had been met with nods of resigned acceptance. The council members knew they would face an angry electorate at the polls next year, but they also recognized that it was their job to prepare the city for emergencies.

As he approached the sidewalk, Flint knew he had to set Robin straight. She needed to get her irresponsible impulses under control immediately.

The sight of her blue eyes wide with shock did nothing

to soften his temper. What else had she expected when she chose to confront him this way?

"Dr. Harris, this is my fault." The quavery voice came from a red-haired woman whom Flint recognized as Robin's mother. Her instinct to spring to her daughter's defense might be admirable, but it was misplaced.

"This is between me and your daughter." He caught Robin's arm and pulled her aside so abruptly that the sign fell to the pavement with a clank.

"Flint, that's not mine." How could she feign innocence when she'd been caught red-handed?

"You must have been taking lessons from Brick," Flint snapped. "He can come up with an excuse for anything. You honestly expect me to believe that you were just holding that sign for someone else?"

"My mother." Robin winced, and Flint realized he must be pinching her arm. He let go.

"Your mother forced you to join her in a protest at City Hall?" The flimsy excuse made Flint even angrier. Why couldn't the woman take responsibility for her own actions?

To make matters worse, the protesters were closing in fast.

"I know it looks bad." Robin's voice was low and earnest. "She doesn't have a car...."

"So you had to give her a ride?" Flint wasn't buying it. "She forced you into it over your objections? And, I presume, you let my children see the signs on the way over. Making them think their father is some kind of a villain!"

"They couldn't see the signs." Robin seemed to be having trouble finding words. "Those were in the trunk."

A disturbing picture flashed into Flint's mind. "And meanwhile the five of you were crammed into that sardine can you call a car? How many people is it designed to carry, Miss Lindstrom? Four, if I'm not mistaken."

She made an ineffectual gesture in midair. "We all wore seat belts, except for Gigi. There's room for a fifth person in the middle of the back, and that *is* the safest seat in the car, you know. Besides, she's an adult...."

A rotund man who owned a local dry cleaners thrust himself partway between them. "Dr. Harris, I'd like to know whether you have any experience whatsoever with retail business. Do you realize we're being regulated into the ground?"

"You're going to be shaken to the ground if you don't take proper precautions." Flint had no patience for diplomacy at the moment.

"That's easy for you to say!" cried a woman whose nametag identified her as the owner of a video store. "No one's going to snatch away your signs and cut into your business! You're just doing this to make money, aren't you?"

"Yeah," said a younger man. "You've got to justify your big consulting fee by recommending changes whether they're needed or not."

"That's right!" Flint could hear his voice boom across the parking lot. "I'm trying to run you all out of business so I can take over your stores and make a fortune! I have no motive but to line my pockets at your expense! I don't give a damn if an earthquake flattens every one of you, which it almost certainly will! Now leave me the hell alone!"

Everyone stared in astonishment, and then they backed away. Robin's jaw dropped open, but she had the good sense not to argue.

On a roll, unable to stop even if he wanted to, Flint roared at her. "If I catch you in any activity like this again—do I need to spell it out? You are expected to behave with the dignity befitting a person entrusted with the care of children. Is that clear?"

Robin's eyes glittered with restrained tears as she spat out, "Perfectly!" and walked away.

Flint stood motionless on the sidewalk, fists clenched, wondering why he felt like such an idiot. After all, he was right, wasn't he?

"The spirits are most unhappy," said the red-haired woman near his elbow. Her name popped into his mind— Gigi. He supposed it must have suited the tiny baby on whom it was bestowed, but it didn't fit the eccentric adult she had grown to be.

"I apologize if I've disrupted your spirits." Flint had no quarrel with this woman, even if she had produced the most perverse daughter in the history of womankind.

"It really is my fault," Gigi said as the protesters drifted away. "There I was on your front lawn with those heavy signs and no car. And I knew she had to drive to the community center."

Flint's stomach twinged uncomfortably. "Are you saying you dumped these signs on my front lawn?"

Gigi's cheeks flushed even redder than her rouge. "I admit, I was trying to persuade my daughter to join me. But she refused. She's terribly stubborn, you know. She almost wouldn't bring me here at all. And then she made such a fuss about disloyalty and how much she owed you."

"Are you sure you aren't shading the truth a little?" Flint hadn't forgotten how Gigi had pretended the spirits were throwing Robin's clothes out the window. A woman capable of that much deception was capable of anything.

Besides, he could hardly bear to believe he'd wronged Robin that badly.

"Your children can confirm it," Gigi pointed out. "Oh, dear. I'm so used to depending on my daughter, you see. That's why I never learned to drive, because she was always around to give me a ride. I'm even the one who persuaded her to throw the stars at you. She thought it was a foolish idea, but she went along for my sake. I do take advantage of her, but I never meant it to come to this."

"She received a well-deserved scolding," Flint said. "Nothing more."

"Well, she's very upset." Gigi twisted her hands together. "I can tell. The spirits will never forgive me if I've ruined everything. They didn't put me up to this today. It was my own idea, and a bad one."

Flint wished the woman would quit babbling about spirits. In fact, he wished she hadn't talked to him at all. He couldn't help but believe in her sincerity, and that meant he'd been unforgivably rude to Robin.

He'd also made a damn fool of himself in front of half the business community of Beachside.

Well, what was wrong could be put right. "Excuse me," Flint said, and stalked across the parking lot toward the community center.

He hated apologizing, but sometimes it had to be done. Maybe he could even offer to buy dinner tonight.

On the other hand, he couldn't be blamed for misjudging the situation. It had appeared so clear-cut. How else could Robin have expected him to behave?

Politely, he conceded, gritting his teeth.

Flint checked his watch as he neared the building. Almost three-thirty, and he had a four o'clock appointment with the principal of Serena Academy. That left just enough time to talk to Robin.

Inside the building, he dropped by the children's gymnastics class. Caitlin was trotting confidently along a mock balance beam set on the ground, while Brick and Aaron watched with varying degrees of disgruntlement. Their stances reflected their personalities—Brick with arms crossed and legs apart, Aaron biting his lip and jamming his hands in his pockets.

No sign of Robin.

Flint wandered down the hall and paused outside the ladies' room. He supposed she might have gone inside, so he waited a while, but then he caught the custodian giving him a suspicious look and decided he ought to continue his search.

Around another bend, he heard a piano pounding out some music that he couldn't identify. Flint went to investigate.

On the door, which stood ajar, a placard read, Modern Dance, Advanced. Tony Garcia, Instructor.

He peered inside. Four couples, who looked about college age, were executing a series of lifts with varying degrees of proficiency. As he watched, one young man almost dropped his partner, while another couple couldn't seem to get their movements in sync.

"No, no, no!" The music stopped and a man of about thirty stepped into view from the sidelines. He had a compact, muscular build and bristled with disapproval. "You're not counting properly! And where is the feeling? The artistry? Gentlemen, these are not sacks of flour you're lifting! Ladies, you are not competing for a gymnastics medal!"

The dancers clustered in one corner, looking suitably abashed. Flint felt a twinge of sympathy. How was a person supposed to be athletic and graceful at the same time?

"Let me demonstrate." Tony gestured to someone on the sidelines.

A familiar slim figure stepped forward, stripping jeans off to reveal her leotard. Robin, of course.

She wasn't going to let this man pick her up and manhandle her body in midair, was she? Flint could feel his fists clenching. Hovering discreetly behind the half-closed door, he watched with mingled skepticism and readiness.

At a signal from Tony, the pianist hit the keys. Music echoed off the walls as Robin pirouetted forward and flung herself into space.

The man caught her without a sign of strain, as if she weighed no more than a feather. Slender as Robin might be, Flint knew from experience that she weighed more than a feather. He supposed he could fake the same effortlessness if he practiced long enough, though.

Her body formed a fluid line, curling around Tony's shoulders. The man paced forward, carrying her as if they formed a single unit. When he swung her almost to the floor, Flint became aware that the two dancers were cutting shapes in space, making designs with their bodies that vanished in a heartbeat.

Even though his aesthetic sense appreciated their craft, he didn't like what was going on. He didn't like the confident way Tony gripped her thigh and swung her up. He didn't like the way Robin entrusted herself fully to her partner, without a sign of resistance. Why couldn't she treat *him* that way?

Flint reminded himself that he *wanted* her to resist him. In fact, he wanted her to keep plenty of distance between the two of them.

But he wanted her to keep even more distance from this Tony fellow.

The guy didn't have to look as if he were enjoying the experience so much. Robin didn't need to wear that blissed-out expression on her face. Anyone would think the two of them were lovers.

How did they keep from getting turned on, anyway? Flint devoutly hoped the man was gay. Or planning to enter a monastery and renounce all worldly temptations. Or, to be charitable, about to be offered a major position with a ballet company in Timbuktu.

Flint supposed a person who didn't know him well might guess he was jealous, but that wasn't the case. Well, maybe a little. He would admit to being physically attracted to Robin. Who could help it? So, of course, seeing her physically involved with another man, even in the course of a dance class, naturally annoyed him.

Annoyed him? It ticked the hell out of him.

Now what was the guy doing? Hadn't he demonstrated his technique sufficiently for his students? Did he have to scoop Robin into a kind of arrested swan dive that pressed her breasts into his arm?

Damn it, why should Flint care? These past three years, he'd developed a self-image as a man who stood alone, on his own two feet, the perfect model of a father and grieving widower. If he got involved with a woman again, he expected it to be with someone businesslike, crisp and well-ordered.

Yielding to his impulses where Robin was concerned would be like jumping off a pier into a raging flood. Flint wasn't afraid. He almost relished the challenge. But he'd never been a fan of white-water rafting and he wasn't about to start now. He had children to think of.

The music thundered to a stop and the students burst into applause. Robin took a modest bow and turned to put on her jeans.

Her face registered dismay as she caught sight of Flint. He waited, trying to maintain a blank expression, until she came over.

"Very nice," he told her. It wasn't much of a compliment, but it was the best he could manage with that Tony person watching. "By the way, I'm sorry about what I said. I was wrong." He tapped his watch. "Got an appointment. See you at dinner."

He walked off without waiting for her reply. An apology had been made. What more could a woman ask?

ROBIN STALKED down the hall toward the gym. The children would be coming out in a few minutes, heading off to change for swim lessons. She wanted to make sure they ended up where they were supposed to be.

In the meantime, she could feel her blood boiling over Flint's arrogance. Did he believe an offhand apology would compensate for the way he'd humiliated her in public?

And he had some nerve, spying on her. Robin had been relieved to discover her friend Tony was teaching a class in the same building—she'd needed a distraction from her outrage at Flint.

Watching the dancers had reminded her of how much she loved to teach, and to perform. It had been a rare treat, to be asked to help Tony demonstrate technique to his students. When he lifted her in his arms, Robin had forgotten everything except the joy of movement, the sense of lightness and power that seized her in midair. All the troubles and worries of her life had vanished for those few minutes, only to come crashing around her when she saw Flint. The man was impossible.

Suddenly the gym door banged open and children ran out, giggling and shrieking. A small knot of mothers had gathered, and each collected her offspring with hugs.

Caitlin trotted out ahead of her brothers, blond hair swinging, face shining with excitement. "That was fun!" she cried. "Oh, Robin, did you see me? I could be a dancer like you, couldn't I?"

"Of course you could," Robin said.

Aaron rushed toward her, flinging his arms around her waist. "I missed you," he said.

Brick stood a few feet away, ignoring his siblings. "Where's Granny Gigi?"

Robin spent the next few minutes answering questions and assuring them that their father hadn't gotten *very* angry. By the time they raced away to put on their swimsuits, she knew she loved these little guys more than she would ever have believed possible.

A maternal instinct she'd never known she possessed had burst into full bloom. Even if somehow it turned out the medical clinic had been wrong and the triplets hadn't been conceived with her eggs, they had still become her children during the short time she'd known them.

Flint might never understand, but Robin had the feeling Kathy would. For the children's sake, she was going to bite her tongue and try to be nice to her employer.

But not any nicer than she had to be.

THE CHILDREN DAWDLED after swim class, joking with their friends and taking ages to dry off and change. Robin wasn't sure why she felt so impatient, except that if Flint arrived home and found dinner not ready, he was sure to blame her.

She didn't think she could put up with his rudeness again without exploding. Who did the man think he was? Granted, the sign reading Embarrass Harris had been tasteless, at best, but that didn't give him the right to bawl her out in public.

Then they had to make two circuits of the City Hall parking lot at Brick's insistence, to make sure Grandma Gigi wasn't standing around waiting for a ride, but apparently one of her friends had taken her home. By the time they parked in front of the Harris house, it was after five-thirty. Dinner at six looked like the impossible dream.

Robin staggered toward the steps with an armload of wet bathing suits and towels. When the children ran ahead and found the door unlocked, she knew with a sinking feeling that Flint had gotten here first.

She stepped inside and paused in surprise. At first whiff, it smelled like someone was cooking. At second whiff, she identified the tantalizing aroma as Chinese food—of the take-out persuasion.

Still not ready to face her employer, Robin lugged her load into the laundry room and dropped everything into the washer. Swimsuits had to be cleaned in cool water with little agitation. Towels needed hot water and lots of stirring. She settled on warm water and a medium spin.

Robin stood at the sink brushing her hair and listening to the children chatter to their father in the kitchen. They sounded so happy together.

Back in the familiar surroundings, she decided her earlier conclusion that the children had become hers seemed self-indulgent and premature. Yes, Robin had grown to love them. It was hard to imagine not seeing them every day. But wasn't it pride that made her search for ways in which they resembled her? Wasn't it arrogance to think she could assume the same importance in their lives as the man who had loved them from birth?

Robin had never known her emotions to take such a roller-coaster ride. It must have something to do with her feelings about Flint. She couldn't even begin to sort them out.

What are you doing here? she asked her face in the mirror. *You're a dancer and a teacher, not a nanny. This job is a stopgap, nothing more.*

Then her heartbeat sped up as fog crept across the mirror. Robin gripped the edge of the sink, telling herself that, after all, she *was* hungry, so that might explain any visual disturbances. But it didn't explain the overwhelming sense she had of another presence in the room.

Robin felt bathed in positive emotions that she could have sworn came from a woman—encouragement and reassurance. She fought to sort out her confused impressions. Based on her previous experience, she expected to see Frederick's face, but the only eyes meeting hers in the mirror were her own.

Robin took another look and realized the glass was spotted with water droplets. There was nothing supernatural about it—she'd left the washer lid open while it filled, and the air had become humid.

Walking over to the machine, Robin saw that she had accidentally pressed the button for hot water instead of warm. That accounted for the steam.

No one had entered the room. No one had been trying to reassure her. It must be simply her own edgy emotions playing tricks.

Scoffing at her foolishness, Robin switched the water temperature and closed the lid, then continued on to the kitchen.

White cartons perched on the table, which the children were busy setting. Flint was opening packets of soy sauce.

"I hope you like Chinese food," he said.

"I love it." Had there ever been such an unpredictable man in the history of the planet?

"I gave your mother a ride home," Flint added.

"What?" She and the children stared at him.

"I got paged. My appointment was postponed until tomorrow. Then when I went to the car, I saw her standing around looking lost." Flint shook his head ruefully. "She was holding a sign that said Want a Quake Forecast? Ask a Fortune-Teller."

Robin laughed. "That's my mother."

"She even made me carry the sign into her shop. It *was* kind of heavy." Flint filled glasses with ice water. "Who is that guy with the toga? He asked me if I had any beer, as if I would carry it around in my pocket. Anyway, then I saw the Chinese place on the way home and thought you deserved a break, and here we are."

"Wow! Kung pao shrimp!" Caitlin hopped into her chair.

"Egg rolls!" said Aaron. "And those crunchy things!" Brick grabbed the carton of sweet-and-sour pork.

They devoured the meal in relative silence, given the children's usual tendency to talk all at the same time. Apparently Chinese food was a favorite.

Robin couldn't figure this man out. It had been kind of him to give Gigi a ride. And thoughtful of him to bring dinner. Was this his way of making up for the tongue-lashing earlier? The idea that Flint might feel contrite softened her anger.

She knew many men had trouble expressing their feelings. Flint seemed so articulate and self-possessed that it was hard to imagine he, too, might speak gruffly to cover embarrassment. Perhaps that's why his apology had sounded so ungracious.

Or was she giving him more credit than he deserved?

Flint insisted she remain seated after dinner while the children cleared the table. He even went to move the laundry to the dryer.

Impressive, Robin thought, but kept up her guard.

After dinner, Flint played War with Brick and Caitlin, and sure enough, Brick won. Then came Uno with Aaron, who trounced his father. Robin suspected Flint had purposely given his son the advantage a couple of times.

She enjoyed seeing the children so relaxed with their father. Tonight Flint was showing another side of himself, a side she liked very much.

And didn't trust as far as she could throw a seismograph.

Finally the children were tucked into bed, read to and kissed. Worn out from a busy afternoon, they fell asleep instantly.

Robin emerged from folding towels to find Flint fiddling with the tape player in the den. "I've been waiting for you," he said.

"Why?" She clutched the towels in front of her.

Flint lifted them away and set them on the couch. "I'm going to teach you a lesson."

"Oh?" Robin's chin came up.

"I'm going to teach you," he said, "that I can dance as well as that Tony person. Probably better."

Chapter Eleven

Robin couldn't imagine that Flint meant to whirl her onto his shoulders, even though she knew he was physically capable of it. "Excuse me?" she said.

"We're talking popular dance here," he amended with a sheepish grin. "Of course, with a little practice, I could do what that fellow did today."

"Of course," Robin repeated. From most men, the claim would have been empty bragging, but she had a suspicion Flint could pull it off. What he might lack in grace, he would make up for in sheer power. "What did you have in mind?"

"I found a party tape I made a few years back. When we used to give parties." Flint reached out and pushed a button on the player. A tantalizing beat filled the room and the room filled with the mock-Fifties vigor of "Crocodile Rock."

Flint certainly knew how to rock and roll. Robin had almost forgotten the steps, but they came back to her as Flint caught her hand and twirled her around.

She found herself smiling at the bounciness of the music and the infectious youthfulness of the dance. For someone so tall, Flint moved with surprising speed, and she relaxed in the security of his partnership.

Dancing with Tony this afternoon, Robin had enjoyed detecting the subtle pressures that indicated which way he was going to move next. But her enjoyment had come from the experience itself, not from any personal contact with Tony.

Dancing with Flint was another matter entirely. Despite the energy of rock and rolling, which sent them flying around the family room to the imminent peril of Caitlin's computer, Flint's concentration seemed to focus entirely on Robin. Where Tony had projected himself toward the watching students, Flint drew her into a private universe that shut out everything but the two of them.

He twirled her around, and Robin laughed with sheer exuberance. The air shimmered as Flint met her, released her, then caught her again. Robin's breath came quickly and her heart thudded.

When the music ended, Flint kept hold of her hands. "I'd almost forgotten," he murmured.

"How to dance?" she asked.

"How to have fun."

She feared for a moment that he would remember the photograph of Kathy and withdraw as he had before, but then a slow dance came on the tape and Flint drew her into his arms.

This might not be such a good idea, Robin thought, but she didn't care. Why shouldn't they have fun? Why shouldn't they enjoy a rare moment with their defenses down?

The room around them had fallen into darkness. A single lamp cast a glow, like the radiance of a private moon. She no longer worried about the photographs. They lay in deepest shadow.

Caught close against Flint, Robin could feel the pounding of his heart and smell his masculine fragrance. With restrained gentleness, he guided her along the star-lighted paths of a galaxy that belonged to them alone.

Robin closed her eyes and rested her cheek against Flint's shoulder. She didn't have to think about her movements—they floated naturally with his as she instinctively followed the shifts of his muscles.

The soft air soothed away ordinary sensations. She no longer felt the floor beneath her feet, only the warmth of Flint's arms. In three-quarter time, they moved into a slower, more languorous world where the air seemed to thicken and support them like the currents of deep space.

Robin's skin became acutely sensitive to the touch of Flint's legs as they brushed hers, to the pressure of his hand on her waist, to the hardness of his shoulder beneath her cheek. Her mind tried to warn that this could be dangerous, but the warning went hurtling away through space like a shooting star.

Flint halted and his hands framed her face. With slow deliberation, his mouth closed over Robin's. For an instant, she couldn't react. Then her lips opened to his.

She couldn't miss the change in him as his tongue gained entry. His entire body became taut and supercharged. Where they touched along his powerful frame, she could feel his arousal. The man wanted her in an elemental way and Robin, lost among the stars, felt his desire reverberate through her bones.

Flint switched off the music. Before Robin could regain her composure, he lifted her and carried her down the hall to his room. Their mouths never parted. They swept through the house in a single, uninterrupted motion.

The bedroom door closed behind them. Flint must have turned on a lamp, because Robin could see him clearly in its gentle light as he lowered her to the bed.

From the far recesses of the universe, she heard a voice whisper that she ought to find her way back to earth. She couldn't remember why, and it didn't matter. The voice faded into a distant echo.

Flint leaned over the bed, and Robin's fingers reached to his shirt, slipping the buttons free and finding the furred expanse of his chest. There was no hurry at all, she thought dizzily as she arched up to explore his chest with her lips.

Flint let her slide away his clothes and touch him all over. Robin wanted to experience every part of him like an undiscovered planet filled with wonders. She reveled in his shuddering responses, in the barely restrained ferocity of his sinews and synapses. He held himself above the bed, inches from her clothed body, as she bared every inch of his naked male potency.

Even though she'd seen him jogging in the mornings and knew he worked out at the gym several times a week, Robin had rarely caught more than a brief glimpse of Flint when he wasn't buttoned up and businesslike. Now, unclothed, he radiated raw virility, from his muscled arms to his slim hips.

Flint lowered himself to the bed beside her. His eyes locked into Robin's, transfixing her, as if claiming her soul. Strong hands removed her jeans and pulled down her leotard. Before she knew it, her breasts lay bared to him.

Flint's tongue covered the quivering tips, rousing them into hard peaks. He kissed her mouth, then claimed her breasts again, then traced a line down her flat stomach. A moment later, Robin realized he had removed every stitch of her clothing. She must have wriggled, must have helped, but she hadn't been aware of it.

His next kiss was tender but distracted, and she realized why when he launched himself into her, exploding the two of them off the launching pad with a burst of fire and velocity.

Robin gasped at the sensations careening through newly awakened nerve endings. Flint had become a driving force of nature, overwhelming, awe-inspiring. At the speed of light, he carried her into ecstasy.

They merged and parted, then merged again. Robin had never dreamed she could be lifted out of herself this way, flung into a swirling array of stars.

She had no desire to resist, only to match his fierce thrusts with an equal passion. How could she have lived in a house with this man, been angered and amused and annoyed and charmed by him, and never realized that he had been created to fill this void in her?

With a moan deep in his throat, Flint drew himself out of her for one agonizing moment. Robin reached for him, and he grasped her buttocks and united them with a flash of pleasure so overwhelming that she cried out. In the fire of an expanding sun, she welcomed Flint's explosion within her and then the long, quiet drift that followed.

They lay together in a silence that stretched into eons. Robin knew they should speak. Tonight they had left their old world and entered a new one. Neither of them had given any thought to the aftermath.

She wished she didn't have to face the complications. She knew now that she'd been denying the attraction between them from the beginning. But it had persisted and tonight had taken on a life of its own. Still, she and Flint existed as separate people, very different people, and they would need to resolve those differences.

Before Robin could figure out how to begin, Flint sat up, his back rigid against the headboard. "I take responsibility for this. I knew you were vulnerable. What I didn't realize was how vulnerable I was."

Why couldn't he say tender, loving things? Why couldn't he admit how much he needed her? Robin hauled herself up to a sitting position. "Flint, it isn't just a matter of you being lonely and me being naive. I'm not naive and I don't believe you're all that lonely. This was meant to happen."

"I don't buy that," he said. "We make our own decisions and we control what we do."

She could feel anger bubbling up at his stubbornness. "I don't know what kind of relationship we can have, but I think we ought to give it a chance."

Flint slipped his arm around her shoulders. "Robin, we're always fighting. We don't view life the same way. If we keep matters platonic from now on, I think we can go on living together, for our sakes and the children's sakes. But if we keep this up, this—this passion—sure, it's amazing. But how long will it last? We'll end up fighting and hating each other."

"Do you have to be so damn logical?" she pleaded. "Was what happened tonight logical? Do you honestly believe logic can keep it from happening again?"

"I don't want you to leave." She could see the conflict in his eyes. "But I have to do what's best for the children. Robin, let's try to keep this platonic. I think we can make it work."

The idea was outrageous. Only Flint, deluded into the conviction that his rational mind could rule his emotions, would even propose such a thing. But Robin could already see him opening a gap between them. She had to break it down quickly, before the division widened.

"It isn't that simple." She plunged ahead before she had time to think. "There's something I haven't told you."

He tipped his head and watched her, saying nothing.

"This is going to sound—kind of strange," Robin admitted. With half her mind, she wanted to backpedal. Originally, she'd thought it didn't matter whether she was the triplets' mother. After all, she'd planned to work here for a few months and then vanish from their lives.

But now she could see that everything fit a pattern. She hated to admit her mother might be right. Even now, Robin didn't believe spirits had guided her here, only that nature abhorred a vacuum. She'd been pulled here, and she was going to stay.

Haltingly, she told Flint how she'd donated her eggs when she was in college. As she talked, expressions registered on his face—doubt, skepticism, disbelief and then, slowly, anger. "You should have told me at once. You should never have taken the job."

"I'd already signed the contract." Trying to recall her thought processes that dizzying morning when she'd learned the truth, Robin knew her position sounded weak. "I was worried about who would look after the triplets. I told myself it didn't matter, that I was only going to be here on a temporary basis. I knew you'd be angry. I just— Flint, I never expected us to get involved."

"You should have told me," he growled. "You had an obligation to be honest." He stopped, his eyes clouded.

Dismay dimmed Robin's confidence that they could work this out. In her world, wrongs could be righted and errors forgiven. But Flint was a rigid man, and that harshness separated deeds into darks and lights, with no gray area in between.

"I'm sorry," she said. "Flint, I didn't have to tell you now, but I wanted you to know. I wanted to show you why it's so important that you give our relationship a chance. For the children's sakes."

He rolled away from her and lay staring into space. Robin wanted to clear the air, but she knew that she could never justify herself to Flint. She could only hope that, after thinking the matter through, he would find it in his heart to forgive her.

If only she could be sure he had a heart.

FLINT AWOKE in the early morning hours. At first, he thought it was just one of those momentary drifts into consciousness that occur most nights, but then he heard a whimper coming from the boys' room.

Aaron must be having one of his bad dreams.

Slipping out of bed, Flint pulled on a robe. He paused to gaze at Robin, hair tangling across her face, expression peaceful as a child's.

He'd never expected a bombshell like this. How could it have happened?

In Aaron's room, he found the boy already slipping into a deeper sleep. In the past week, Flint had to admit, the boy's nightmares had became fewer and farther apart.

They'd been intense after Kathy's death. All three of the children had suffered sleep disturbances. Within six months, though, the dreams had faded, but Aaron's had returned a few months ago. Their doctor explained that children go through physical and emotional stages, and that a new one is entered about the age of seven. Apparently this had triggered the nightmares of loss and abandonment in Aaron, but not in his sturdier siblings.

Would they get worse if Robin left? Possibly, Flint thought, but how could he let her stay? His rational mind told him this relationship would never last. The longer Robin remained, the worse it would be for the children when she departed.

No longer sleepy, he went into the kitchen and pulled some notes from his briefcase. Work was picking up since the government had reported that shoddy construction had contributed to damage in the Northridge quake. Cities and institutions were worried that even if they appeared to have met quake standards, the contractors might not have constructed the buildings correctly. A number of them had asked Flint to prepare proposals.

He rubbed his forehead, feeling the beginnings of a headache. He had so much to do. The last thing he needed was nanny problems.

Not just nanny problems, damn it. Robin. Robin with her mischievous eyes so much like Brick's. Oh, Lord, he'd never made the connection before. Of course her eyes looked like Brick's. She was his mother.

Flint remembered sitting with Kathy at this same table, discussing the possibility of an embryo transfer. They'd mulled so many issues—would the mother be healthy and intelligent? How could they be sure the children would resemble them enough so no one would ask questions? Should they tell their relatives?

Kathy had insisted on secrecy and on choosing a donor with her coloring and blood type. The only thing they hadn't considered, because they'd never thought it would matter, was that the woman lived in the same town and someday they might actually meet her.

They should have gone to a clinic in Los Angeles, Flint thought. But that would mean not having Caitlin and Brick and Aaron. He couldn't imagine any other children. He knew he owed their very existence to Robin.

But how could she have hidden the truth from him? How could she have deceived him all this time?

Trying to keep his anger in check, he allowed himself to remember their lovemaking last night. He hadn't experienced anything like it since the early days with Kathy, before the financial pressures and time shortages and infertility problems. He'd never expected to discover such happiness again.

If he allowed himself to be purely selfish, then he would take as much as Robin could give, and damn the future. Damn the pain it would cause when their arguments overwhelmed their attachment and the children once again lost a mother.

But to do that went against everything Flint believed. Everything.

He walked into the family room and turned on the light. He wanted to look at Kathy's photo for reassurance, but it lay in shadow. Annoyed, Flint angled the lamp shade, trying to cast light on the picture, but it stubbornly remained obscured.

The blurred image made him feel as if he, too, was losing his sharp sense of Kathy's presence. He couldn't allow that to happen.

He must send Robin away before the children learned the truth. And he owed something to Kathy, as well. She'd wanted to keep the triplets' parentage secret, and secret he would keep it.

Flint turned off the lamp and went back to the kitchen. He might as well work—he certainly wasn't going to sleep again tonight.

IN ROBIN'S DREAM, she wandered through the community center looking for the children. She could hear them whispering, but every time she opened a door, she found only another empty corridor.

At the sound of a car starting, she ran out into the parking lot, but Gigi and the other protesters blocked her way. "Embarrass Harris!" they cried, and, "The big one won't be our fault."

She woke up, startled by the quiet around her. The voices had reverberated so loudly, she could have sworn they were real.

Robin knew at once that Flint wasn't in the room. From the sunlight slanting through the window, she realized she'd overslept.

She put on yesterday's clothes, hoping the children wouldn't get suspicious when they saw her. Then she realized that despite the lateness of the hour—seven-thirty by the bedside clock—she didn't hear any voices. The kids never slept past six.

Robin emerged from the bedroom into a silent house. Despite the welcoming sweep of sunlight, it had a curiously empty feel as she walked through.

"Where is everybody?" She could have sworn her voice echoed.

The absence of the Harris clan gave Robin an uneasy feeling. It certainly wasn't the kind of greeting she had hoped for after her tryst with Flint.

Darn it, what did she expect? She wished she knew. He'd snapped back to form as soon as his passion was spent, as unyielding as ever. She knew her revelation about the children had affected him strongly, but she'd hoped he would mellow after a night's sleep. In the cool stillness of the house, however, her hopes waned.

She found the door to her bedroom shut, as if she lay sleeping inside. That was probably what Flint had led the children to believe.

Robin stepped in and caught her breath. Her suitcase lay atop the bed, neatly packed. There was a note on it.

> Robin,
> I'm taking the children out to breakfast to give you time to make a getaway. I'm sure you'll agree that the best thing is for you to leave at once. Please don't contact me again.
>
> Don't worry about the children. Maureen will be back in two days and I can manage until then.
>
> I apologize for my lack of chivalry, but I believe I've treated you at least as fairly as you've treated me.
>
> Flint

Beside it lay a check for the remainder of her salary.

Robin's first reaction was a cold, heavy feeling in the pit of her stomach. She'd lost them. Flint, the children, everything.

She sat on the edge of the bed, trying to absorb the shock. She tried to imagine how the children would react when they returned and found she'd gone. She could picture the hurt disbelief on their little faces as they listened to Flint manufacturing some excuse.

She couldn't bear it. And she didn't intend to.

Robin pressed her lips together angrily. If Flint insisted on firing her, then she had to leave. But she didn't have to go without saying goodbye to the children. He wasn't going to like it when she showed up, but at least he wouldn't make a scene in public.

Where would he have taken them? To persuade the triplets to sneak out quietly first thing in the morning, he would have had to promise something special. Robin doubted the pizza place opened this early. That left a nearby McDonald's.

She carted the suitcase to her car, trying to figure out what to say. She could tell the children she'd had a job offer. But why leave so suddenly? She supposed she'd have to accept whatever excuse Flint had already dreamed up. She hoped it made sense.

Robin tried not to think about the closeness they'd shared last night. She'd never cared this much about a man before. She knew it would take a long time to get over him. But she couldn't worry about that now.

Gritting her teeth, she started the car and drove to the restaurant.

At this hour, it was nearly empty. She saw at once that Flint and the children weren't there. Robin was on the verge of leaving when she scanned the parking lot and caught sight of the familiar Volvo.

She turned back and made her way through the restaurant to the outdoor playground. As soon as she pushed open the door, she saw Flint sitting at a table, reading the newspaper. The children must have disappeared into the mazelike tangle of tubes and slides. Otherwise, the area was deserted.

Robin took a deep breath and went to join him.

Flint's brow furrowed as he glanced up. She could see him getting ready to chew her out.

"Hold on." Robin slid into a chair. "I just want to tell the kids goodbye. Otherwise they're going to think women vanish into thin air. They'll never trust anyone again."

"Maybe they shouldn't," Flint muttered.

She ignored his churlishness. "Let's get our stories straight. Why am I supposed to be leaving? Have you already told them?"

He shook his head. "I forged a note. We're supposed to find it when we get home. You got a job offer out of town. You have to catch a flight immediately."

"What happens if they run into me at the beach?"

He snapped his paper shut. "All right. I guess I hadn't thought it through. What would you suggest?"

Robin couldn't formulate anything, not with Flint sitting so close. Even though she wanted to shake him for his stubbornness, she missed the warmth of his arms. She wanted to see his expression soften. She wanted to hear him laugh. She wanted to bury her nose in his neck and inhale.

"My brain doesn't function this early in the morning," she said.

"You should have considered that before you barged in here."

"*You* should have considered that before you invented such a ridiculous excuse."

They glared at each other. At that moment, Aaron barreled toward them from the slides. "Robin! Robin! Hey, guys, Robin's here!"

The other two triplets materialized in a flash and raced to hug her. "We were afraid something was wrong," Caitlin admitted, and Robin saw tears sparkling in her eyes.

"You kids were upset?" Flint asked in surprise. "You didn't say anything."

"She never sleeps this late," explained Caitlin.

"We figured she might be sick," Aaron added.

"Or hung over," Brick said.

"What?" Robin stared at him in astonishment. "Where did you learn that phrase?"

"A kid at school used it," Brick admitted. "It means you have a headache, doesn't it?"

Caitlin snorted, but didn't correct him. "Anyway, we're glad you're here."

"Actually..." Robin took a deep breath. "Kids, I hate to tell you this, but I have to leave."

"Just for today?" asked Aaron.

"No. I, uh, well, I've been offered a job." She hated lying to them.

"School doesn't start for six weeks," Caitlin challenged.

"I have to have some minor surgery first." Robin wished she didn't have to make up stories like this.

"There's nothing wrong with you, is there?" Aaron said.

"Nothing serious."

"It's Dad, isn't it?" Caitlin fixed her father with an accusatory glower. "He's sending you away and he doesn't want to take the blame. Shame on you, Flint."

Robin bit her lip. Flint would never forgive her if she laughed, but Caitlin was too perceptive for anyone's good. Darn it, Robin loved this little girl, and these two boys, too, who at the moment wore identical expressions of confusion.

"This is a matter for grown-ups," Flint growled. "Believe me, Caitlin, I have good reason."

"But you can't send her away," Aaron cried. "She's our mother!"

"I know you miss your mom, but you can't put Robin in her place," Flint said.

"Doesn't he know?" Caitlin asked Robin.

"Know what?"

"That you're the egg donor," the little girl said.

The distress on Flint's face mirrored Robin's own. "You told them?" he demanded.

"Of course not!" She turned to Caitlin. "How did you find out?"

"We knew all along," the girl said. "Why do you think we worked so hard to get Flint to hire you as our nanny?"

Chapter Twelve

Robin knew her mouth had fallen open, but she couldn't seem to force it shut as Caitlin calmly explained about the letter from the clinic and her research in the computer.

"We figured if Flint met you at school, he'd fall in love," the little girl announced as the five of them crowded around the table. "Then when he messed that up, Aaron had a stroke of genius. You know, about hiring you for our nanny."

Aaron grinned. "Yeah. Genius."

"Dumb luck," grumbled Brick.

"Don't call me dumb!"

"Would you guys shut up?" demanded Caitlin. "We're talking about our mother!"

Flint raised his hand for quiet. "Let's get one thing straight. Kathy was your mother."

Seeing Caitlin's face start to set in stubborn lines, Robin said quickly, "Yes, she was. If not for her, you wouldn't be here."

"Can't somebody have two mothers?" Brick asked.

"What about adopted kids?" said Aaron. "They have two mothers."

"So why can't we?" Caitlin pressed.

Robin and Flint exchanged glances. This issue obviously wasn't going to be resolved with a few minutes' conversation.

"I'm already behind in my work for today," Flint said. "Robin, if you don't mind, I'd like you to stay on for at least the rest of the day, until we can work out a sensible solution."

Flint must be an incurable optimist if he thought this situation could be resolved in one day, Robin reflected, but she knew better than to say so. "I'd be happy to."

He gave her a short nod, kissed the kids and strode out the exit into the parking lot.

"Wow," said Caitlin. "He gave in."

"Not exactly," Robin warned.

"Well," Caitlin said, "it's a start."

Aaron examined his Power Rangers watch. "It's time for projects."

Robin sighed. She didn't want to ignore Flint's schedule, even though her instincts cried out to let the children enjoy the playground a while longer.

"Let's go home," she said.

"The Anders kids are visiting their grandparents today," Brick suggested. "Could we play with them instead of riding bikes?"

"Sure." Robin shepherded the kids to her car, listening with half an ear to their eager chatter. They seemed almost to have forgotten the exchange of a few minutes ago, which weighed so heavily on her mind.

After all, from their point of view, they'd won the battle. But what about the war? she wondered.

FLINT REACHED the office before he realized he'd left his briefcase at home. He'd intended to pick it up when he took the children back, and then to work out of the kitchen all day while supervising them.

Before he could swing home to pick it up, a series of phone calls pinned him to the office. One client had a dozen questions about his recommendations; another insisted he make a proposal immediately on an industrial park.

It was almost noon before he could take a break. Advising his secretary that he would return promptly, he hurried out the door.

Damn his forgetfulness about the briefcase, Flint thought irritably. Damn the way business ran hot and cold, leaving him twiddling his thumbs one month and overwhelmed the next. And damn all the complications in his private life.

He'd been angry at Robin for intruding at the restaurant this morning, but he was glad now that she had. Who would have guessed the children already knew the truth?

He'd always been proud of Caitlin, but lately her intelligence had proven more a liability than an asset. It amazed Flint how quickly the children had transformed from helpless toddlers into independent children. They needed a firm hand and a lot of structure. How was he going to manage that by himself?

When he switched on the car, the radio was tuned to an all-talk station. He listened critically to a public service spot about earthquake preparedness. The information was valid—keep plenty of food and water on hand, maintain a first-aid kit and a radio with batteries—but hardly enlightening.

Then the talk-show host returned. "We're chatting today about boarding schools. With us in the studio is Dr. Samuel Jameson, principal of Heights Boarding Academy. Tell me, Dr. Jameson, what kind of parent would send a young child away to school?"

"A parent who wants the best for his child." The principal had a casual, friendly tone. "A parent who's tired of seeing the moral breakdown of our society, who wants his child to focus on his or her studies. . . ."

As the voice droned on, Flint realized the philosophy had a certain appeal. After all, he'd been worrying about what would happen as the triplets grew into adolescence. With a boarding school, he'd never have to worry about supervision.

According to the principal, the school—located an hour's drive north of Beachside—offered horseback riding, tennis, swimming and soccer, along with a personal computer for every child and instruction in the arts. It sounded perfect.

This afternoon, Flint decided, he'd have his secretary call the school and get further information. He suppressed a guilty twinge at the prospect of sending his children away. They hardly saw him during the week anyway, and he could spend extra time with them on weekends to make up for it.

He supposed he might allow Robin to visit the children occasionally. It was far from an ideal solution, but she wouldn't have any choice but to go along with it. And the kids would never forgive him if he barred her company altogether.

As he pulled into the driveway, Flint glimpsed Brick dashing through the Anders' front yard with his siblings and the Anders' grandchildren in pursuit. The group raced around the side of the house and disappeared into the back. Good—that meant he could fetch his briefcase and disappear unnoticed.

Flint found it on a kitchen chair and was about to leave when he heard a noise from Robin's room. She must have come into the house for some reason. He didn't see any point in letting her know he was home, but then he heard the noise again, more clearly. It sounded like a moan of pain.

"Are you okay?" He hoped she wasn't crying because of his cold treatment this morning. Flint didn't relish the thought of dealing with a hysterical female.

"Not really," came her strained voice.

Flint set the briefcase down. In Robin's room, he found her standing with one foot elevated on a step stool, examining her bare thigh beneath a reading light. She had removed her jeans and wore nothing but a T-shirt and panties.

"Sorry." Flint started to back out. "I didn't realize you were undressed."

"Oh, for Pete's sake!" Her blue eyes sparked at him. "You saw a lot more than this last night!" Before he could object, she continued, "I was trying to get the kids' ball out of the Anders's rock garden and I fell on a cactus. One of those low-growing kind that don't look like much, but—ow!"

He could see now that she held tweezers in one hand and was pulling something out of her skin. When Robin looked up, tears glimmered in her eyes. "I don't like to ask for help, but I can't reach them all."

"I'll be right there." Flint went to wash his hands, then returned. "Just relax. I'll get them out."

He knelt and touched her knee to steady himself. She trembled but didn't protest as he pressed the tweezers against her skin and plucked out an all-but-invisible sticker.

"Thanks." Robin's voice had a rueful note. "I felt so stupid, falling like that."

"I'm glad you didn't let the children go after the ball," Flint said. "Now hold still."

Examining her thigh with methodical thoroughness, he removed several more prickles. This was proving more difficult than he had expected. He could hardly see the damn things, and he hated hurting Robin.

"I'm not sure if I've got them all," he said.

She flinched. "There's more there. Are you sure you can't see them?"

Flint opened the blinds wider, but even with full sunlight, he couldn't spot the tiny spikes. From childhood campouts, he knew there was one almost foolproof way to get all the thorns out, and he didn't intend to shrink from it now. "Hold on." Bending close, he ran his fingers lightly up Robin's leg.

He discovered the prickles quickly. The blunt ends didn't hurt his fingertips, and he was able to remove the last of the prickles. In a few minutes, Robin was able to confirm that he'd caught them all.

The only problem, Flint discovered, was that tracing his fingers along Robin's naked thigh was an intensely personal form of contact. It made him remember all too clearly how their bodies had felt last night.

He moved away quickly. "Glad I could help," he said when she thanked him.

"Flint." Robin chewed on her lip. "Listen, about the kids..."

"I'll take care of them," he said. "I think I've got a solution." He described the boarding school. "They'd be well taken care of, and once they've adjusted, I think they'll be happy there."

He wished she wouldn't stare at him with that expression of disbelief. "What about Aaron?" she said. "Who's going to comfort him when he has nightmares?"

"They must have some kind of house mothers or something."

"And Caitlin?" Robin said. "You know how she hates restrictions. She'll turn that brain of hers to beating the system. The whole trick is to make her take responsibility for her own actions. But how can she do that in an institution?"

"They have a personal computer for every child." Flint clung to logic. "She'd have plenty of opportunity to do the things she likes."

"And Brick?" Robin pulled on a clean pair of slacks. She'd tossed her jeans in the trash, Flint noticed, and assumed they were full of stickers. "He has a tendency to be macho. In the wrong situation, he could turn into a bully. He needs to be handled carefully."

"The school stresses moral education." Wasn't that what the principal had said?

Robin ran a brush through her hair with short, fierce strokes. "Flint, moral guidance doesn't just mean imposing rules, it means listening to the children, helping them find their own way to be good citizens. They need individual attention, and a lot of love."

"I don't need you to tell me about love." He moved toward the door. "However, I promise to give the matter more thought. I haven't investigated it yet, anyway."

"Listen to your feelings," Robin said.

"I'd rather listen to my logic," Flint replied, and strode away with such speed that he was halfway to his car when Robin came running after him.

"Your briefcase," she said, and handed it to him. Then, to his astonishment, she planted a kiss on his cheek before darting across the street to the Anders's house.

AFTER LUNCH, while the children were filling in workbooks, Robin called several of the schools at which she'd applied. None of them were hiring.

She saved the experimental school, A Learning Place for Children, until last. As she tapped the number into the phone, Robin realized she had put it off because of her mixed feelings.

She felt as if she ought to want the job. After all, it would remove her from a difficult situation. And she certainly did love teaching. But love wasn't a simple thing, not a simple thing at all.

Robin chewed on her lip, determined not to let sentiment get the better of her. Flint might be the best lover she'd ever found. He might be capable of great tenderness, as he'd shown when he'd removed the cactus spines. But overall he was wrong for Robin, and she didn't intend to waste time worrying about him.

"Miss Lindstrom?" The principal picked up his phone, snapping her back to the present. "I haven't forgotten you. I'm sorry about the delay. The fact is, getting a school like this off the ground is tricky. We have an endowment but there've been some unexpected costs in the start-up. We have to leave the theater and art program up in the air until we're sure we can fund it."

"Of course," Robin heard herself say.

"Why don't you try us back in a week or two?" he said. "Naturally, if you get another job offer, I'll understand, but we were impressed with your credentials and you seem like the type of person who would fit in here. Please bear with us."

"Certainly," Robin said. "I hope it works out."

She hung up feeling like she'd eaten jumping beans for lunch. Her stomach didn't just have butterflies, it had grasshoppers.

The principal wanted to hire Robin, she could tell. If only the finances worked out...

The buzz of the doorbell startled her. The boys abandoned their studies in the family room and pelted through the house, shouting, "Who is it? Who's there?" As Robin hurried toward the front, she heard Brick call, "It's Aunt Maureen!" and fling open the door.

Robin stopped in the middle of the living room. "Maureen! We weren't expecting you back until Friday."

The tall woman drew herself up, even more imposing than the first time they'd met. The Hawaiian vacation had left a sprinkling of freckles on her nose and lightened her gray hair a shade, but the easygoing island attitude clearly hadn't rubbed off.

"It was a great disappointment," Maureen announced. "The festivities were not authentic, if you ask me. Honolulu is overcrowded, the souvenirs are overpriced, and there were spiders in my hotel room. My lady friend ran off with a ukelele player, and then I hadn't even a companion to tour with."

"I'm sorry to hear that." Robin wouldn't have let a few setbacks force her home early from Hawaii, but she could see how they might upset Maureen.

"I'm glad to see you haven't quit in a huff, at least." Maureen marched inside, letting the boys close the door behind her. "Where's Caitlin? Still alive, is she?"

The girl poked her nose out of the hallway. "Hi, Aunt Maureen."

"I hope they were suitably punished for that stunt they pulled on me." The older woman walked into the kitchen and set her purse on a chair. "What tricks have they been up to today?"

"Daddy took us to McDonald's for breakfast," Aaron volunteered.

"We got to play at the Anders's house," said Brick.

"That isn't what I meant." There was a glint in Maureen's eye as she turned toward Robin. "They haven't set your hair on fire? Put snakes in your bed? Cut holes in your stockings?"

Robin shook her head in amazement. "They actually did those things? No wonder the nannies left."

"We would never do that to Robin," said Caitlin. "She's our mother."

"Don't be ridiculous," Maureen said.

"She really is," Aaron told her. "Honest."

"It's a long story." Robin hadn't meant to broach the subject, but now it couldn't be avoided. "Kids, this is something grown-ups need to talk about privately."

The children grumbled, but then Maureen produced a box of oatmeal cookies from her purse and they settled into a snack. As usual on Wednesdays, they had a two-hour computer class at the Boys and Girls Club, and Maureen insisted on driving the five of them in her Cadillac.

"Much safer," she observed with a nod toward the green compact. Robin knew Flint would agree.

The club occupied a bungalow a few blocks from the Beachside Pier. Once the kids were absorbed in their class, the two women headed for a beachfront restaurant.

At this hour, the place was nearly empty, and they snared a table by the window. This part of town, a mile or so south of Gigi's shop, offered a tidier assortment of palm trees and more upscale sunbathers, Robin noted. She kind of missed the kooky characters like Julius Caesar, though.

"Now what's this business about you being their mother?" Maureen asked when they had been served coffee.

Robin took a deep breath and the story spilled out. She kept it as simple as possible, omitting any mention of her relationship with Flint.

"I wouldn't have told you this without his permission," Robin said at last. "But once Caitlin brought it up, the cat was out of the bag."

"It certainly was." Maureen sniffed at her water glass, which came with a twist of lemon. "Would you look at this? They go to all the trouble of adding lemon and then use plain tap water."

"You have a keen nose," Robin said. "I wouldn't know what kind of water it is."

"A person has to be careful." Maureen set the water aside and signaled the waitress for more coffee. "People are always willing to take advantage if you let them."

It struck Robin that in a few years Flint might become like his aunt, so mistrustful and disapproving of the world that he couldn't even enjoy a vacation. Losing his wife had given him a dark outlook on life, but what had caused Maureen to feel this way?

"Forgive me for prying," she said, "but is there some reason you're so suspicious of people?"

"Well..." Maureen paused while the waitress filled her cup. "I suppose I stopped trusting people the day my marriage plans broke off. My fiancé was not an honorable man, as it turned out."

"I'm sorry to hear that." Robin waited, hoping the other woman would say more.

Outside the window, sailboats dotted the horizon. It was a sunny day, so crystal-clear she could see Catalina Island two dozen miles away. On the beach, toddlers chased an enormous ball, while on the pier, fishermen dangled their lines into the surf.

The cheery world of the present passed unnoticed before Maureen's eyes. Judging by her faraway expression, her mind had traveled nearly forty years into the past.

"I was twenty-eight," she told Robin. "In those days, that was old to be getting married. I wanted a career, but then I met the right man, or so I thought.

"He was three years older than me, a junior executive. We met at a party, at a friend's house. He was courteous, well-mannered and handsome. I thought I'd found Prince Charming."

It was hard to picture the Maureen of forty years ago, but watching memories play across her face, Robin began to imagine the romantic young woman she must have been.

"We set our wedding date," Maureen said. "A big church affair. I had the loveliest gown you ever saw, handmade lace and a long train. People said I looked like Princess Grace."

Everything had been in place, that fateful day—the organist, the bridesmaids and Maureen's father in a tuxedo waiting to escort her down the aisle.

"The groom never showed up," Maureen said. "Can you imagine? Later, it began to make sense. He'd told me he was an orphan and had grown up abroad. He didn't have any family or old friends. He must have been hiding something, but we never found out what."

"Are you sure something didn't happen to him?" Robin asked.

"My mother never trusted him." Maureen spoke tightly, as if the wound had never quite healed. "I tried to make excuses for him but she pointed out how weak they were. Finally I had to accept the truth, that he'd abandoned me at the altar because he didn't love me."

"That's awful." Still, Robin wished Maureen hadn't become so embittered. "No one ever heard from him again?"

"Not a soul," Maureen said. "I suppose it is something of a mystery, but I refuse to fool myself. I made a poor choice, and I paid for it."

Robin rested her chin in her palm, staring out the window. Something in Maureen's story nagged at her. She was trying to focus on what it was when Maureen resumed speaking.

"I sold my rings," she said. "I insisted on reimbursing my parents for the cost of the wedding, even though it took me years. They weren't the ones who made idiots of themselves over Freddy, and I wasn't going to let them suffer for it."

Freddy, Robin thought. As in Frederick.

She knew what Gigi would make of all this. She would insist that Maureen was the ghost's long-lost lover and that the spirits had guided Robin into the nanny job to make this connection.

Well, the spirits hadn't guided her—the children had. And if there was anything Maureen didn't need, it was to have a kook like Gigi meddling in her painful personal memories.

Maureen picked up the tab, brushing away Robin's offer to pay. "I'm glad we had this chat. I wanted to get to know you better as soon as I saw the children this afternoon. They behave differently with you than with any of the other nannies. Even Caitlin is attached to you, and I'm glad to see it. This egg donor business, well, I don't like it, but what's done is done. I hope you and my nephew can make some sensible arrangement for the future."

"I hope so, too." Robin accompanied her out of the restaurant. It was nearly five o'clock. Soon Flint would be home, and she hoped he'd come up with a better plan than boarding school.

IT WAS ALMOST SIX and Flint hadn't had time to think straight all day. He'd returned from an appointment only a few minutes ago and picked up a typed sheet his secretary had prepared regarding the boarding school. She'd also given him a message saying Aunt Maureen had returned early.

From a logical point of view, his options were clear. He could enroll the children in the boarding school or he could put them into day care and ask Maureen to help on weekends.

He couldn't keep on employing Robin. The situation was impossible, his logical side insisted. The longer she stayed, the harder it would be to separate her from the children. And the harder it would be to separate Flint from her.

He had never denied the attraction between them, Flint reminded himself as he halted at a red light. But he'd also never denied that they were completely unsuited.

Waiting for the light to change, he glanced at the typed paper. The academic offerings were impressive—foreign languages at all grade levels, advanced classes in math and composition, two hours of homework per night. The secretary had also taken down phrases apparently mouthed by whomever she'd spoken to. "Healthy minds in healthy bodies.... Group mothers act as surrogate parents.... Children learn to function in a group...."

Unbidden, another phrase flashed into Flint's mind. "Abandon hope, all ye who enter here."

This was absurd, he told himself. Youngsters in Japan studied six days per week and had many hours of homework besides. His kids would benefit from the rigorous discipline.

Trying to reassure himself that he'd reached the right decision, Flint pulled into the garage. Briefcase in hand, he entered the hallway.

He could hear voices, calm and upbeat, coming from the kitchen. Parking his briefcase on a table, Flint slipped into the family room where he could see what was going on through the doorway.

No one noticed him. The children, each wearing an apron, were helping Robin prepare dinner.

"Can you read the recipe, Aaron?" she was asking. "That abbreviation means teaspoons, okay? Brick, can you measure two tablespoons of margarine for the vegetables?"

"The muffins are almost done," Caitlin advised. "I think I'll reset the timer for three minutes."

Flint stood in the dusk, watching his family. Each person concentrated on his own task, and each, Flint could see, was learning something in the process. This was the way children were meant to absorb information, in the natural course of their lives.

Warmth glowed from Robin's face as she supervised the triplets. She seemed to thrive on keeping tabs amid the organized chaos, darting in to clean a mess before it spread and guiding Aaron as he measured spices into a dish.

"Okay, time to microwave the fajitas," Robin said, and then she spotted Flint. "Oh, hi. Your father's home." Uncertainty glimmered in her eyes.

The children greeted their father with shouts of glee. Enthusiasm bubbled as they tumbled over each other to describe what they were cooking.

An image chilled Flint's mind, of coming home to an empty, silent house. He could picture himself sticking a frozen dinner in the oven and sitting alone at the table, reading reports while he ate.

Scratch the boarding school. And he wasn't so crazy about the day-care idea, either.

The idea that came to him was irrational, yet had a distinct appeal. Oh, hell, Flint thought, why not give it a try?

"I've been doing some thinking," he told Robin as the children returned to their tasks.

"I'm afraid to ask," she admitted.

"We seem to be turning into a family," he said. "And if that's what we're going to do, then let's act like one. A real family."

Chapter Thirteen

The children were in bed before Robin had a chance to speak privately with Flint. She found him in the living room, staring out the front window.

What a peaceful neighborhood, Robin thought, following his gaze. Lights gleamed through curtains down the street and from decorative lampposts set along walkways. Once, she had thought of this development as too uniform to be interesting, but now she knew that each house held its own joys and shadows.

She hated to interrupt Flint's reverie. He sat lost in thought, leaning back on the sofa. Like the rest of the family, he rarely came into this room, and she wondered why he'd done so tonight.

"I want to thank you," she said at last, perching on an armchair. "I appreciate your letting me stay."

Flint's gaze shifted in her direction. "You understand, we're going to function as a family where the children are concerned. I wasn't referring to our personal relationship."

"Of course." Robin bit back the urge to say she didn't expect to get blood from a turnip. She doubted Flint would appreciate being referred to as a vegetable.

"It's important for the children's sake to create warm memories," he went on. "You're better at that than I am. And you manage to educate them in the process."

"Two for the price of one," Robin murmured. "Very efficient."

He shot her a suspicious look but she kept her expression bland.

"On the other hand, I'm still in charge here," Flint said. "If we're going to fulfill parenting roles, we have to make sure we set some ground rules."

Robin had a good idea what he meant. "Keep to the schedule," she recited. "Maintain discipline at all times. Noses to the grindstone. Did I miss anything?"

Flint's mouth worked, and she realized he was stifling a chuckle. At least the man had the grace to laugh at himself. "How about a trip to Disneyland?" he said.

"For their birthdays? They'd love it!"

"So would I." Flint allowed himself a grin. "I haven't been there in years. They've got some new attractions I'd like to try out."

"You're actually looking forward to it?" Robin teased. "You're not going to wear a Scrooge costume and walk through the park muttering bah humbug?"

"Am I that bad?" His mouth twisted wryly. "Robin, I want what's best for my children. Life is difficult, and they need to be prepared for it. But I don't want to spoil all their fun."

Robin wished she dared cross the living room and take this cantankerous man in her arms. Right now, the harshness that bothered her had fled, leaving the delightful Flint who had thrilled her last night.

Maybe she hadn't given him enough credit. Maybe the man had possibilities in Robin's future, if she could only break a few more pieces off his shell. But it wouldn't be easy.

"I'm going to ask Maureen to come with us," he went on. "We're the only family she's got, and she deserves to be part of the celebration."

"I'd like that," Robin said. "I suppose you know about her fiancé, the one who abandoned her?" He nodded. "Do you think he might have met with an accident?"

"I'm sure someone would have notified her if he had." Flint stretched his legs along the couch. His jeans and maroon polo shirt made a dark splash against the white cushions. "Frankly, I wish he had died. If that was the case, I think Maureen would have recovered much faster."

If Frederick really was the lost fiancé, would that help Maureen? Robin wanted to reflect on that possibility, but now wasn't the time. She wanted to learn more about Flint while he was in such an open mood.

In response to her questions, he described his childhood. His mother had been ill much of the time and died when he was twelve. An only child, he'd been unable to turn to his workaholic father for support, so he'd learned to rely on himself. Maureen had done the best she could to help out.

After Flint finished talking, they sat for a while in companionable silence. The living room, with its remoteness from the rumble and tumble of their everyday activities, was the perfect retreat, Robin thought.

Something else struck her a few minutes later as she switched off the lamp and followed Flint to the family room to watch the evening news.

He'd stopped preserving the living room the way Kathy had, as if expecting her to return at any moment. Was it possible he might finally be letting go?

THEY ARRIVED at Disneyland early on Friday morning. Flint had decided it was worth taking a day off work to avoid the weekend crowds.

Buoyed by the children's excitement, even Maureen wore an expression of happy anticipation. Robin, who had visited the park many times over the years, always got a childlike thrill as she saw the park's gates, the Matterhorn and Sleeping Beauty's castle towering ahead.

She sneaked a glance at Flint, but he was absorbed in following the parking attendant's directions. Nothing was left to chance at Disneyland, including a well-ordered pattern of parking in the huge lot.

The children had said the park was special to their mother, and that Flint hadn't brought them here since Kathy's death. Robin couldn't shake the feeling that she was treading on eggshells today.

Well, she didn't plan to keep the kids at arm's length to avoid comparisons to their mother. Flint could react any way he liked. At least Robin would find out whether he really was recovering from his wife's death.

Besides, she intended to enjoy herself.

They joined throngs of people, many speaking foreign languages, but didn't have to wait more than a few minutes at the pay booths. Soon they were hurrying behind the eager children to catch a trolley down Main Street.

As the six of them crowded to the top of a double-decker, Robin's heart lifted. She could have credited the sunshine, or the bright colors of their surroundings, or the sight of Winnie the Pooh signing autographs on a street corner.

But she knew it was because Flint sat beside her, absentmindedly humming the Mickey Mouse Club theme. His usually stern face beamed as he watched his children bounce up and down in their seats.

"Eight years old! We're eight years old!" sang Aaron.

"I'm going on the Indiana Jones ride first thing!" announced Brick.

"Then Pirates of the Caribbean!" said Aaron.

Caitlin wore a grin like the Cheshire cat. "And then the Haunted House. I want to see how they create the illusions."

"I guess that settles the question of where we start," Flint said.

Maureen frowned at her shoes. They had low heels but didn't provide much support compared to Robin's Nikes. "I didn't realize the place was so large. Are we going to do a lot of walking?"

Flint spread out a map of Disneyland and showed Maureen where everything was. The two of them plotted a course that would take them around the park without any wasted motion.

Robin didn't care how much motion she wasted. She wanted to dance to the Dixieland band that was playing as they climbed from the bus. She wanted to buy everyone an ice cream bar and bounce beside Tigger, who was entertaining a crowd of toddlers near the bridge to Fantasyland.

Flint grinned at her. "You look like a kid yourself."

Giving Aaron a hug, Robin said, "I feel like one."

"Of course you do. You can't be more than a few years out of college," Maureen pointed out.

As Flint shepherded the children in the direction of the park's latest attraction, the Indiana Jones Adventure, Robin dropped back to join the older woman. "If you get tired, there's a train that runs around the park. You could make a circuit or two and meet us at another station."

"I'll be all right." Maureen surveyed the offbeat architecture and bright shops as she walked. "I'm enjoying this. I feared it would be too commercial, but it is rather fun."

"You haven't been here before?" Robin couldn't disguise her astonishment. The park was more than forty years old. How could anyone live in Orange County all that time without visiting it?

"Oh, when it was first established, I thought I'd wait until I had children." They strolled past a souvenir shop. "When I realized I would never have any, well, it didn't seem worth coming here by myself."

"You never got over him, did you?" Robin blurted before realizing how tactless that sounded.

"What do you mean? Of course I got over him," Maureen retorted. "Rather quickly, as a matter of fact. Why should you think otherwise?"

Robin spotted Flint and the triplets waiting in line. "Sometimes I make false assumptions, Maureen. I apologize."

"No harm done." But a thin crease across the older woman's forehead indicated she hadn't stopped thinking about Robin's remark.

As they reached the line, Flint reached out and drew Robin close. "They all want to sit next to you, but I told them I had dibs."

"I want to sit next to you, Dad!" Brick protested.

"I choose Aunt Maureen." Caitlin's kindness made Robin proud of her.

"I want Robin," Aaron said. "In case I get scared."

The new ride proved to be like a video game, a roller coaster and an exotic adventure rolled into one. "It's like being inside a movie!" crowed Brick.

"I want to ride it all day!" announced Aaron.

Being assaulted by deadly spears, a giant boulder, a one-hundred-foot cobra, bubbling lava and assorted fireballs made Robin's head start to throb. She was glad to hear Flint announce that they were moving on to the more familiar Pirates of the Caribbean.

"There's plenty to see," he told the kids. "And there's no reason we can't come back again every year, is there?"

The kids grumbled a little, but forgot their complaints when they reached the next ride. Soon the air filled with pirates' singing as they boarded boats for their underground cruise.

"Everything appears so lifelike," Maureen said as they set sail beneath an artificial sky.

She didn't look so thrilled a moment later when they plunged down a steep descent and water splashed around them, but the sight of Animatronic pirates firing at each other across the bow of the boat quickly distracted her.

Before they knew it, the ride had ended. Everyone spilled into the sunshine and headed for the Haunted House.

Even Caitlin couldn't figure out how the ghosts managed to insinuate themselves beside the visitors in their carts, but she enjoyed the ride all the same. And so did everyone else.

Next they headed to Toon Town, which was crowded but fun. With its crazy buildings and rubbery furnishings, it reminded Robin of a cartoon come to life. After that, everyone enjoyed It's a Small World, despite Brick's protest that his friends considered the attraction corny.

"That's the catchiest song I ever heard," Maureen complained as they floated out. "It won't stop echoing through my brain."

To compound matters, Caitlin remembered every one of the lyrics from when she'd sung the song in a first grade play, and she insisted on singing it over and over as they waited in line for pizza.

But it was Flint whose reaction fascinated Robin. He spoke very little, letting his family's reactions bathe him in a cheerful glow. He stared at each new sight, from the children's jail with elastic bars to a marching band playing Disney tunes, as if he'd just awakened from a long sleep.

About three years long, Robin thought.

Watching him fetch the children extra drinks and buy them trinkets, she realized with a start that she hadn't argued with the man all day. When he was in this mood, it was hard to imagine arguing with him about anything. He was considerate and spontaneous, qualities remarkably lacking in his everyday life.

Would she ever understand Flint? Robin wondered after lunch as he trotted beside the children toward a Toon Town roller coaster, leaving the two women to enjoy their coffee.

"They've missed a lot, these past few years, all of them," Maureen said. "I don't think Flint realized how much until today."

"Was he like this when Kathy was alive?" Robin asked. "Relaxed and happy?"

"When they were dating, yes." Maureen slipped off a shoe. "But after they got married, well, they had to live on a shoestring, as people used to say. They both worked very hard, especially after the triplets came."

"Three at once must have been difficult," Robin agreed.

"Kathy didn't get to enjoy herself much during their marriage. At least, not in terms Flint would understand." Maureen rubbed her foot discreetly. "Actually, she loved every minute with the children, but he saw her in the evening when she was exhausted from a long day. I think that's why he's felt so guilty."

"Guilty?" Robin said in surprise.

"That might be one of the reasons he's had trouble accepting her death," Maureen explained. "Grief isn't a simple thing, you know. I also believe, although he'd never admit it, that after the shock of Kathy's death, Flint felt angry at times. He was left alone with three preschoolers, and that could be overwhelming even for a strong man like him. Sometimes we resent people who abandon us even when we know it's not their fault."

How could a woman possess so much wisdom and not see that she had held onto her own anger for forty years? Robin wondered.

Flint and the children returned a few minutes later. The triplets all talked at once as they described the exciting twists of their ride.

"On to the next adventure!" declared Flint, and they set off with high spirits.

The afternoon passed in a blur of lines, rides and ice cream bars. The children ate too much junk food but appeared no worse for wear, and Flint didn't bother to chide them.

About five o'clock, the group landed in Fantasyland, where Maureen insisted on taking the children on the Peter Pan attraction. "That's always been my favorite story," she said. "I want to enjoy it with my great-niece and nephews. Go on, the two of you. I'm sure you can keep out of trouble until we get back."

As the foursome departed, Flint stood in the middle of Fantasyland wearing a puzzled expression.

"What's the matter?" Robin asked.

"I just realized I don't know what to do with myself without the children," he said. "That's not exactly what I mean. I can think of plenty of things to do, but none of them at Disneyland."

"Well, it *is* a kids' amusement park." Robin stepped aside to let a woman push a stroller past.

"It's more than that." Flint glanced at the Mad Hatter's teacups whirling off to their left. "I haven't taken any leisure time away from my family for ages. I don't know how to play without them."

Robin inspected their surroundings, rejecting the Dumbo attraction because of its long line and Mr. Toad's Wild Ride because it looked too juvenile. "This isn't the right section for you. You're more the Tomorrowland type, I'd say."

Late afternoon sunlight gleamed across Flint's eyes. "I just got an idea," he said. Before Robin could quiz him, he caught her arm and pulled her onto King Arthur's Carousel.

"You're kidding," she said.

Flint directed her onto a golden horse and flung his leg over the fierce stallion beside her. "Why? It's the only merry-go-round I know that's big enough for grown-ups."

"Yes, but I haven't ridden one of these in years."

Music drowned her out as the carousel began to accelerate. Robin clung to her horse, realizing the ride was faster than she'd anticipated. She also noticed that they weren't the only adults riding.

She caught her bearings after a moment. Between the music and the flashing circular view of crowds, the castle, the teacups and the flying Dumbos, Robin abandoned her reservations and settled down to enjoy herself.

Flint rode his stallion with devil-may-care grace, the wind whipping through his hair, his mouth twitching with delight. Reaching over to touch Robin's cheek, he called, "See? One-handed!"

"My prince!" Robin called back.

Flint's gaze locked with hers. His hand traveled up her cheek to her temple and brushed her hair.

A sense of comradeship flooded through Robin, as if they really were riding together through a magic kingdom. They had left their ordinary world behind, and she wished they could stay this way always. She wanted to travel with Flint into new worlds, new experiences, new pleasures. From the intensity of his sidelong glances, she gathered that he felt the same.

Alarm fluttered in Robin's throat as it struck her that she was falling in love. For so long, she'd been convinced that Flint was wrong for her. Was she letting the enchanted surroundings overwhelm her good judgment?

But if he was really willing to open his life to her and start over, maybe dreams could come true. Maybe that wasn't just a slogan for children.

The music ended, and Flint lifted Robin down, his hands lingering on her waist. She drew away when she saw Maureen and the triplets returning.

They raved about the Peter Pan ride with its flight over London and Neverland. *We've been to Neverland, too,* Robin thought. *I wish we could stay there.*

The family ate dinner at the Blue Bayou, a restaurant overlooking the pirate ride. Flint insisted they needed a leisurely meal if the children were going to stay up for the parade and fireworks later that night.

Dinner passed in a blur of childish chatter. Aaron and Brick couldn't agree on which they'd enjoyed more, driving cars at Autopia, riding with Indiana Jones or twisting down the Matterhorn. Caitlin preferred the Haunted House. Maureen's favorite, of course, was Peter Pan.

Robin was about to observe that she liked the carousel best when Aaron blurted, "Why haven't we ever come here before?"

"We used to come here," Caitlin said reprovingly. "Didn't we, Dad?"

"Yes, of course."

"I don't remember it, either." Brick blew bubbles through his straw into his drink.

"The Pirates of the Caribbean scared you the first time you rode on it," Flint said. "You cried the whole way through."

"No way," said Brick.

"With Mom?" Caitlin asked. "Was she there?"

Flint's mouth tightened. Then Maureen said, "What's important is that we're having fun now."

"Absolutely right." Flint smiled at his family. "I'm glad we came."

The admission warmed Robin almost as much as their encounter on the carousel. The man might actually be emerging from his emotional hibernation.

After dinner, they rode around the park on the train, then listened to a rock band in Tomorrowland. The children's faces took on the hollow look of near-exhaustion, but they refused to leave before the parade and fireworks.

When darkness settled, Disneyland changed its appearance. Despite the bright lights and ever-present music, Robin couldn't help being aware of dark corners and confusing pathways. Concerned about the children getting lost, she made a point of keeping them close.

Flint didn't seem troubled. He walked ahead with Maureen as the little group prowled down Main Street in an ever-thickening crowd. If she was tall enough to see over people's heads, Robin thought, she might not feel so uncomfortable.

"When is the parade going to start?" Aaron asked.

"Soon," Robin said. "Maybe we should go find a place to stand along the route."

"It starts near Small World," Caitlin said.

Brick groaned. "Isn't that the other side of the park?"

"We could take the train. Or figure out some other place along the route," Robin suggested, and looked around for Flint and Maureen.

In the glare of lights and the shifting shadows, she couldn't spot them. More and more people seemed to be pouring into the park, pressing shoulder to shoulder as they headed toward Fantasyland.

"Better hurry," someone said nearby. "We don't want to be late." Robin had the confusing impression she was listening to the White Rabbit.

"Where's Dad?" Aaron asked.

"We need to find him," Robin agreed. "It's time to line up for the parade."

"There's too many people." Caitlin caught her hand. "Robin, I want to go home."

"Let's find your father first." Robin knew he had to be around. Had he and Maureen gone into a shop without telling her? Why didn't he realize that she couldn't spot him amid all these people?

"Where's Brick?" Aaron said.

Robin realized she was clutching two children but hadn't seen or heard from the third for several minutes. "Caitlin, have you seen him?"

"He's always wandering off," the little girl said. "He thinks he's Superman."

"Superman's out of date," sneered Aaron. "Nobody wants to be Superman."

"What about Johnny Ferguson?" Caitlin replied. "He was Superman last Halloween."

"He was Batman," said Aaron.

"Would you two be quiet?" Robin didn't like snapping at them but her nerves had begun to fray. She couldn't see Brick anywhere. She started calling his name, but her voice got lost in the hubbub.

The crowd carried them deeper into the park. It took all Robin's strength to force her way to one side, hauling Aaron and Caitlin along.

"I don't know where he went," Caitlin said. "He's gonna be in trouble now."

"I need to go to the bathroom," Aaron whined.

"You'll have to wait." Robin gazed frantically down the sidewalk. "Maybe he went into a store. Is there a video arcade?"

She pulled the children with her, calling until her voice grew hoarse. Suddenly a figure loomed from the crowd— Flint, clutching Brick by the arm.

Anger flashed across Flint's eyes. "I found him in the ice cream store, practically in tears. What the hell is going on here?"

"We got separated," Robin said. "Brick, are you all right?"

"He wandered off," Caitlin said.

Flint's rage focused on Robin. "It was your responsibility to watch the kids. Can't I trust you even for a few minutes? The child was terrified."

"I'm okay now," Brick protested.

"That isn't the point." Flint's baritone carried over the noise. "I expect more maturity and reliability from the woman I hire to take care of my children."

"If you hadn't gone wandering off yourself, this wouldn't have happened," Robin flared. "We searched everywhere."

"Not everywhere enough, apparently," Flint snapped.

"I'm not tall enough to see over this crowd!" She wasn't going to let him lay the blame on her. "I've only got two hands. That isn't enough to hold onto three children. Where were you?"

"Please don't fight," Caitlin said.

"I'm sorry." Brick chewed on his lip. "I didn't mean to cause trouble."

Flint glowered, but bit back the angry words. "Let's not make an issue of this right now. It's time for the parade."

A moment later, Maureen appeared, holding a package. She seemed unaware of the disturbance, and Robin didn't want to fight any more, either.

She understood why Flint would be upset, but couldn't he give her a little more credit? At least he should have asked for her side of the story.

He'd described her as the woman he hired to take care of his children. As they made their way toward the parade route, Robin realized that she'd come to believe she meant more than that to him.

Perhaps she was being unfair. Seeing Brick lost and tearful must have struck at Flint's heart. He'd misdirected his concern into anger, and Robin had been the obvious target.

Sometimes, she reflected, it was easier to understand a man than to forgive him.

She hadn't been honest with herself earlier when she'd decided she was falling in love with Flint. The truth was that she had fallen in love with him a long time ago. She loved him, but she didn't know if she could live with him. Not unless he stopped lashing out at her whenever his temper was aroused.

She needed to set the man straight. And he needed to apologize. But now was obviously not the time.

They found a place where the children could sit down in front of the crowd lining the street. The parade began, a riot of lights and music slipping by with favorite Disney characters in costume. It had been updated since Robin saw it last, but she had to force herself to register what she was viewing.

The parade ended and fireworks blazed through the sky, amid earsplitting booms. The children cheered, although some younger kids clung to their parents in alarm.

Caitlin stood up to get a better view. She leaned against Robin, who slipped an arm around her. A moment later, Brick pressed close and claimed the other arm. Aaron had wedged himself between Flint and Maureen and was accumulating lots of cuddles.

They didn't have to act like a family—they *were* one. But Robin wondered what it would take to make Flint see that.

Chapter Fourteen

By Monday, Robin still hadn't decided what to do about Flint. He hadn't mentioned the incident with Brick again, but the memory of his angry words lingered.

They apparently lingered for Aaron, too. He suffered one of his bad dreams Friday night, and Robin spent an hour cradling and reassuring him until he fell back to sleep.

On Saturday, she baked three birthday cakes and the children invited friends from the neighborhood. Later, they delighted in their presents—books from Flint, gift certificates from Maureen and, from Robin, a late-afternoon shopping trip to a toy store. Flint had to work most of the day, which came as a relief to her.

Robin spent Sunday at the beach and was amazed how much she missed the children. In an odd way, she missed Flint, too—at least, she missed the warm side of him.

Monday morning, she arrived at Flint's house to discover that Aaron had sprained his wrist the previous day, pretending to be an acrobat in the Disneyland parade. In addition, Brick had finally stopped toughing it out and revealed that he'd incurred major blisters at the amusement park. These had burst open on Sunday and left him hobbling around.

"They can skip their classes today," Flint instructed as he strode out the door. "But I want them productively engaged."

"Absolutely." Robin repressed an impulse to add, "Sir!"

Then he was gone, without a single word of apology for Friday's outburst. The man needed a good shaking, Robin thought.

The morning passed smoothly. Since bike riding and gardening were out of the question, she let the children choose their own activities. They spent a couple of hours sacked out in front of the television, which would have driven Flint into a rage. But Robin judged that, after so much excitement, the kids needed a little downtime.

By later in the morning, Aaron had dived into one of his new books, Brick was playing with a science kit he'd picked out at the toy store, and Caitlin was on-line, eavesdropping on electronic conversations.

"Don't ever give anyone your name or address," Robin warned as she brought the triplets' sandwiches into the family room. Flint had forbidden the children to eat anywhere other than the kitchen or patio, but today Robin felt like flouting him wherever possible. "And never arrange to meet anyone you've contacted through the computer without telling your dad or me."

"I know that." Caitlin picked up a sandwich, checked to make sure it was cream cheese and took a bite. "I'm not stupid." She talked with food in her mouth. Today, Robin didn't reprove her. "Half these people make up their names. They lie all the time. There's two guys right now bragging about some stock that's going to make them rich. They're just trying to drive up the price."

"Isn't that illegal?" Robin said.

"It's almost impossible to catch them." Caitlin went back to her high-tech snooping, leaving Robin to provide fresh sandwiches to the ever-hungry boys.

By mid-afternoon, though, the kids had grown bored and begun picking fights. The second time Robin had to send them all to their rooms, she heard her voice approaching a shriek. When Maureen called to check on Aaron's wrist, Robin invited her over for a snack.

"I could use the adult companionship," she admitted. "I need to cool off."

"I'll pick up some fresh pretzels at the bakery on the way over," Maureen said. "The kids love them."

And there would be no sugar to launch them into hyperspace, Robin reflected. "I'd appreciate that. Thanks, Maureen."

When the doorbell rang a few minutes later, she hurried to open it before realizing that it was too soon for Maureen to arrive.

Gigi stood on the porch, colorfully clad in a Gypsy-style scarf, an embroidered peasant blouse and stirrup pants. "Hey, kid."

"Hello, Mom." Robin wished her mother hadn't disobeyed for the second time and come to Flint's house, but she didn't want to be rude. "I'm afraid I'm expecting company, so..."

"It's only for a little while," Gigi said. "I want to see my grandchildren."

Robin wished she hadn't told her mother the truth yesterday. Now Gigi must have come on the bus and wouldn't be able to catch a return ride for an hour.

Robin knew she would just have to make the best of things. Besides, with luck, Flint would never find out.

On the other hand, when did she ever get lucky where Flint was concerned?

The triplets poured out of their rooms as soon as Robin gave them permission. "Grandma Gigi!" Caitlin called in delight.

"Happy birthday!" Gigi produced a large shopping bag. "I'm a few days late, but I only learned yesterday that you were my grandchildren."

"What did you bring us?" Aaron peered into the bag.

"Some special things from my shop." Gigi produced three packages wrapped in glittery paper.

"Wow." Caitlin accepted her box with a reverent expression. "This is beautiful."

Before they could litter the floor with torn paper, Robin steered everyone into the kitchen. Soon the youngsters had shredded the wrappings and were admiring their acquisitions beneath Gigi's approving gaze.

She'd given Aaron a children's book on unexplained phenomena. Robin skimmed it, afraid Flint might find it objectionable, but it took a well-reasoned, scientific approach.

For Brick, Gigi had selected a magic set featuring marked cards and others tricks to entertain his friends. He was delighted.

Both gifts seemed appropriate to Robin, but she wasn't so sure about Caitlin's. Gigi had given her granddaughter a crystal ball.

"Mom, what do you expect her to do with that?" A cloudy globe about the size of a bowling ball, it didn't appear to have any practical use.

"I expect her to develop her psychic abilities." Gigi scraped her chair closer to Caitlin's. "My sensitivities may have skipped your generation, but that doesn't mean she hasn't inherited them."

"What do you mean, sensitivities?" Caitlin peered into the ball.

"My ability to commune with spirits, to access the future and the past," Gigi intoned. "It goes through the female line, since women are more sensitive than men."

"I'm sensitive," said Aaron.

"Me, too." Brick looked dubious. "Can you be sensitive and still play soccer?"

"Mom, this is all nonsense." Robin refused to consider the image she'd seen in Gigi's mirror, or her sensation in the laundry room of another woman's presence. There was no such thing as psychic ability.

"Maybe it's not nonsense," Caitlin said. "You should see the stuff they talk about on the science fiction and fantasy bulletin board. In the computer."

"Science fiction is make-believe." Robin gathered the wrapping paper and thrust it into the trash. "It may be based on real principles, but the stories are imaginary. And fantasy, well, that's not even based on science."

Aaron glanced up from his book. "I don't know. There's some strange stuff in here. Stuff nobody can explain."

The doorbell rang. "That's Maureen!" Robin sang out, and ran to answer it. She could use an ally. Gigi had, as usual, managed to get the upper hand, and Robin wasn't about to let her keep filling the children's minds with foolishness.

Amid the flurry of introductions and the smell of fresh-baked pretzels, the issue of ghosts was soon forgotten. The two older women hit it off immediately, despite their different personalities. Or perhaps, Robin mused, opposites really did attract.

Look at her and Flint, for instance.

She didn't want to think about him, but it was hard not to. Every now and then, she caught a whiff of his scent and images slammed into her mind—Flint taking her in his arms to dance, Flint bending over her on the bed, Flint driving her to ecstasy with his lovemaking.

Robin snapped back to the present. She and the other two women were reclining in lounge chairs on the patio while the children sat around a table playing with Brick's marked cards.

"You must come by my shop," Gigi was saying. "I tell fortunes, you know."

"How amusing." Even in a chaise longue, Maureen sat rather stiffly. "I've always thought it would be fun to have my fortune told."

"Give me your palm," Gigi said.

"Oh—I couldn't."

"Yes, you could." Gigi took Maureen's hand and laid it on her lap, examining it closely. "Your lifeline is long and steady, but your heartline has a break in it. Did something go wrong for you?" Before Maureen could answer, Gigi's breathing sped up. "He's here. He wants to talk to me...." Her eyes lost their focus, as if staring into another dimension.

"Is something wrong?" Maureen asked. "Is your mother ill?"

"I don't think so. Mom?" Robin moved to the foot of Gigi's lounge chair. She recognized the signs of a trance, which she'd always believed resulted from her mother hypnotizing herself. But this had come on too quickly, without the usual hocus-pocus.

Gigi's jaw twitched as if she were talking with someone. Expressions of disbelief and dismay flitted across her face.

"We'd better call a doctor," Maureen said. "Does she have heart problems?"

"I don't think she's in any danger." Robin glanced at the children, but they were absorbed in their play. "She does this sometimes during séances, except then she talks out loud."

"Nevertheless, it could be a symptom of something serious." Maureen jostled Gigi's arm. "Can you hear me? Do you need to go to the hospital?"

Gigi blinked and slowly came out of her trance. "I'm all right."

"What happened?" Maureen asked.

"He needed to talk to me, urgently." Gigi shuddered. "I'm afraid it wasn't good news."

"What wasn't?" Robin couldn't keep the skepticism from her voice. "And who is he?"

"Frederick, of course." Gigi turned to Maureen. "He's a restless spirit who's seeking his lost love. She's in some kind of danger. He just told me that the danger is greater than he thought. She must come to a séance on Wednesday morning. He insists on it."

Maureen had flinched on hearing the name Frederick. Now she rapped out the words, "Why are you telling me this?"

"Surely you guessed," Gigi said. "The woman he's looking for is you."

Maureen glared at Robin. "You've been telling tales."

"I haven't. Please believe me." Robin could feel herself blushing. She couldn't bear to have Maureen believe she would tell her intimate personal story to anyone, even Robin's own mother. "I didn't say a word."

"A word about what?" asked Gigi.

"Her former fiancé, Freddy," Robin said. "Maureen mentioned him last week."

"Oh, Frederick's been pestering me since long before Robin came to work here," Gigi assured Maureen. "I have witnesses."

Maureen clamped her lips together and studied the two of them. "All right. I'll let Robin off the hook. But as for attending a séance, I simply can't. I've put the past behind me, and I intend to leave it there."

"But the danger!" Gigi caught Maureen's shoulder. "He was beside himself with worry."

"I can take care of myself, thank you." Maureen shook herself free and stood up. "I'm sure you mean well, Gigi, but you have no business interfering in my private life. If I wanted to tell the world about my personal trials, I would go on one of those daytime talk shows. At least I'd be paid for my troubles.''

With a quick nod at the women, she stalked into the house. The children didn't notice her departure, too absorbed in a device that split a rope in half and then reassembled it as if by magic.

Robin got to her feet. "It was kind of you to bring the gifts, Mom, but it's time for your bus.''

"Oh, dear." For once, Gigi didn't spring to her own defense. "I didn't plan it this way. Robin, I know I try your patience. I do exaggerate and I do manipulate you sometimes, but only for your own good.''

"Like those spirits who threw my clothes out the window?" Robin demanded.

Her mother nodded ruefully. "I'm afraid so. But I didn't intend for Frederick to show up today. Maureen really *is* the woman he's searching for. And he's so frightened for her. Couldn't you talk to her? Persuade her to come by my shop Wednesday morning—out of curiosity if nothing else?''

"Maureen has a right to keep her personal business to herself," Robin said. "Now I'd better go make sure she's all right.''

She hurried through the house and onto the front porch. Maureen stood on the sidewalk next to her Cadillac, talking to Flint. As Robin watched, he caught her eye. Anger simmered at her.

Robin's stomach sank. What had seemed a moment ago an awkward moment among the women was about to turn into a confrontation with Flint. She knew he'd never believe she had been an innocent bystander.

She waited, palms damp, as Maureen drove off and he started up the walk. Sharp words sprang to her mind, defending her actions. But would they do any good?

When he arrived, however, his reaction surprised her. He simply paused a few feet away, then nodded to her and walked inside.

Robin followed. Before she could question him, however, Gigi entered from the backyard with the children pelting after her.

"Daddy, look!" Brick showed off his rope device. Aaron and Caitlin, too, insisted on retrieving their gifts for Flint's inspection.

While he was occupied, Gigi said a subdued farewell and headed for the bus stop. Apparently her mother realized that today she'd gone too far.

Flint kept busy playing with the children while Robin prepared dinner. She wished she knew what he was thinking. But then she decided not to torture herself. No doubt he would let her know in due time.

Alone in the kitchen cooking chicken fajitas, Robin found herself reflecting on Gigi's trance. How had her mother made the connection between Maureen and Frederick? Robin had purposely avoided mentioning the story of the faithless fiancé.

She supposed Maureen was simply the most eligible prospect Gigi had encountered: the right age, unmarried, likely to have been involved with a man at some point in her life who fit Frederick's general description. The similarity in names must be a coincidence.

The children arrived to set the table, and dinner passed amid their usual babble. Flint asked a few questions, but didn't say much.

It seemed like ages before the children went to sleep. Caitlin dozed off with the crystal ball next to her bed. Aaron's eyes drifted shut while he was reading his book on unexplained phenomena, and Brick snored softly with the marked cards jutting from beneath his pillow.

When Robin emerged after checking them, she found Flint in the kitchen, wiping the counter. "If you want to chew me out, go ahead," she said. "I swear I didn't invite my mother here and I certainly didn't put her up to involving Maureen in anything."

"I'm sure you didn't." Flint spoke the words with measured calm. "Besides, I know the children enjoyed today."

"But Maureen didn't." Robin stood with the counter separating them.

"Maureen's a grown woman. She can take care of herself."

If he wasn't upset, why did stern lines mark his face? Why wasn't he meeting her gaze?

"Flint?" Robin said. "What's wrong?"

The deep intake of breath told her she was on the right track. "I've been reviewing the last few days," he said. "I've come to the conclusion that I made a mistake."

Relief flooded through her. "You were concerned about Brick. I know you didn't mean to yell at me that way."

With a flicker of surprise, he replied, "I wasn't referring to that. But you're right. I did overreact."

"If you didn't mean that, what did you mean?" Robin said.

Flint cleaned the counter with precise movements, as if readying it for military inspection. "It was a mistake to say we should act like a family. I gave you the wrong idea."

Robin felt her chest squeeze. "I have no intention of moving into your bedroom. If you think otherwise, you're kidding yourself."

Flint reached across the counter and caught her arm. His hand felt large and protective. "I'm not making myself clear. Robin, I care for you very much. More than I should. But ever since I absorbed the fact that you were the egg donor, I've been trying to fit you into Kathy's place. Only you're not her."

"Of course I'm not." She bristled, less for her own sake than for Kathy's. "I would never try to replace her. But the kids need a mother."

"Lots of children have only one parent, and do fine," Flint corrected. "But that isn't the point. The point is, it's wrong for me to try to fit you into a mold. Our relationship should remain that of employer and employee. That way, your mother doesn't feel free to involve my aunt in her shenanigans, and you don't treat the children as if they were your own."

"They are my own," Robin said.

He withdrew his hand. "You may be the biological mother, but you have no legal standing. Don't try to fight me on this, Robin, because I'll win."

"It never even occurred to me—"

"These are my kids." Flint regarded her with a frostiness that gave Robin a chill. "They're my responsibility and mine alone. You make an excellent nanny, but any relationship beyond that is off-limits. I accept the fault for suggesting otherwise."

Robin couldn't believe the man's callousness. "Just like that?" she cried. "The children's feelings don't matter? My feelings don't matter? Just because I'm not Kathy's twin sister, you're shutting me out?"

"I wish you would learn to control your outbursts." Flint's beeper went off, and irritation tightened his mouth. "Perfect timing, as usual." He checked the phone number on the device. "I'd better return the call."

Left alone, Robin clenched her fists in frustration. How could she go back to being nothing more than a nanny after everything that had happened between her and Flint?

"I've got an important meeting that's been moved up to tomorrow." He appeared in the doorway. "I have to go work on a report at my office. I'll see you later."

Robin nodded, not trusting herself to speak. She didn't want him to see her turmoil.

After he left, she went to check on the children again. Aaron tossed restlessly, and she hoped he wasn't going to have another of his bad dreams. Robin sat beside him for a while, and gradually his breathing calmed.

An intense swell of tenderness washed over her as she watched him. How did the children manage to resemble angels while asleep when they could be such imps during the day?

Walking from the boys' bedroom to Caitlin's, Robin again sensed how powerful the connection was between her and the children. She knew she would give her life to save them from danger.

She wished she could understand why Flint kept retreating into a shell. Every time he started to open up, he flipped right back into a defensive stance that closed her out.

He couldn't mean what he'd just said, not deep inside. Gazing at Caitlin, so innocent in slumber, Robin thought of the warmth Flint was capable of showing.

That night when they'd danced and made love, he hadn't behaved like a man incapable of committing himself to another woman. He hadn't been trying to put Robin in Kathy's place, either.

If only he weren't so stubborn, she knew they could work things out. She refused to give up this easily.

Leaving Caitlin's room, Robin pushed back an errant lock of hair. As her fingers brushed her scalp, she was startled to feel something gritty. Sand.

After spending yesterday afternoon at the beach, she'd taken a long bath at Gigi's apartment. To her embarrassment, Robin realized she'd become so involved in reading a novel that she'd forgotten to wash her hair.

Flint had an important meeting tomorrow, which meant he might need to leave early. He wouldn't appreciate it if Robin lingered in the bathroom, washing and drying her hair.

Well, she had a long, solitary evening ahead. Now she knew what to do with it.

As she started to her room, Robin heard Aaron muttering. She hurried in and found him tossing, but he quickly settled down.

She didn't want to be on the other side of the house if he started screaming with a nightmare. Aaron needed her. The other children needed her, too. Once awakened, they'd have trouble getting back to sleep and would be cranky the next day. With a shrug, she fetched her towel, shampoo, mousse and hair dryer. She would use the children's bathroom.

After only a moment's hesitation, Robin left the door ajar. Otherwise, she'd never be able to hear Aaron over the sound of the water.

The oversize tub didn't have a curtain. Despite Robin's doubts, the children had proved that the water didn't spray out even when they took showers. And she wasn't worried about modesty. Flint wouldn't be home for hours.

Soon the hot water was soothing away her anxieties. Maureen would recover from Gigi's foolishness. Flint would realize that he didn't need a clone of his late wife in order to make a new family.

Surely things could be worked out.

HE WAS SURE he'd done the right thing.

Staring at his report without seeing it, as he'd been doing for the past ten minutes, Flint kept replaying tonight's conversation in his mind. He hadn't tried to blame Robin for her mother's behavior. He hadn't criticized her in any way. He'd stated his case in a calm and rational manner.

Then why did his brain keep riding a roller coaster?

He admitted the fault was his, that he kept wanting Robin to be like Kathy—steady, reliable and organized. At least, that was the way he remembered her.

It bothered Flint that Kathy kept slipping away. Sometimes he had to consult her photograph to remember exactly what she'd looked like. Other times, he would discover he'd gone for days without thinking about her. He was losing her all over again.

And now he was losing Robin, as well. He'd seen the dismay in her eyes, this evening in the kitchen. She wouldn't stick around forever. Sooner or later one of those schools would hire her. And eventually she'd fall in love with someone, maybe one of those scruffy fellows that were always hanging around the beach. They could read tarot cards and play pickup volleyball together.

Flint slammed his fist onto his report. Darts of pain shot up his hand. Why on earth had he done such a stupid thing?

He had to review this report to make a presentation tomorrow. Fortunately, the written part had been completed. He just needed to prepare mentally to address the board of a commercial leasing firm about why they needed his services.

Sitting in the office wasn't creating the right atmosphere. Flint decided he could concentrate better at home.

With a grimace, he stuffed the report into his briefcase.

Chapter Fifteen

Robin didn't believe in wasting water, but the hot stream across her tight shoulders felt wonderful. She allowed herself to relax for several minutes, then slowly began shampooing her hair.

She closed her eyes, arching against the soothing warm flow. Beneath her fingertips, sand loosened and washed away. She couldn't imagine how she'd managed to get so much of it into her hair, until she remembered a toddler running on the beach, waving a plastic shovelful of the stuff. Robin had ducked and shielded her eyes, but she hadn't considered the effect on her hair.

If she didn't rinse out the tub properly, the kids could build a sand castle in here tomorrow.

Smiling at the notion, Robin began to hum. The song that came to mind was "I Will Always Love You," and as she mouthed the words, scenes from the movie *The Bodyguard* flashed through her mind. Beautiful Whitney Houston, maddeningly remote Kevin Costner. Danger, passion and above all, beautiful music.

Suddenly Robin had the sensation that someone was watching her. Amid the steam, she caught a flicker of movement in the mirror. Could she be hallucinating again?

She swung toward the door and caught her breath. Flint stood in the hall, his expression a mixture of surprise and longing.

She could feel his gaze travel across her body, lingering on her mouth, her breasts. He moved into the doorway, his hands flexing as if ready to touch her.

Relief tingled through Robin. Flint hadn't lost his desire for her. His words tonight about keeping their distance had been part of an outdated defense system. Now surely he would realize that.

And then he changed. Narrowed eyes masked the hunger she'd witnessed a moment before. His jaw tightened and he turned away, his back stiff with resolution.

In a rush of humiliation, Robin saw that she'd been wrong. She'd believed Flint did care for her, and that sooner or later he would discover that fact. Now she couldn't avoid facing the truth that Flint's feelings for her were purely sexual and nothing more.

Cheeks burning, she finished her shower and wrapped herself in a towel. Flint had disappeared.

Robin grabbed her gear and hurried to her room.

FLINT SHUT HIMSELF in his bedroom, spreading the report on a small desk by the window.

He couldn't believe he'd stood there gawking at Robin like a schoolboy, but she was so incredibly beautiful. He hadn't meant to invade her privacy. He'd assumed one of the children must have decided to take a bath at this unusual hour and had peered in to make sure everything was all right.

The effect of long hair sweeping across her nude body had given Flint the impression of a nymph bathing in a waterfall. Robin possessed such natural sensuality, he'd almost ripped off his own clothing and joined her.

He couldn't let himself yield to this passion. To abandon his inhibitions, to fling his reservations aside, meant plunging into a future that he couldn't control. It meant a free-fall through life.

Robin's vitality fascinated him, and her kindness softened his heart. But there was something dangerous about her, as well. For himself, Flint wouldn't have minded, but he had to think about the children.

He wished he could identify what it was that troubled him. He'd told himself it was Robin's unpredictability. He'd even accused her more than once of being irresponsible. But something else worried him even more, something he hadn't been able to put into words.

Flint had only his instincts to rely on, although he hated to admit it, because he thought of himself as a rational man. He simply knew that he must never again yield to his longing to possess Robin and let her possess him, or something terrible might happen.

And now, like it or not, he had to get through this damn report.

THAT NIGHT, Flint did something he hadn't done since high school—he fell asleep at his desk. Morning light awakened him.

He ached from the uncomfortable position he'd been hunched in. And he couldn't remember anything about what he'd read. He would just have to wing it today.

His mood didn't improve when the phone rang, and the secretary to the firm's president informed him that her boss's airplane had been delayed arriving from New York last night. The meeting had been moved back to its originally scheduled time, tomorrow afternoon.

"I'll see you then," Flint growled. He'd wasted an entire evening for nothing.

He put on his jogging clothes. He needed a morning at the gym to work off last night's strained muscles. He wouldn't mind taking out his frustrations on a weight machine, either.

Coffee was ready in the kitchen. Robin, blond hair floating around her like a halo, was fixing scrambled eggs for the kids. She didn't look dangerous in the least.

She gave him a short nod. "Morning," Flint muttered. "Meeting's postponed."

"I heard the phone ring. I figured it was something like that." Robin set the pan aside and dropped whole-wheat bread into the toaster. "Breakfast!" she hollered so loud Flint's head ached.

"Gotta go." He set the half-full cup aside and shuffled toward the garage.

The triplets nearly bowled him over as they raced in. "Eggs! Eggs!" screamed Aaron in delight.

"Can I have chocolate milk?" Brick demanded, about two inches from Flint's ear.

Caitlin let out a shriek that could have awakened the dead. "Brick stepped on my foot!"

Flint wished he'd drunk something alcoholic last night. At least then he'd have an excuse for suffering a hangover.

He had almost reached the garage when the doorbell rang. Vowing to strangle any salesman who would disrupt the family at this hour, he thrust open the door.

There stood Aunt Maureen, bandbox perfect in a navy skirt and white blouse. "I've come to talk to Robin," she said.

"She realizes her mother was out of line." Flint stepped aside as his aunt stalked past.

"Maybe yes, maybe no." Maureen disappeared into the house.

He was definitely losing control, Flint told himself grimly as he got into his Volvo. But he was going to take it back, starting today.

Only first he had to get these kinks out of his muscles. And out of his brain.

"I SUPPOSE it's a harebrained idea, but I'm going to call your mother. I think I should go to the séance tomorrow."

Maureen and Robin sat on the front steps, watching the children ride their bikes. The kids were pretending to be the Pony Express, delivering imaginary packets of mail from one end of the block to the other.

Caitlin had insisted it was unfair to make bad guys out of make-believe Indians, so instead they feigned being under attack by pirates. This might be the first time, even in fantasy, that pirates had attacked the Pony Express, Robin mused.

"Are you sure you want to do this?" she asked.

The older woman blinked against the sunshine. "For forty years I've hung onto my anger. Oh, I denied it. I thought I got over Freddy long ago, but you were right the other day. I've never trusted a man again. I suppose I felt I wasn't worthy of love or he wouldn't have abandoned me. It's foolish, but that's the way I felt."

"You think the séance will help?" A car approached, and Robin leaned out until she saw all three children move to the side of the road. As soon as it passed, they resumed their cycling.

"I consider it a form of exorcism," Maureen said. "Either this so-called spirit really is Freddy, or he's a fake. In either case, I think I'll finally be rid of him."

"We all have to know when it's time to move on," Robin mused.

Maureen gave her a curious look. "You're not thinking of leaving, are you? The children adore you."

"I feel the same about them," Robin said. "But from the way Flint acts, my days are numbered."

Maureen shook her head but said nothing. The fact that she approved of Robin was gratifying. Maureen's good opinion clearly wasn't easy to come by. But Maureen didn't know the whole story of Robin's relationship with Flint, and Robin wasn't going to tell her.

She knew what she had to do. After Maureen had gone and the children were busy with their workbooks, Robin called the director of A Learning Place.

"Perfect timing," he said. "I was just about to call you myself."

Robin's pulse throbbed in her throat. "Good news, I hope?"

"Excellent." His smile transcended the phone lines. "We've got full funding for a theater and dance program. We'd like you to come on board."

She could hardly believe she was hearing those words. "I'm—delighted. I accept."

Robin couldn't concentrate on what he was saying for a moment through the buzz in her mind. Then she realized the director was giving her the fall schedule.

"Classes start August twenty-eighth," he said. "That's a bit earlier than the public schools, but our parents like the idea of a longer academic year."

She made mental calculations. The twenty-eighth was not quite three weeks away.

"We're going to have two weeks of faculty orientation and planning," the director continued. "That may seem excessive, but we have an entire new school to get organized. I want you to put your head together with our art and music teachers, to coordinate your productions."

Robin studied a calendar hanging near the refrigerator. "That means I start next week."

"Actually, a lot of the teachers are getting their offices and classrooms ready this week," the director advised. "I know this is short notice, but I didn't get the okay until yesterday."

So many things to do, Robin thought. She would need to make up a list of supplies, go shopping, decorate her classroom....

"Could I come by tomorrow and pick up a key?" she said.

"Certainly. I appreciate your willingness to hit the ground running," the director said.

Robin leaned against the counter, her emotions slamming into each other. She had landed her dream job. She had a ton of work to do. This provided a perfect excuse to leave Flint's house, as she knew she must.

But she hadn't expected change to arrive this suddenly. She hated to break it to the children. And how could she bear not seeing them every day?

Operating on automatic pilot, Robin went to the laundry room to transfer a load of wash into the dryer. She was thrusting in an armful of whites when a sock leaped out of her hand almost spitefully and landed behind the machines.

With a grimace, Robin peered into a maze of pipes. The narrow space resembled a jungle into which socks might disappear forever.

She couldn't let the darn thing go without a fight. Besides, help was at hand. On a shelf above the washer lay an old toy of the children's, an eighteen-inch mechanical arm that could pick up objects at a distance.

Robin seized it and began probing for the sock. She felt the arm bump something soft and pulled a lever so its jaws closed on the object.

What came up wasn't a sock, however. It was a pink sweatband.

Dropping it on the dryer, Robin probed some more. Eventually the sock yielded and she retrieved it, covered with dust and a trace of grease. It would have to wait for another load of wash.

The sweatband must belong to Caitlin, Robin thought as she picked it up. Then she saw that it bore the initials KLH.

She didn't know what the L stood for, but the band had obviously belonged to Kathy. It must have lain there undiscovered for more than three years.

Robin was surprised that it looked neither dirty nor greasy. As she held the feather-light stretch fabric, she thought about Kathy standing in this same room, performing these same tasks.

I wish I could bring you back, Robin thought. *I have to leave these children, and they need a mother. I would give you Flint and the kids and everything, just so you could keep them safe and happy.*

In the silence of the room, Robin's ears hummed. She had the odd impression that she'd been listening to someone else's thoughts instead of her own. Could she be getting ditsy like her mother?

Shaking her head, Robin switched on the dryer and left the sweatband to be washed another day.

SHE WAITED until everyone finished dinner before she broke the news. They took it in stunned silence.

The children sat around the table staring in disbelief. Robin felt her heart sink as she took in Caitlin's shock, Brick's crumpled face and Aaron's brimming tears.

"I'm sorry," she said. "I applied for the job before I started working here. Besides, you guys will be off to school soon yourselves."

Flint hadn't mentioned any more about boarding school, and to her relief, he didn't now. "No long faces," he said. "I can arrange day care after school and I'm sure Maureen will fill in on weekends."

"Couldn't Robin come?" Brick asked. "On Saturdays, I mean?"

Robin caught a warning gaze from Flint. "I'd like to stay in contact, but..."

"You all knew that Robin's position here was temporary," Flint added.

"Couldn't we go to Robin's school?" said Aaron. "Then we could see her every day."

"I'll take it under consideration." From Flint's chilly tone, Robin knew he meant no.

Still, she had nothing to lose, so she plunged ahead. "You *were* considering a change of schools. Why not enroll them at A Learning Place? Their program is very exciting and advanced."

"I've heard about it," Flint ground out. "Child-oriented, isn't that what they call it? Kids work at their own pace. Flexible classrooms. All that experimental stuff. My kids need more discipline, not less."

"Do they?" Robin felt as if she was taking her life in her hands, but she didn't care. "They're bright and they've been very well-behaved these last few weeks. I think they could benefit from an unstructured, creative environment."

"An environment that throws them into contact with you on a daily basis? Isn't that what you really want?" Flint grabbed his plate and carried it into the kitchen.

"What's wrong with that?" Robin gathered some glasses and followed. "Maybe you can put your heart in the deep freeze, but I can't. And neither can the children. They need nurturing."

Flint clapped the plate onto the counter so hard the cutlery danced. "I'll expect you to leave as soon as possible."

"Tomorrow will be fine." Robin turned away.

"I've got a full schedule," Flint warned. "I'm expected at City Hall in the morning to meet with the planning director, and I've got a proposal to present tomorrow afternoon."

"I'll call Maureen." Then Robin remembered that the older woman would be attending the séance. "She's tied up in the morning, so I'll stick around until she's free."

"I'd appreciate that." Flint busied himself with the dishes.

Robin retreated to her room. She wanted to shake that stubborn man. Why was he so dead set on closing her out? If he would only loosen up a little, the children would benefit.

Woodenly, she began folding clothes into her suitcase. As she lifted a blouse from the hanger, she noticed the old-lady-style dresses hanging at one side of the closet.

At least she hadn't fled like the other nannies, leaving her possessions behind. The only thing Robin would leave at Flint's house was her heart.

With the children, of course.

BY BEDTIME, the atmosphere in the house had become oppressive. The children avoided Flint as much as possible, even passing up his offer of a bedtime book.

"We can read our own books," Caitlin said.

"Yeah, we've outgrown that stuff." Brick folded his arms.

"Me, too," said Aaron.

Watching them head off to brush their teeth and put themselves to bed, Flint experienced a sense of loss. He tried to tell himself that it was about time the kids developed more independence, but he wasn't sure he liked it.

Robin had retreated to her room and stayed there all evening. She hadn't been sulking, though. At some point she must have emerged and finished cleaning up the kitchen. Flint had left a pot soaking and forgotten to wipe off the stovetop. He discovered them later, all cleaned up.

Did she have to behave so responsibly when he wanted to stay mad at her? Not that he blamed her for leaving, but she'd had no business suggesting he enroll the children at her school. And it certainly wasn't her place to accuse him of being hard-hearted.

He walked onto the front porch to gaze at the stars. The house felt stuffy tonight, and he needed the fresh air.

A part of him didn't want Robin to go. Hell, if he let himself, he might beg her to stay. But if he did that, he would undermine everything he'd built up these past three years.

Again, Flint wished he could nail down exactly what bothered him about her. He felt a vague sense of threat that grew stronger the closer they became.

Maybe it was simply that Robin was the wrong woman for him and the children. The fact that he would see her eyes every time he looked at Brick, and her sweetness in Aaron, and her feisty temperament in Caitlin, was an issue he would simply have to live with.

"Not so many stars tonight, but you find them very interesting?" asked a voice from the sidewalk.

With a start, Flint realized one of his neighbors was walking her pet poodle. He'd seen the woman before, an older Chinese lady, but didn't know her name.

"Just doing some thinking," he said.

"Nanny trouble?" asked the woman.

He stared at her. "Excuse me?" Now what would have given her that idea?

"You have many nanny troubles, I think." The woman extended her hand. "I am May Sung. I think you have beautiful children."

"I'm Flint Harris," he said. "Thank you."

"They look like their mother."

Flint digested that observation for a moment. "You knew Kathy?"

"I'm sorry. I am confused. The minute I saw her, I believed Robin was their mother." May continued to regard Flint, not at all concerned about the unwritten social code that barred strangers from probing into their neighbors' lives. "You have trouble with her?"

"She's leaving," Flint said. "She got a better job."

"Taking care of your family is not a job to her." May clucked at her poodle to still its fidgeting. "You should ask her to stay."

"I don't mean to be offensive, but exactly when did this become your business?" Flint snapped.

The woman shrugged. "I have lived too many years not to say what I believe. What you fear most comes from within yourself. Your chance may not come again."

"Thanks for the advice," Flint said.

His neighbor nodded, tugged on the leash and went on her way. Mist, closing in from the ocean, hid her from sight before she'd gone more than half a dozen steps.

Damn it, since he met Robin his well-ordered world had fallen apart. The children had turned down their favorite bedtime ritual, Maureen was acting emotional, and now a mysterious Chinese lady was meddling in his business.

The sooner matters got back to normal, the better, Flint told himself as he turned and went inside.

Chapter Sixteen

"We've got to come up with a plan." Caitlin had called this meeting of the triplets in her bedroom the minute Flint walked out the door. Robin was busy writing out a list of instructions about the vegetable garden, the week's meals and several other items that Caitlin had suggested.

"Let's run away from home," Brick said.

"Robin would make us go back." Aaron picked up a take-apart plastic skeleton and held it on his lap like a doll. "Besides, I'd miss Daddy."

"How could you miss Daddy? He's never here." Caitlin knew she was being unfair, but children had a right to be. Especially when someone else was so unfair to them.

"We could live in a boxcar, like the Boxcar Children," Brick suggested.

"Yeah, and we could fly to the moon like Dr. Dolittle, too," snapped Caitlin. "Get real."

"We are getting real," said Aaron. "We're just kids. We can't run away by ourselves."

"I know who would help!" Caitlin couldn't believe this brilliant idea hadn't occurred to her before. "Grandma Gigi!"

"Yeah!" Brick's face lit up. "And she lives at the beach! I love the beach!"

"How do we get there?" asked Aaron.

"On the bus." Caitlin didn't like the idea of sneaking out on Robin, though. "We could leave a note."

"Then they'll find us," Brick said.

"We could just say we were safe." Caitlin knew that wouldn't be enough. Robin would worry herself sick, and Flint would be furious.

"We could leave clues," Aaron suggested. "You know, like in a mystery. So they could figure out where we went, but not right away."

Caitlin gazed at her brother in surprise. "That's a good idea."

"Of course it's a good idea," Aaron said.

They didn't have much time. Robin trusted them to play quietly for a while, but sooner or later she would check.

Caitlin got out a lined sheet of paper and the three of them gathered around. "What kind of clues?" she said.

"We could draw a picture of the beach," Brick said.

"Too obvious."

"Maybe we could write a lot of capital letters, doubled up, like TT and SS, and we could sneak a GG in there," offered Aaron. "That would be a good clue."

Caitlin thought of another problem. "Does anybody remember exactly where Grandma Gigi lives?"

"That's easy," said Brick. "Over the fortune-telling shop. It's near the end of Beachside Avenue."

Caitlin gave him a brisk nod, pretending not to be impressed. Her brothers were getting smarter, now that they'd reached eight years old. "If we're going to come up with clues, we'd better get started."

Together they wrote the letter.

"Dear Robin and Flint."

They agreed not to call him Daddy, because then Caitlin insisted they had to call Robin Mommy.

"We have run away to a safe place. Here is the first clue— TT. SS. GG.

"We are going there on a Magic Vehicle. That's the second clue. Like in the books."

"That's the Magic School Bus," Aaron pointed out. "We're not riding a school bus."

"It's close enough," Caitlin said.

"When we get there, we will find even more magic stuff. That's the third clue. Don't be mad. We just want Robin to stay."

They all signed it. Brick suggested pricking their fingers and writing in blood, but the other two nixed that idea. They settled on ballpoint pen.

Then they dug around in their drawers to find fares for the bus. Their money jars hadn't yet recovered from the pizza incident, but they scraped up about five dollars, which Caitlin figured was enough.

From the kitchen, she heard Robin call, "Are you guys still breathing in there?"

"We're fine!" Caitlin responded.

"Ready to ride your bikes?" came the response.

"We're going out right now," Caitlin called. "See you in a while!"

"I'll be out in a few minutes." Robin sounded distracted.

"Perfect," muttered Brick. "We'll be long gone before she catches on."

Caitlin had to argue Aaron out of taking the bikes and leaving them at the end of the block. "We don't want them to get stolen," she scolded. "Come on. We'll have to move fast."

As they went out through the garage, she wished she had a bus schedule. Well, they'd just have to start walking and hope for the best.

ROBIN PREFERRED to keep a close eye on the kids when they were playing outside, but this morning things kept popping up. The dentist's office called with a reminder of checkups the next day, and she had to leave a note for Flint. Then he got a business call at home—this afternoon's meeting had been postponed yet again—and she had to call and leave word at his office.

After that the secretary at A Learning Place phoned to say they would be closing at one o'clock today, so Robin needed to come by before then to get her key.

There were so many things to do, and none of it could block out the realization that today was her last one as the children's caretaker.

En route to the front door, Robin paused to scoop a book of Aaron's and a pair of Brick's socks off the floor. The children scattered their possessions throughout the house in ways that weren't even logical. How had the book ended up on the floor? Why were Brick's socks in the living room?

As she carried the items to the boys' bedroom, tears pricked Robin's eyes. It was going to take all her strength to walk out of here this afternoon.

The children weren't possessions. Flint had no right to shut her out of their lives, not when she loved them so much.

Her thoughts in turmoil, she went onto the porch and surveyed the street. There was no sign of the kids.

That wasn't unusual, since they were allowed to venture onto surrounding residential streets. Robin decided to straighten out the gardening tools in the garage until the youngsters showed up. At least she could leave the place in apple-pie order.

This morning, the garage struck her as unusually cluttered. The reason didn't register at first, until Robin began wending her way toward the tool shelf and had to skirt a bicycle.

What was a bike doing here when the children were supposed to be out riding?

Maybe the kids had gone across the street to play. But the Anderses usually opened their garage door when the grandchildren were on the premises, and today it was shut tight.

Worried, Robin went to check their rooms. On Caitlin's bed, she spotted the note.

As she read it, Robin began to smile. Their intent was unmistakable.

Then she stopped smiling. She didn't like the idea of eight-year-old kids, even very bright ones, running around Beachside unsupervised. And Flint would like it even less.

She went to her room to get her purse, dropping the note onto the kitchen table. If she were lucky, maybe she'd catch the runaways at the bus stop.

"I'M TIRED of waiting." Brick swung his legs as he sat on the bench. "We've been here forever."

"Almost ten minutes," Aaron corrected. He was the only one of the three who wore a watch.

Caitlin glanced across Beachside Avenue toward the side street that led to their housing development. "Robin could be along any time now."

"If she figures out the note," Brick said.

"She'll figure it out." Aaron drummed his fingers on the bench. "We shouldn't have left so many clues."

Caitlin wrinkled her nose at the exhaust fumes from the traffic. She'd never noticed how busy Beachside Avenue could be. When she was riding in a car, it seemed nearly empty, but now she couldn't believe the number of cars and trucks stinking up the air.

"Do we have time to go in that store?" Brick indicated a hobby shop in a strip mall half a block away. Model airplanes hung in the window.

"No," Caitlin said. "Would you stop fidgeting?"

"Is that Robin's car?" asked Aaron.

They followed his gaze to the side street. There, halted at a red light, sat a familiar green compact.

"I think that's her driving," Brick agreed.

"There's too much glare on the windshield." Caitlin knew she was grasping at straws. "You can't possibly see her."

"But she could see *us,*" Aaron pointed out.

A loud wheeze blotted out the other traffic noises, and a bus pulled to a halt in front of them. It blocked their view of Robin's car.

"Come on," Caitlin said.

"I don't know...." Aaron remained sitting until she grabbed his arm and yanked him up.

"We might as well go." Brick gave them both a grin. "She won't be able to stop us until she gets to the beach. Once we're there, maybe we can stay for a while."

"All right." Aaron stopped resisting and followed his siblings up the steps.

Caitlin handed the driver their money, which left a pitifully small amount of change. The bus was full of beachgoers, picnic baskets and surfboards, and she and her brothers had to sit separately.

The door groaned shut and the bus cranked itself into motion. The great adventure had begun. Caitlin only hoped it wouldn't end with the three of them being grounded for the rest of the summer.

ROBIN GRITTED her teeth in frustration as the bus pulled away and she saw that the children had left with it. She'd had them in her sights and that darn red light had held her back. Now she would have to follow them to the end of the line.

She appreciated their desire to hang on to her, and their resourcefulness in going to Gigi's, but it wouldn't do any good. She also hoped they wouldn't pull any stunts like this after she was gone. She would have to alert Maureen.

Thinking about Maureen reminded Robin that the older woman would be visiting Gigi herself. Since séances were usually held at night, it was odd that Frederick had specified this morning. He must have had some reason, Robin supposed.

Maureen had seemed convinced that attending today's séance would relieve her mind, no matter how it turned out. Sometimes, Robin remembered reading, people needed rituals in order to resolve their feelings of grief and loss. There was no ceremony to acknowledge a broken heart. Maybe that's what Maureen had needed forty years ago.

Robin hoped the séance could fill that need. At least then Gigi's meddling would prove itself worthwhile.

Meanwhile, she needed to round up the kids and get to A Learning Place in time to pick up her key.

THE PLANNING DIRECTOR, Everett Zane, ushered Flint into his office and introduced a tall African-American woman, Shirley Greene, as his new assistant.

"Shirley will be in charge of implementing your recommendations and I want to be sure she understands your points," said Everett, a short, round-faced man who looked almost comical beside his statuesque assistant.

"I've read your report," explained Shirley in a throaty voice, "but it always helps to discuss things in person."

"Absolutely," Flint agreed. The City Council was scheduled to vote on his recommendations next week. With all the protests, they might approve it or table it for further study. However, the planning staff was gearing up, just in case, and he liked that approach.

He led the two planners to a topographic wall map of the city. The ocean slashed across at an angle, from upper left to lower right, forming the southwest border of Beachside. The city stretched from flat beach through the higher ground where Flint lived to Beach Heights, a region of ancient sea cliffs that offered spectacular views.

"The biggest problems will come along the beach," Flint explained. "In an earthquake, sandy soil magnifies the shaking. If the tremor is severe, you can get a condition called liquefaction, in which the soil turns into a form of quicksand."

"Is that just a theory, Dr. Harris?" Shirley asked.

"No, it's been demonstrated. It started to happen during the Long Beach quake of 1933," Flint said. "Fortunately, the shaking stopped before it got too bad."

"How long a time period are we talking before the next big one?" Everett asked. "A decade? Two decades?"

"I wish I knew," Flint said. "California has hundreds of small earthquakes every year. It's not unlikely we'll get one in the five point zero to five point five range during the next couple of years."

"Excuse me, Dr. Harris, but I'm from Milwaukee," the assistant explained. "That sounds like a pretty big earthquake to me."

"In parts of the world where people live in mud huts on ungraded slopes, absolutely," Flint said. "That's why soil preparation and building standards are so important. Around here, we've had earthquake standards for sixty years, but we're learning more all the time. And merchants love to put up shaky signs and facades that could break loose."

"So there's a real urgency to your recommendations," said Ms. Greene.

Flint hoped the City Council would agree. He didn't like to think about the facade on that store Gigi owned, or about Robin walking in front of it. It was exactly the kind of peril he hoped to eliminate.

"Let's get down to the details, shall we?" he suggested, and the two planners nodded.

ROBIN GOT CAUGHT in a traffic jam near the beach. In this hot August weather, half the population of Orange County seemed to have headed for the ocean.

By the time she reached the bus, the passengers had departed and it was reloading. A quick check of the area showed no sign of the triplets.

Gritting her teeth, Robin spent the next ten minutes searching for a parking space. That task accomplished, she wedged herself out in the six inches between her car and a van that had parked over the line. Banging her hip, she fought down the urge to curse.

Anxiety had made Robin's temper short. Although the children planned to visit Gigi, they might easily get lost. Bright as they were, the kids tended to overestimate their own abilities.

She hurried through the parking lot, dodging teenagers on Rollerblades and beachgoers carrying sun umbrellas. On the boardwalk, she couldn't see more than a few feet ahead of her because of the crowd.

Gigi's shop was only a block away, but today that distance felt more like a mile. Robin kept trying to scan the beach to see if the kids had wandered out that way, but the sand was swarming with sunbathers. She'd forgotten what August could be like, especially since temperatures in the high nineties had been predicted for today.

When she reached the fortune-telling shop, Robin jerked on the door so hard she nearly dislocated her shoulder. It was locked.

She muttered under her breath as she noticed the Gone to Commune With Spirits sign. Gigi must be upstairs holding the séance. But what about the kids?

If they'd arrived to find the store locked, they wouldn't have waited around. But where could they have gone?

Robin sought clues in the bright kaleidoscope of swimsuits and towels dotting the beach. She couldn't spot three eight-year-olds in street clothes.

"Going to the séance?" Julius Caesar appeared out of the mass of people moving along the sidewalk. He had traded his toga for a shabby centurion's costume. The cloth was shredded, the fake body armor broken and the plastic helmet missing its plume. Catching her gaze, the man said, "I decided to honor Frederick with a full-dress uniform."

"Have you seen three children?" she asked. "Two boys and a girl, eight years old?"

The old man shrugged. "Probably heading for the mime show. Down that way." He pointed farther along the boardwalk.

"Thanks." Robin took off at a rapid pace.

She spotted Caitlin first, blond hair like spun sugar in the sunlight. She stood between her brothers in a bunch of children, watching two mimes juggle beach balls.

Coming up behind them, Robin waited until the show ended. There was no harm in letting them watch, now that she had arrived to keep an eye on them.

"I guess we'd better..." Brick swung around and bumped right into her. "Oops."

"She's been standing there for five minutes," Caitlin said.

"Hi." Aaron gave Robin a relieved smile. "I'm glad you're here."

Robin felt her annoyance dissolve as she surveyed the children. As long as they were safe, she couldn't stay angry at them. But she did need to go pick up that key.

"You're coming with me to my school," she said. "I need to go over there, and this way I can show you my classroom."

"Can't we stop and say hello to Grandma Gigi?" Caitlin queried as the four of them started back. "We don't know when we'll see her again."

"It's nice to have a grandmother," Aaron said. "We want to keep her."

"Family is important," Brick noted.

Robin thought at first they might be parroting lines they'd heard on television, but they appeared sincere. All three children had grown attached to Gigi. She wondered if Flint realized how painful it would be to cut the children off from their newfound family.

"All right," she said. "We can say hello if the séance hasn't started."

At the shop, they marched up the outside staircase. Robin gestured the children to silence while she slipped open the door and peered inside.

Irma was laying out a tablecloth, Julius sat on the couch eating potato chips, and Maureen fiddled nervously with a pair of candlesticks on the sideboard.

Robin ushered the children inside. "They just want to see their grandmother for a minute."

Gigi emerged from the kitchen with a tray of cookies. "I knew it! I knew my grandchildren would show up!"

With whoops of delight, the youngsters descended on the treats. Gigi beamed.

"I'm sorry," Robin told Maureen. "We didn't mean to interrupt your plans. We'll only be here a minute."

"Not at all. They must stay for the séance," Gigi announced. "It will be an educational experience."

"Oh, please! Can we?" Brick begged.

"He doesn't know what a séance is," said Aaron.

"Neither do you," said Brick.

"It's where we get to meet ghosts." Aaron radiated pride at knowing more than his brother. "Isn't it, Grandma Gigi?"

Robin shook her head. "Flint would be furious."

"I want them to stay." Maureen's response caught her off guard.

"But why?"

"I want them to understand that people shouldn't hold feelings inside." The older woman tugged at the tablecloth, straightening it a fraction of an inch. "After forty years, think of all the anger I'm still hanging onto. I want them to understand that that isn't the way to handle disappointment."

"And it will be good for Caitlin to see me in action," said Gigi. "For the boys, too. You never know what abilities they possess."

"That's what I'm afraid of." Robin checked her watch. It was past eleven-thirty. "I have to go by my new school before one." She told them about the job and her need to fix up the classroom.

"All the more reason to leave them here," Gigi said. "They'll be out of your way."

"I'll take responsibility for them." Maureen spoke with an air of finality.

If it hadn't been for Maureen, Robin would never have agreed. But she didn't relish spending the next hour trundling the children around and listening to them complain about missing the séance. "If it gets scary, I want you to stop," she told her mother.

"Believe me, we will," Maureen said.

As she hugged the excited triplets and departed, Robin realized it wouldn't matter how Flint reacted when he heard about the séance. She wasn't going to be working for him after today, anyway.

IT WAS HALF PAST noon by the time Flint emerged from the planning office. He was startled to see five business owners carrying protest signs in front of City Hall.

"What are you doing here today?" he asked one of them.

"We've decided to march every day until the council drops this insanity," she answered. "Besides, we've got our names on our signs. It's good advertising."

Flint knew he should leave, but since his afternoon meeting had been canceled, he wasn't in a hurry.

"Wouldn't it be better for business if you showed more concern for the safety of your customers?" he asked.

He regretted the remark instantly as the five barraged him with barbed comments. One accused him of making a profit at their expense. Another claimed the whole issue was overblown. A third charged that overregulation was ruining the business climate in California.

A low rumble obscured their words. Flint wondered if an airplane had wandered off course and was flying too low. Then he felt a wave of dizziness and nearly lost his footing on the steps.

Palm trees were swaying across the street. "Sit down before you fall down!" he snapped at the protesters. "It's an earthquake!"

They stood glaring for a moment as if he were trying to trick them, and then the trembling intensified into a jolt. They all sat, Flint among them.

Across the street, a shop window rattled in its frame and a sign overhead tipped sideways. A green traffic light flickered, then switched to flashing red.

The shaking stopped. No one moved for a moment, and then the merchants stood up.

"That was scary," admitted the woman, brushing off her dress. "But not that bad."

"I've felt worse," boasted one of the merchants.

"You see?" said another. "There's hardly any damage and that must have been, what, a five point five?"

"Possibly." Flint couldn't hazard a guess without knowing how far away the epicenter was and how deep in the earth the quake had occurred. "Remember, there will be aftershocks...."

As if the earth were determined to prove him right, the ground shuddered, forcing the woman merchant to clutch a railing. Across the street, the heavy sign tore loose and crashed to the sidewalk.

It could have killed someone, Flint thought.

Then he realized that although the quake had ended, he could hear the rush of blood loud in his ears. His palms felt sweaty, and he was breathing faster than normal.

He'd been through quakes before, but they usually struck early in the morning while Flint was in bed. It was rare to find himself outdoors witnessing nature's fury as far as the eye could see.

He instinctively took a survey of his surroundings. Except for the damage across the street, nothing major had given way, although he was sure closer inspection would reveal some cracks.

But the main thing on his mind was his family. It was just past twelve-thirty, so they might be eating lunch. Their often-rehearsed plan called for everyone to duck under the table where they'd be safe from falling objects. Besides, his house was located on solid ground on the north side of the city, a good distance from the beach.

Feeling slightly reassured, Flint went to his car and put in a call on the cellular phone. To his surprise, no one answered.

He waited a few minutes and dialed again, in case they'd been outside. Still no answer.

There must be a reasonable explanation. Maybe they were visiting the Anders family, or Robin had taken the kids to a fast-food restaurant.

Despite this rational conclusion, Flint's body refused to relax. There was always a small chance that something had fallen on them, or that the quake had started a fire.

Three or four sirens wailed in the distance. They might be responding to fires but more likely to heart attacks.

The merchants were picking up their placards and heading away, Flint noticed as he backed up the car. He wondered idly whether their disputed signs had survived the shaking.

Maybe now the good people of Beachside would see the wisdom of Flint's recommendations. But at the moment, that was the last thing on his mind.

He drove home as quickly as circumstances would allow. Palm fronds littered the road, along with strips of bark that had shaken off the trees. Halfway home, a fallen tree blocked part of Beachside Avenue, jamming traffic.

Taking side streets, Flint had to make his way around a street flooded by a broken water main. This shaker might not have been as severe as the Northridge quake, but it had still left a considerable mess.

As he pulled up in front of his house, Flint saw that Robin's car was gone. He hoped she'd had the foresight to leave a note.

Inside on the kitchen table, he found the children's scribbled message. The meaning sent a wallop of anxiety through Flint's stomach.

The kids had run away to the beach. Robin must have gone after them. They couldn't have gotten much of a head start, since she checked on them frequently.

He found Gigi's telephone number and dialed it. The phone screeched in his ear and a mechanical voice announced, "We're sorry. All circuits are busy. Please try again later."

As usual after a quake, people were calling each other to check on injuries. In addition, the shaking had probably knocked phones off the hook, tying up the lines.

Flint tried not to think about the flimsy facade and sign on Gigi's shop. He tried not to think about a beach jammed with panicky people or about the way sand magnified the shaking.

He willed himself to remain calm as he got back into the car and headed south. Flint tried dialing Gigi on his cellular phone, since cellulars sometimes worked when regular phones didn't. It rang through, but all he got was her answering machine. Were the children there? Could they be lying in a heap of rubble?

As he drove, he felt panic threaten his self-control. He had never experienced such a deep and overwhelming sense of dread before, and yet some part of his mind recognized it at once as the terror that had lain hidden inside him for three years.

Now, maybe too late, he knew what it was.

Chapter Seventeen

Robin was standing in her classroom when the trembler hit. Through long training in earthquake drills, she ducked under the desk.

Nothing fell, since the room was bare of decorations, but she could feel the floor rolling beneath her. It was like riding a ship, except that this ship was sitting on supposedly solid ground.

After the shaking, she sat motionless for a few minutes to calm her breathing. She hadn't been aware of being frightened during the event, but now, in the stillness, alarm tingled through her, mixed with relief. The thing was over and she had survived.

Then the aftershock struck. When the rocking started again, Robin thought, *I don't need this. But then, who does?*

Afterward, she waited several minutes before emerging from the building. A Learning Place was composed of new structures built to the latest standards, and she saw no signs of breakage.

The airy campus was deserted when she crossed it. Robin found a pay phone, but the circuits were busy and she couldn't get through to her mother's apartment. Still, with Maureen and Gigi both on hand, she thought the children would be safe.

Earthquakes were always frightening. Growing up in Southern California, Robin had experienced several shakers larger than this. They always unnerved her briefly, but she had decided they were no worse than tornadoes, blizzards, hurricanes, floods and the other perils that threatened the planet.

At least the sun was still shining, the birds had resumed singing, and the air was no smoggier than usual.

The drive to Beachside should have taken less than half an hour under normal circumstances. Today, however, fallen objects slowed her drive to the freeway. Then, when she reached it, Robin got stuck again. According to the radio, the jam was due to a chain-reaction crash caused by an inexperienced driver who slammed on his brakes when the quake started.

She decided to get off the freeway as soon as possible and take an alternate route home.

THE STREETS around the beach were packed, Flint found when he reached the area. People seemed in a hurry to get home, or perhaps they were afraid of a tsunami.

The huge waves, formerly known as tidal waves, could be generated by quakes deep in the ocean floor. However, according to the radio, today's quake had been centered in the desert.

The preliminary rating was five point four. There were no reports of deaths, which failed to reassure Flint. He knew how sketchy information would be for hours yet.

At least he had no trouble parking. Cars were pouring out of the beach lot in droves.

As he strode toward the shop, Flint took in evidence of the quake's power—cracks in the sidewalk, bits of plaster and stucco broken off buildings, palm fronds littering the ground.

Gigi's wooden facade had withstood the shock, but her sign hung at a rakish angle. It would have to be pulled down before it fell down, Flint noted as he reached for the door. He tugged twice before he realized it was locked.

Then he saw the sign. What were his children doing communing with spirits?

At the top of the stairs, he knocked twice and waited. After a moment, Flint rapped again. He could hear voices. Why weren't they answering?

Annoyed, he threw open the door.

Startled faces swung toward him. The scene might have been a tableau from an old painting. In the dim light filtering through the curtains, Gigi, Maureen, the white-haired man and another woman sat around the table holding hands. Nearby, the triplets were lined up on the couch, watching.

A pole lamp had fallen onto the floor and a heavy mirror had skewed crazily. "Is anyone hurt?" Flint demanded.

"Hurt?" Maureen said. "Flint, you're interrupting us."

Gigi released the others' hands. "The spirit has gone."

"But he must return!" cried the third woman, who looked about the same age as Gigi. "He hasn't told us why he thinks Maureen is in danger!"

Flint stared at them in disbelief. "We've just had an earthquake. Are you people nuts?" He gestured toward a chandelier overhead. "One more aftershock and you could be wearing that thing for a hat."

"An earthquake?" Gigi blinked as if awakening from a nap. "Oh, my goodness. I thought it was the spirits shaking things up."

"And rapping on the door, too, I suppose?" Flint snapped.

"They do stomp around sometimes," said the white-haired man. "Make a lot of mischief."

"There are ghosts, Dad!" Aaron jumped off the couch. "One of them talked to us!"

"It was really Grandma Gigi who talked," Brick explained.

"Are you kids all right?" Flint gathered the boys into his arms. Caitlin sat motionless on the couch. "Honey?"

She expelled a long breath. "Dad, I could feel him. He was here. Aunt Maureen's old boyfriend."

"His name was Frederick," Aaron said. "He wanted to warn her about some terrible danger."

"But you interrupted before he could tell us what it is," Brick scolded. "Couldn't you have waited a few minutes, Dad?"

"You don't really believe this." Flint turned to his aunt.

Maureen folded her hands on the table. "I know it sounds odd, but I do. It was Frederick. He remembered things no one else could have known—a password we used in our notes. It was silly, but we used to enjoy having a secret code."

"Can't imagine why the fellow took forty years to come back." The white-haired man adjusted his helmet.

"It's because of the danger," said the third woman. "Oh, dear. I wonder if I should ask Mortimer to find out what it is."

She didn't explain who Mortimer was, and Flint didn't care. An earthquake had just endangered these people's lives, and all they could talk about was some idiotic séance.

Maureen held up her hand and the others fell silent. "At least they've solved my mystery," she said.

In spite of himself, Flint was curious. "You've found out what happened to your fiancé?"

"Apparently so." His aunt explained that Frederick had been walking to a florist's shop the morning of the wedding to pick up his boutonniere. As he passed a brick building, it exploded on top of him.

"I remember reading about it in the paper," Maureen said. "There was a break in a gas line. But apparently they never found his body."

"He didn't abandon her," Gigi added. "It was a misunderstanding all along."

"The whole thing could have been solved with a psychic reading forty years ago," said the third woman with a sniff.

Flint couldn't focus on their chatter any longer. He had been watching the doors to the kitchen and the bedroom, waiting for one more person to appear. "Where's Robin?"

"She went to her school to pick up a key," said Gigi. "I expect she'll be back soon."

"Has she called?" Then Flint remembered the phone lines were tied up. "I'd better go look for her."

"Where?" said Maureen. "Flint, be realistic. You're more likely to run into trouble yourself than to find Robin."

The white-haired man began stuffing cookies in his mouth from a plate on the sideboard. "She's a big girl."

Flint knew it was unlikely Robin had been injured in the quake. He also knew she was perfectly capable of finding her own way home.

And none of that meant a damn.

The terror that had struck him on the drive over, he realized now, was the reason he had avoided getting involved with Robin in the first place. It was the unthinkable dread that he would love again, only to lose her to another of fate's blind cruelties. In all these years since Kathy died, Flint had never realized until today that he was living in fear.

It hadn't stopped him from falling in love with Robin. And it wouldn't stop him from going in search of her now.

"Maureen," he said, "please take the children home with you. I'll pick them up as soon as I can."

"Of course." There was an unfamiliar air of calm about his aunt, a subtle difference in muscle tone. He could have sworn she had lost ten years off her age.

Flint headed for the door.

"Dad," Caitlin said. "There was something else."

"Yes?" Thinking she referred to Robin, Flint swung around. "What, Caitlin?"

"At the séance," she said. "Someone else was watching us. I think it was Mommy. I could—I could feel her."

"Really?" said Gigi. "I kept sensing another spirit but I couldn't get a grasp on her. I'm proud of you, Caitlin!"

"So am I." Flint gave his daughter a quick kiss and hurried out the door. He was glad she had found comfort in thinking about Kathy in the middle of a near disaster. He just hoped this garbage about spirits wouldn't give the children silly ideas.

Flint performed rapid mental calculations on his way to the car. He'd seen the blockages on Beachside Avenue and heard on the radio about a mess on the freeway.

Coming from the school, Robin would probably have exited earlier than usual, onto a road called Palmdale. The odds of spotting her weren't great, but Flint wouldn't rest until he'd checked out the grounds of A Learning Place. He could imagine her lying in her classroom with a broken leg, her shouts echoing unheard across an empty campus.

Flint couldn't say why he felt such urgency. He just couldn't stop thinking about the day he'd lost Kathy and the anger and pain at knowing he hadn't been there to help.

For three years, without realizing it, he'd built walls around himself to prevent such a thing from happening again. Now that it might have, he wasn't going to sit by and wait for the worst.

He loved Robin. Damn it, he loved her more than he would have believed possible. He would do anything in his power to keep her safe.

Flint refused to dwell on the possibility that fate might blindside him again. He had to keep his wits alert and his eyes sharp for any sight of her in the oncoming lanes.

The Volvo made good time until he reached Palmdale. Then he discovered that, like the other major thoroughfares, it had been brought to a standstill. In this case, the problem appeared to be a fallen power line.

Flint wrenched the car onto a side street. Two blocks over, a residential street paralleled Palmdale most of the way to the freeway. In fact, it ran right behind Serena Academy, he realized, his heartbeat accelerating. If Robin were seeking an alternate route, she probably would choose this one.

The speed limit was low and there were half a dozen stop signs, but Flint saw to his relief that the way was clear.

Then, as he came over a rise, he made out a welter of green several blocks ahead. On approach, it resolved itself into the massive branches of a fallen tree.

A few cars were skirting the mess, which lay undisturbed. With all the tie-ups on major arteries, this blockage might not even have been reported yet.

As he waited for a sports car to pass and then eased the Volvo into the open lane, Flint caught sight of a glint of glass beneath the branches. The flicker of reflected light set his heart pounding.

It looked as if a small car might be trapped beneath the branches.

He parked in a clear space and dialed 9-1-1 on his car phone. After reporting the accident, Flint opened his trunk and pulled out some tools.

Because he drove to out-of-the-way places in his work, he carried not only the usual jack and screwdrivers but also an ax. It wasn't as big as he would have liked, but it would have to do.

At the edge of the branches, he called out several times, but got no answer. Whoever was in the car was either unconscious or unable to respond.

Flint attacked the branches with an intensity that came from some unknown power source. He didn't even know if it was Robin in there, but right now, nothing mattered except clearing the wood and freeing the victim.

Sirens wailed toward him, but they were a long distance off. Working with such ferocity that he feared he might smash into the car itself, Flint had to temper his chopping as he neared the door.

He could see the color of the paint now. It was green, like Robin's compact.

The roof appeared partially collapsed. Flint could see a patch of blond hair pressing against the side window and guessed the driver was wedged there.

He couldn't lose her. The danger had been greater than he knew, all these weeks, but it hadn't come from Robin. He should have protected her, even though Flint knew he could hardly be expected to foresee an earthquake. But he would never forgive himself if she died without knowing he loved her.

With a burst of adrenaline, he cleared away the last heavy tree limb and wrenched open the door. The occupant sagged, but something held her in place.

"Are you all right?" Flint crouched down and smoothed away the tumble of golden hair.

It was Robin. He knew it even before he saw the curve of her cheek. He could tell by the sweet, light fragrance that filled the space around her.

She stirred, then coughed. "Flint?"

"Are you hurt?" he said.

"A little." Her voice came out whispery with shock. "Something's pressing on my chest."

The caved-in roof had trapped her. Even with his adrenaline pumping, Flint couldn't pull away the hunk of metal. No wonder she hadn't answered him. It must hurt her to breathe.

In his concentration on Robin, he didn't even realize the firemen had arrived until one of them touched his shoulder. "Sir?" the man said. "Would you step out of the way, please?"

Flint moved off, but not far. For the next half hour, he answered a policeman's questions and called reassurances to Robin as the firefighters brought in equipment to claw open the car.

When they freed her, the onlookers burst into applause. Paramedics tried to whisk her onto a stretcher, but Robin declined. "I'm just bruised," she said.

At Flint's insistence, she let the paramedics check her. They confirmed that except for some bruises and minor cuts, she appeared fine.

"It'll hurt like hell in a few hours," one of the men warned. "You need to keep her warm and watch for signs of shock."

"I'll take good care of her," Flint promised as he steered her to the Volvo.

Robin slumped into the car seat. As he started the motor, Flint wondered if perhaps she needed medical attention after all.

Then she said, "Are the children all right?"

"They're fine. So are Maureen and Gigi, except their brains must be addled. They kept yammering about some ghost."

Robin gave him a weak grin. "How on earth did you find me?"

"I'm not sure." Now that he thought about it, Flint realized how lucky he'd been. "Maybe one of your mother's spirits was guiding me."

Robin let out a low chuckle. "Wouldn't Gigi love to hear you talk that way!"

They were passing the academy, only a couple of blocks from the accident. The ground around the theater building was littered with debris from heavy roof tiles.

Robin shuddered. "You were right about that place."

"I was wrong about a lot of other things, though," Flint said.

He didn't speak again for a while. He wanted to be able to concentrate fully on Robin when he said what he had to say.

Instead of heading for home, he drove up a winding road to the heights. Although some dirt had slid loose on the cliffs, the rocky soil up here appeared to have withstood the shaking with little damage.

Flint stopped at a turnout that overlooked the city. From here, they could see all the way to the ocean.

Afternoon sunlight revealed a town battered but unbowed. Traffic moved in antlike lines along the major arteries, and Flint could make out a few fallen trees. But he saw no black smoke from fires, no blocks of collapsed buildings as there had been in Northridge.

In the sweeping panorama below, Flint felt as if he could see his entire life laid out before him. There was the neighborhood where he lived, off to the right. Farther south lay City Hall, where he'd spent this morning, and then the beach, where he'd found Maureen and the children.

"We got off easy," he said. "This time."

"It could have been a lot worse," Robin agreed.

He wasn't sure how he would have survived if he had lost her. Deeply as he loved the children, Flint knew he had to let them grow up and lead their own lives. He needed Robin to fill his future with joy.

He slipped an arm around her and drew her against him. Her head rested on his shoulder. "Thank you for saving me. Flint, I want you to know, I don't have any hard feelings about your kicking me out."

"You don't?" he said.

"It's not your fault you're stubborn and pigheaded and a pain in the neck," Robin murmured against his jacket. "But if you think I'm going to walk away and never see the children again..."

"I think you should have custody of the children," Flint said.

That stopped her cold for several seconds. Then she asked, "You mean it?"

"The children need a mother," Flint said. "You seem to be the logical choice."

"They need a father, too," she pointed out.

He gazed over the town below, registering the flashing red lights of rescue vehicles in half a dozen spots. "Then we'd better get married."

Robin straightened, then groaned. "That paramedic was right about my muscles— Did you say, get married?"

Flint nodded. "Married, hitched, man and wife. As a matter of fact, I think we should have three ceremonies, one for each child, just to make sure the thing is well and truly done."

"But you can't stand me," Robin said.

He burst out laughing. "You can't stand me, either. What better reason to get married?"

"I like you most of the time," she protested.

"You just called me pigheaded and stubborn."

"Well, you are!" She regarded him dubiously. "Come on, Flint. What's this all about?"

"I love you," he said. "I'm tired of fighting my feelings out of a misplaced sense of loyalty. I wasn't really being true to Kathy, I was trying to protect myself against ever again losing someone I love. Well, to hell with that. I want every minute I can have with you, no matter what."

Robin's expression hovered between a smile and pure incredulity. "Flint, ever since I've known you, you've held me at arm's length. Any minute now, the defenses will go up again. I just know it."

Flint couldn't believe this was happening. He'd finally realized how much he loved Robin, and she didn't believe him.

"I'll show you," he said.

Sliding out of the car, he strode toward a nearby house where he'd noticed a rose garden in full bloom. A woman answered the door on the second ring.

Flint pulled out his driver's license and credit cards. "I'm sorry to disturb you," he said. "My name is Flint Harris. I'm not selling anything and I'm not a crook. I nearly lost the woman I love in this earthquake and I'm trying to persuade her to marry me. Could I buy a huge bouquet of those flowers from you? I'm desperate to make a good impression. If you have any better ideas, I'll pay for those, too."

The woman gazed from him to his driver's license. Then she said, "Oh, I've seen your picture in the paper. You're that earthquake expert."

"That's me," he said.

She invited him inside and asked his opinion about a couple of cracks in the living room wall. Fortunately, the damage was only superficial.

In return for his assessment, the woman refused any payment. She fetched a garden clipper and in minutes had assembled a gorgeous riot of blossoms, interspersed with ferns. The woman wrapped the cut ends in wet paper towels and covered them with aluminum foil.

"That way they'll last longer," she said. "And good luck with your young lady."

"I can't tell you how much I appreciate this," Flint said as he went out the door.

"I love romance," said the woman.

Robin was dozing in the front seat when Flint opened her door. "What on earth were you doing?" Then she saw the flowers. "Where did you get those?"

"The barter system," he said. "I just did a little earthquake consulting." He handed her the flowers and knelt on the pavement beside the car. "Robin Lindstrom, will you do me the honor of becoming my wife?"

"You can't be serious!" she said.

"That isn't the way you're supposed to answer," he complained.

She took a deep whiff of the flowers. "These are fabulous."

Flint gritted his teeth. "I hate to mention it, but this position is murder on the knees."

Concern darkened her eyes. "Oh, Flint, I'm sorry. Please get up."

"You haven't given me an answer," he said.

Robin stared at him through the roses. "Yes. I absolutely insist on marrying you. Will that do?"

"Just fine." Flint got up and brushed bits of gravel from his pants. "I'm holding you to it."

"I hope that's not the only thing you're holding me to," she said.

He got inside the car and made it perfectly clear that he planned to hold her as often and as close as possible.

Chapter Eighteen

Maureen's house was located a few blocks from Flint's in an older neighborhood. Built in the California bungalow style of the 1930s, it had a covered front porch, double-hung windows and roses climbing over a trellis that spanned the front walkway.

As she got out of the car, Robin took a last whiff of her bouquet and left it on the seat.

She still hadn't absorbed the fact that Flint loved her and they were getting married. She was really going to be the children's mother, in every sense of the word.

As Flint helped her out, pain throbbed up Robin's back. The muscles were protesting their long stint of being held immobile while she was trapped, and she could feel bruises turning black and blue on her chest.

Robin had been frightened during her ordeal, but not panicky. She'd been driving along the quiet street when she saw the tree begin to sway. Apparently the ground around it had been overwatered and the quake had weakened the roots.

She hadn't expected it to flop into the street. When she heard the crunch of branches against her car, Robin had assumed a limb had fallen and that she would drive clear.

The crash seemed in retrospect to have happened in slow motion. The seat belt had saved her from hitting the windshield, and she'd had time to dodge to one side as the roof caved in.

Even when she'd discovered she was trapped, Robin had expected help to arrive at any moment. She had been in a familiar setting, and somehow she had known Flint would come. She hadn't even felt surprised to see him.

Her thoughts broke off as Maureen ushered them into the house. Light washed through open curtains, illuminating a living room filled with antiques. The children sat on flowered carpeting, playing cards around a mahogany coffee table. They waved as Flint and Robin came in but were too intent to interrupt their game.

A large seascape depicting a storm had been removed from the wall above the settee, Robin noticed. At first, she thought it might have fallen in the quake, but then Maureen pointed out two bright posters leaning against a chair, both Hawaiian scenes.

"I'm tired of living with dark colors," she said. "I brought those back to give to friends, but I'm going to put them up so I can enjoy them myself."

"That's the first time I've seen your curtains open," Flint noted.

"You'll be seeing a lot of changes around here," said his aunt.

She gestured them to follow her to the dining room. When they cleared the door and got a view of the table, Robin gasped. A huge china cabinet had collapsed across it, smashing plates and cups to splinters.

"How awful!" she said.

"I always sit there to eat my lunch," Maureen said. "I eat between twelve and one. If I hadn't gone to the séance, I would have been killed."

Flint gave his aunt a hug. "Thank goodness you're safe. Here I am an earthquake consultant, and I didn't make sure the thing was fastened to the wall."

"You warned me plenty of times," Maureen said. "I'm capable of fastening it myself, but I never bothered."

Something clicked in Robin's memory. "Frederick wanted to warn you about some danger."

"This must be why he set the time of the séance when he did," Maureen said. "He came back after all these years to save my life. He must have loved me a great deal." Her eyes brimmed with tears.

Flint stared at the fallen cabinet. "As a scientist, I have to call this a coincidence. But as your nephew, I wonder if there aren't some things in life that science can't explain."

"Lots of them." Robin hooked her arm through his. "Are you going to tell her, or should I?"

"No one needs to tell me." Maureen favored them both with a warm smile. "It's obvious my nephew finally came to his senses. About time!"

A few minutes later, they broke the news to the children, who ran to hug them.

No one seemed very surprised, though. "I knew if we went to Grandma Gigi's, everything would be all right," said Caitlin.

Robin wondered if Gigi had been right about Caitlin's psychic abilities, then decided it didn't bear thinking about.

They picked up some fast food on the way home. After a quick meal in the kitchen, the exhausted triplets fell into bed and were asleep almost before their heads hit the pillows.

Except for a few books that had toppled, Flint's house had escaped unscathed. *Not Flint's house, our house,* Robin corrected herself as she walked toward the kitchen to finish picking up the fast-food wrappings.

She was halfway through the family room when she noticed that the earthquake had tipped one of the photographs. As she straightened it, Robin realized it was the picture of Kathy with the children.

The woman appeared to be winking.

Robin rubbed her eyes and looked again. Kathy wasn't winking, but her image gave off a warm glow that Robin could have sworn hadn't been there before.

Flint's footsteps approached from the kitchen. "I cleaned up," he said.

"That's my job."

"You're not the housekeeper any more." His arms encircled Robin. "You're a mother, a wife-to-be and a teacher. If we need to hire more help around here, we'll do that."

She relaxed into his embrace. She felt too sore to make love just now, but that would pass. "I guess we owe a lot to this earthquake."

"There's something else I wanted to say." She felt Flint tense slightly. "I've been thinking that it isn't fair to ask you to move into this house. Kathy picked it out and it's full of her memories. If you prefer, we could start somewhere new."

Robin considered for a moment, but she already knew her answer. "I don't want to get rid of her memories. I'd rather stay here."

She heard Flint's relief in his quick release of breath. "It's a good neighborhood for the children. We've all come to feel at home here."

"So have I," said Robin, with all her heart.

"THAT'S YOUR CUE!" Maureen whispered.

Caitlin bit her lip, her face young and uncertain beneath its circlet of flowers. "I hope I don't trip."

"You'll be fine," Robin urged.

Her bouquet clutched tightly, Caitlin slipped through the doorway and down the aisle. The pink dress had transformed her from a tomboy into a princess, and she walked with head held high.

Next it was Maureen's turn, as maid of honor. Pink flattered her, Robin noticed, and no one could walk with more grace and dignity.

After Maureen left, Robin waited with nerves tingling until the organist launched into "Here Comes the Bride." Gigi gave her daughter a nudge. It warmed Robin to realize that her mother was almost as excited as she was.

They entered together, Gigi in her deep rose cocktail dress and Robin in the ankle-length ivory gown that the children had helped her select. Pink rosebeds trimmed the overskirt and the matching short veil on her ivory toque hat. In her arms, instead of a formal bouquet, she carried a spray of roses in vivid colors.

The guests turned to watch. Without trying, Robin could pick out the faces of neighbors, teachers and friends. Julius Caesar wore a garland of laurel leaves in his hair for the occasion.

By the altar, close to their father, waited Brick and Aaron, solemn in their junior-size tuxedos, and Caitlin, ethereal and pixielike. "Isn't that funny," whispered Gigi. "You had three children before you even, well, *knew* each other, in the biblical sense."

"We'll just have to make up for lost time," Robin whispered back, and saw her mother's delighted grin.

Then she lost all awareness of everything except Flint, standing tall by the altar, waiting for her with love shining on his face.

He was the man who would steady her through any earthquake, rescue her from any danger and let her rescue him from the prison he had once built around himself. He was the father of her children and the friend who would stand beside her for the rest of their lives.

With a sense of bursting into the future, Robin hurried down the aisle to meet him.

UNLOCK THE DOOR TO GREAT ROMANCE AT BRIDE'S BAY RESORT

Join Harlequin's new across-the-lines series, set in an exclusive hotel on an island off the coast of South Carolina.

Seven of your favorite authors will bring you exciting stories about fascinating heroes and heroines discovering love at Bride's Bay Resort.

Look for these fabulous stories coming to a store near you beginning in January 1996.

Harlequin American Romance #613 in January
Matchmaking Baby by Cathy Gillen Thacker

Harlequin Presents #1794 in February
Indiscretions by Robyn Donald

Harlequin Intrigue #362 in March
Love and Lies by Dawn Stewardson

Harlequin Romance #3404 in April
Make Believe Engagement by Day Leclaire

Harlequin Temptation #588 in May
Stranger in the Night by Roseanne Williams

Harlequin Superromance #695 in June
Married to a Stranger by Connie Bennett

Harlequin Historicals #324 in July
Dulcie's Gift by Ruth Langan

Visit Bride's Bay Resort each month wherever Harlequin books are sold.

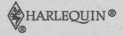

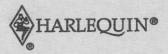

HARLEQUIN®
AMERICAN ROMANCE®

This Valentine's Day, take your pick of the four extraspecial heroes who are coming your way. Or why not take *all* of them?

Four of the most fearless, strong and sexy men are brought to their knees by the undeniable power of love. And it all happens next month in

Valentine's MEN

Don't miss any of these:

#617 THE BOUNTY HUNTER'S BABY
by Jule McBride

#618 THE COWBOY AND THE CENTERFOLD
by Debbi Rawlins

#619 FLYBOY
by Rosemary Grace

#620 THE BEWITCHING BACHELOR
by Charlotte Maclay

With love From HARLEQUIN AMERICAN ROMANCE

This February, watch how
three tough guys handle the

Lieutenant Jake Cameron, Detective Cole Bennett and
Agent Seth Norris fight crime and put their lives on the
line every day. Now they're changing diapers, talking
baby talk and wheeling strollers.

Nobody told them there'd be days like this....

Three complete novels by some of your favorite
authors—in one special collection!

TIGERS BY NIGHT by Sandra Canfield
SOMEONE'S BABY by Sandra Kitt
COME HOME TO ME by Marisa Carroll

Available wherever Harlequin and Silhouette books are sold.

When desires run wild,

Confessions

can be deadly

JoAnn Ross

The shocking murder of a senator's beautiful wife
has shaken the town of Whiskey River. Town sheriff
Trace Callihan gets more than he bargained for when the
victim's estranged sister, Mariah Swann, insists on being
involved with the investigation.

As the black sheep of the family returning from Hollywood,
Mariah has her heart set on more than just solving her
sister's death, and Trace, a former big-city cop, has more
on his mind than law and order.

What will transpire when dark secrets and suppressed
desires are unearthed by this unlikely pair? Because nothing
is as it seems in Whiskey River—and everyone is a suspect.

Look for *Confessions* at your favorite retail outlet this January.

MJRC

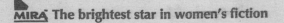